MICHAEL J. BOWLER

I KNOW WHEN YOU'RE GOING TO DIE

ACKNOWLEDGEMENTS

I extend my heartfelt thanks to my editor, Loretta Sylvestre, and to all the beta readers who gave me feedback on this novel along its circuitous path to publication, especially fellow author Huston Piner. I'm especially greatful to the teen beta readers of LitPick.com who read an early draft of this book and provided valuable feedback that I incorporated into the final product.

CHAPTER ONE

MAKE WISE CHOICES

I'M LADLING OUT STEW TO ragged old men, boys in hoodies, and women clothed in layers of dirty, mismatched apparel. They've come to stay the night at one of Skid Row's rescue missions because it's better than a tent or cardboard box on San Pedro Street. I like being here more than I like being at home, so I help out every weekend.

I'm chatting with a skinny boy and his mother passing through the line on their way to scarf a hot meal at one of the foldable tables when one of the mission staff taps me on the shoulder.

"Leo, there's a guy in the sleeping quarters asking for you. Said his name is Franklin."

"Thanks," I reply. I don't recognize that name, but I make my excuses to the boy and his mom and hand over my ladling duties to the girl who'd brought me the message.

To get to the sleeping quarters, I walk down a narrow, dark-paneled hallway with the familiar smell of sweat and unwashed socks. The door to the dorm is open and I step in. It looks like a huge barn with a worn hardwood floor studded with row after row of folding cots. Since it's dinnertime, all the cots are empty except one.

An old man with surprisingly alert eyes lies atop that cot staring at me. Most of the older people who frequent the shelter have rheumy eyes, always moist and often clouded, because they've struggled for so long on the street, and maybe because they have alcohol or drug problems.

"Come here, boy." His voice is raspy and echoes faintly in the cavernous room.

At first, I don't recognize him. True, there are hundreds of homeless on the streets every day, but I've been volunteering on Skid Row since I was fourteen and after almost three years, like I said, I know most of them. I'm thinking that if this guy is a regular, he's passed under my radar.

And yet…

I *have* seen him, I think. Not here at the shelter. Walking to my car…? Yes! Several times over these past two or three weekends, I've noticed him. He's caught my eye because, every time, he's stared at me so intently it made me shiver. He'd be pretending to rummage through a dumpster, but his eyes would follow me until I got into my car. I confess his gaze made me uncomfortable, but I let it go. I've learned to shrug off such creepy feelings because so many of the people I meet down here have mental health issues.

I steel myself and walk between the rows of empty cots—each with its neat bedroll awaiting an occupant—and stop before the stranger with the scary eyes. Unlike most of the people, his clothes aren't especially dirty and he doesn't smell like someone who's been on the streets for a long time. Wisps of gray hair stick out from his head at haphazard angles and his face has so many wrinkles I don't think I could count them if I tried.

I don't make eye contact, but that's because I never do. Not here, not anywhere. People tell me I'm the definition of "shy" and they're right.

"You asked to see me, sir?" I say deferentially, my gaze on his gnarled hands.

He rolls over onto his back. "I been watching you, boy. Seen you on the streets a lot."

I freeze. *So, I didn't imagine it!* "Yeah?"

"Yeah." The voice sounds like sandpaper scraping along a fence. "Rich boy like you helping out poor folk like me. What gives?"

I've been asked this question by all my relatives, so I'm ready with my answer. "I think people like me who are lucky to have a lot should help people who don't. And I hope I'm making the world better instead of worse. The kids I know just party and think about themselves all the time. I don't want to be like that."

A crooked smile cracks the wrinkled face. "You're the one, all right."

"The one?"

With effort, he unclasps his hands with their swollen knuckles and holds his right arm out toward me. It shakes, like he barely has enough strength to keep it aloft. "Take my hand, boy."

Unlike my best friend J.C., who never touches any of the people when he comes with me to the shelters, I usually have no worries about contact. But I hesitate this time. I mean, this guy *has* been watching me on the streets. But kindness makes me swallow my anxiety and I clasp his hand. He squeezes gently.

"Look into my eyes."

Ordinarily, I'd just glance into his eyes and then look away. But that commanding tone compels me. I raise my eyes and focus on his. They're brown and alert and they shimmer beneath the overhead lights. We lock gazes, and I stiffen. Something I can't quite pin down swells within me, like a surge of emotion. I suddenly feel... different.

All the tension drains from his face in an instant. Relaxed, he releases my hand, pulling his arm back with great deliberation. He rests both hands across his stomach and gazes up at me with obvious gratitude.

"Thank you, boy. Now I can die."

I shudder. "Wha-what do you mean?"

The man offers a gentle smile. "I gave you a great gift, boy. Or maybe a curse. Had it so long, I can't be sure no more. But I couldn't die till I passed it on."

I stand frozen in place, my heart thumping, my breathing on hold. A gift? A curse? "Uh, pass what on, sir?"

He chuckles and it's a wheezy sound, like he doesn't have much air in his lungs. "Just you calling an old bum like me "sir" proves you be the one."

I feel different inside and his words scare me because I know he's done *something* to me. "I'm just a regular kid, sir. Nothing special."

That chuckle erupts again, wheezier this time. "Oh, you're more than a regular kid. Like you said, most kids only care about stupid crap like partying. You'll use my gift well." He lapses into a coughing fit that scares me even more.

"Want me to get some help?"

He waves away the idea with one hand. After a few moments, the hacking ceases. "No need. It's my time." He suddenly looks really pasty and gray in the face. "When you find someone worthy, boy, pass on the gift to them," he whispers, his voice very soft and almost inaudible. He closes his eyes and lies still. "Until then, make wise choices."

Then he stops breathing. Literally, just stops. One second his chest is rising and falling and then the next, there's nothing. I want to shake him back to life and ask a thousand questions, but instead I run from the room to get help.

I toss and turn all night, images of the old man's craggy face and piercing gaze filling my dreams. Each time I wake, I hear his scratchy voice repeating the same words over and over again: *I gave you a great gift, boy. Or maybe a curse.*

What does that mean?

The next day, when J.C. accompanies me to the mission, he's dressed in designer jeans and a fancy shirt fit for a dance club. Maybe that's why, before we're even finished serving lunch, everyone clamors for him to perform. He's been dancing since he was little and knows so many styles I can't keep track. Dancing and fashion are the loves of his life. He cranks hip hop on his phone and launches into an awesome routine that includes some cool break dance moves, his ebony hair doing its own dance against his forehead as he spins. Everyone is clapping and cheering within minutes.

As I ladle soup into chipped white bowls and pass out fresh rolls, I keep thinking of Mr. Franklin, the old man who died. Everything about that encounter troubles me and I find my mind wandering from J.C.'s performance. To the regular mission staff, death is a common occurrence, almost a daily one. Even I've seen people die down here, but this time was different. Especially the way I felt when I locked eyes with him.

"Make wise choices."

My thoughts are interrupted by raucous applause. The song—most likely from one of those Step Up movies J.C. adores— ends and my best friend stops dancing. Staff, volunteers, and homeless alike shout and clap with gusto.

Sweat beading his forehead, J.C. looks over at me and grins. I grin back and toss him a thumbs up.

After lunch, we head to a nearby McDonald's and buy bags of hamburgers, chicken sandwiches, and fries to give out on the streets. I make momentary eye contact with each person I hand a bag to because I want them to know they're human like me. But I can't hold it for more than a second until, beneath the dim shade of the freeway overpass on Main Street, this one man grasps my arm as he takes his bag. He's a regular named Hank, an older guy with a limp who always wears a dirty Dodgers cap and mismatched clothes I'm sure he found in a dumpster.

"Thank you, Leo." Hank's voice is strained, but sincere.

I force myself to look into his grateful eyes and our gazes lock. I can't seem to look away. It's like I'm being drawn into Hank's very soul. Then I see it! Gasping, I lurch back and yank my arm away from him.

He recoils, looking stung by my action, and I want to apologize, but no words come. I'm paralyzed by what I just saw and can only offer him a silent nod.

Gripping the bag with gnarled fingers, Hank lurches down Main Street until he reaches the corner and turns out of sight.

J.C. steps around in front of me. "Hey, Leo, you okay? You look like you saw a ghost."

"I know… when he's… going to… die." I barely get the words out.

J.C. stares at me. "Huh?"

I shiver, my hand still outstretched from giving Hank the Big Mac and fries. I look down at it—my fingers are trembling. I pull them into a fist and lower my arm to my side.

"Leo?"

I face J.C., but don't meet his gaze, a chill enveloping my body and causing me to break into a cold sweat. "I-I never look people in the eye, J.C. You-you know that, right?"

He tilts his head like I'm crazy. "Duh! What are you talking about, man?"

I glance again at the corner where Hank vanished. Homeless people lie on blankets and tarps or on the bare gray sidewalks. Others lounge beside colorful nylon tents or shelters made from cardboard boxes. I know many of these people by name and they know me. Several of the women stare at me with concern. I must look as scared as I feel.

"Yo, Leo, anybody home in there?"

I turn back to J.C., but focus on the lower half of his face. His brow is drawn together and his mouth is clamped in a straight line. It's a worried look..

I clear my throat. "I looked into Hank's eyes when I handed him the food."

J.C. punches me on the shoulder and grins. "Awesome. That's progress, right?"

I shiver again. Traffic noise and passing cars distract me for a moment and derail my train of thought. I stare at the dimple in the center of J.C.'s chin and whisper, "I saw him dead, J.C."

His mouth drops open. "Huh?"

I shake my head, those horrific images fixed to the backs of my retinas like photographs. "He-he was all bloody and kind of twisted up. I-I couldn't see how he died, but I knew *when* he died."

He gives me one of his hard looks and then bursts out laughing. "Good one, bro. You had me going there for a sec."

"I'm not joking, J.C. He's about to die!"

I start jogging down Main, but soon I'm running, ignoring the dust I kick up from the sidewalk as I hurry in the direction Hank took. I hear J.C. curse under his breath and then his footsteps as he follows. The homeless ladies touch my shoulder in gratitude as I pass and offer their best, mostly toothless, smiles. I'm too spooked by what I've just seen to return anything but a quick nod.

"Leo, wait up."

I don't slow my stride and feel, rather than see, J.C.'s loping gait alongside me.

As I stop at the corner of Main and one of its busy cross streets, a screech of tires, followed by a loud *thud* and cry of human anguish, pierces my ears. I break into a sprint.

A crowd is already gathering in front of Marguerite's Place, a Mexican restaurant where I sometimes buy food for people on the streets. Traffic at the intersection has momentarily halted and people clamber out of their cars for a better look. I run to the edge of the crowd and muscle my way through.

A man's voice laments, "The light was green. He just stepped out in front of me!"

My heart rate quickens. A large pickup truck, its bed laden with garden-ing equipment, has stopped mid-turn onto Main, a line of cars halted behind it. A body lies in the crosswalk. Sirens assail my ears.

"Hey, kid, watch out!" a man says as I push my way past an inside ring of onlookers. I hear J.C toss out a couple of curse words in Spanish and another voice responding, "*Puta madre.*"

I inch my way closer to the pickup so I can get a clear view of the body. I immediately recognize the ragged jeans and baggy flannel shirt. My heart pounds and I can scarcely breathe.

"Leo, what are you—"

J.C. stops in midsentence and I feel his arm brush up against me, but I don't glance over. My gaze is fixed on Hank's bloody face. The McDonald's bag must've flown from his hand onto Main Street because it's already been crushed by a passing car. Blotches of ketchup adorn the pavement and mingle with the blood pooling from the back of Hank's head. The ratty blue Dodger's cap is splashed with ghastly streaks of red.

"Holy crap," J.C. whispers beside me. "You were right!"

My head feels light. The heat rising from the hot asphalt nearly overcomes me. I foresaw this man's death! My knees grow weak and I grab J.C. by the arm. He wraps his arm around me, gripping my shoulder so I don't collapse. The wail of sirens gets louder.

J.C. leans into my ear, "Come on, Leo. We should jet."

I stare numbly at Hank's dead gaze and twisted limbs. I feel J.C. dragging me back and finally turn to follow him.

We escape the scene just as the police arrive and hurry back to my car, which is parked blocks away in front of the old Hotel Cecil on Main. Unlike all the other kids at La Costa High who have fancy cars, I drive a three-year-old Prius that has visible parking lot dings on the sides and "only" cloth upholstery, all of which embarrasses my mother like you wouldn't believe.

I feel J.C. slip his hand into the side pocket of my baggy cargo pants to pull out my key fob. He opens the door and eases me into the passenger seat.

"Wait," I mumble. "I'm driving."

J.C. shakes his head. "Not spooked as hell like you are. I'll drive."

I nod absently and he sprints around to the driver's side.

He knows me well enough to know I don't want to talk about what happened. Not right now, anyway. We leave downtown L.A. behind us and head back via freeway and palm-lined streets to our beachfront town of La Costa in a heavy silence. He doesn't even crank the mariachi music like he usually does, for which I'm grateful.

My mind replays in an endless loop the encounter with Hank, and the one with Mr. Franklin at the shelter last night—an experience I now *kind of* understand, but don't *really* comprehend. I realize the car has stopped moving and I look around. We're already back in La Costa, parked in a space on East Hanley Street with the well-watered green expanse of Beck Park spread out before us. As I gaze through the dirty windshield, it sinks in that I completely zoned out on the ride back.

J.C. kills the engine and sighs in that very dramatic way he has. "Okay, Shy Boy, what the hell happened back there?"

I guess he thinks my town nickname will draw out a smile, but it doesn't. I'm too rattled. He must sense my fear because his tone changes. He places one hand on my arm so I'll look at him, but I make sure not to do that. Looking at people is the problem. I get that now. I can't look someone in the eye ever again.

Okay, my thoughts are rambling. I take some deep breaths and focus on two young kids tossing around a football in the park, making sure not to look at J.C. "'Member last night I told you about the old guy that died?"

I can almost see him shrug with indifference. "Yeah? That's nothing new for that place."

I nod. "'Cept I didn't tell you what he did first." I pause, the memories flooding in and nearly drowning me under their weight. I tell him everything Mr. Franklin did and said, but J.C. just clucks his tongue in annoyance.

"So, what does that have to do with today?" He obviously hasn't made the connection.

I swallow hard and keep my eyes on that football sailing back and forth across a patch of blue sky between the two boys. "I think he gave me the power to see when people are going to die."

J.C. slaps the steering wheel. "Holy crap!"

I nod.

"We have to test this out." He's acting like I just told him I got a new video game, rather than the power to see death. "Look in my eyes."

I glance over at his eager face in horror and instantly avert my gaze. "Hell, no! I can't know when you're gonna die."

"Why not? If I died today my mom wouldn't even notice."

His voice reeks with contempt and I want to comfort him, but it's the same for me. If I vanished off the face of the earth, my mother might not realize it for months, if ever.

"I'd notice," I whisper, still looking down at the handbrake. "I don't know what I'd do without you."

Silence fills the car. Only the sound of the kids yelling as they toss the football come to my ears. I force myself to look up. J.C.'s mouth hangs open and he has this stunned look on his face. I make sure not to look into his eyes, though.

"Wow," he blurts finally, expelling a gust of air at the same time. "You really mean that?"

I nod.

He breaks into one of his genuine smiles, which he seldom uses for any-one but me, and places a hand on my shoulder. "Thanks, Leo."

Eyes still downcast, I nod again, but I'm too choked up with mixed emo-tions over everything that's happened and don't know what to say next.

"So, we pick a stranger." J.C. returns his hand to the wheel.

"We know everybody in La Costa."

"Then we go to a liquor store in Lawndale and buy a soda. You look into the clerk's eyes and tell me what you see."

J.C. has a way of making everything sound so easy, so simple. Ordinarily, it's one of the things I really like about him. But this is different. I just know—deep down—that there's nothing "simple" about what that man gave me, and I suspect my life will never be the same again. I want to make J.C. understand, but the feeling inside me is too intangible to put into words, so I just nod and he starts the engine.

CHAPTER TWO

WHAT DID YOU SEE?

As J.C. pulls out of the parking lot, I'm still watching those outgoing young boys tossing the football around and showing off for each other. *Why can't I be more like them?* I've been so painfully shy my whole life that I couldn't even stand up in front of the class to present a report until I was in high school, and even now I don't dare make eye contact with anyone in the class when I do because I freeze up and make everyone laugh. I can't even remember how often I've wished to be more like other boys I grew up with, the ones who shout greetings across the playing field and join in pick-up basketball or stand up in front of the class without trembling. I don't want to be selfish and careless like so many of my peers, but I'd give anything to be more confident.

We leave La Costa behind and turn down busy Dogwood Avenue toward the area near Kingston High School. Thanks to urban sprawl along that route, it's got lots of strip malls, gas stations, and convenience stores.

J.C. prattles on as he navigates the traffic. "You're like a freakin' X-Man, dude!"

He makes the ability to see how people are going to die sound like the power to fly or teleport or something actually cool.

I gave you a great gift, boy. Or maybe a curse. Had it so long I can't be sure no more.

We cruise past Kingston High with it's massive performing arts center dominating the campus. It looks so lonely with no kids around. But then I remind myself it's Sunday afternoon, so there wouldn't likely be people there anyway.

"Let's go to that coffee place next to Pet Palace," J.C. says, keeping his eyes on the road.

I nod, even though I really don't want to do this. I just want whatever Mr. Franklin gave me to go away.

"I couldn't die till I passed it on."

Does that mean I have to die in order to get rid of it?

We pass the Arco station and a Baskin-Robbins ice cream place. I have the sudden urge for a double-scoop chocolate ice cream cone. With everything that's happened in the past twenty-four hours, I don't want to be sixteen anymore. I want to be five, with chocolate ice cream dribbling down my shirt.

I watch people on the sidewalk casually going about their business and realize I could tell each of them when they're going to die. Assuming they believed me, how many of them would want to know?

Then another terrifying thought strikes me. *What will happen if I look into my own eyes in a mirror, like when I'm shaving?* I only need to shave maybe once a week at most, but if I accidentally look myself in the eye, will I see my own death? I mentally put my hand over my heart and swear to be really careful not to stare into my eyes next time I face a mirror. I don't want to know the future

J.C. pulls into a parking lot on our right. A Vons supermarket looms dead ahead, but he swings left past Pet Palace and slides into an empty space. He shuts off the engine, pulls the key out of the ignition, and then turns purposefully to face me.

"Okay," he says, the excitement in his voice palpable. "Let's go in the coffee place so you can check out the clerk."

"Okay." Despite my fear at what we're about to do, out of habit I snatch some granola bars from the center storage compartment and slip them into my pants pockets in case we spot any people who look homeless or hungry. We exit the car and J.C. clicks the "lock" button, pocketing my fob.

People come and go from Pet Palace. Right in front of the entrance is a large sign proclaiming, "Adopt A Dog Today!"

J.C. grabs my arm around the biceps and squeezes excitedly. "I got a better idea. We go in there and you look at people checking out the dogs. Piece of cake."

Easy for you to say, I think, while he drags me forward. I don't protest and allow him to lead me inside the store. Dogs barking and birds chirping replace traffic sounds, and musty animal scents assail my nostrils.

Adults and kids of various ages hover around a large temporary pen that houses five dogs. I notice a cool looking German Shepherd and maybe a Lassie-type dog—I've never had a dog, so breeds aren't my specialty. The others look real tiny, like Chihuahua size.

J.C. drags me forward to join the ogling crowd. A perky teen girl wearing a red Pet Palace polo shirt seems to be in charge, hovering about and answering questions in a high, chirpy voice. An old lady who, I swear, looks a hundred and fifty years old, holds a little dog in her arms. Maybe it's a poodle. Like I said, dogs aren't part of my life experience. The girl is saying something about shots and spaying, but I tune her out to lean in closer and check out the little animal. It seems content within the crook of the old lady's arm. She grins at me with yellowed teeth and wrinkles spreading outward around her mouth like cracks from an earthquake.

"Isn't she adorable?" the lady says, I guess because I'm leaning in so close.

I glance up. "Yeah. Real cute." I look into her eyes and see her death. My chest tightens, just as it had when I foresaw Hank's death. I stagger back.

J.C. turns me toward him and mouths, "Anything?"

I nod as someone bumps into me from behind. I turn to apologize and find myself gazing into the eyes of a kid who looks maybe twelve, but easily my height.

"Sorry," the boy says. "Just wanted to check out the shepherd. He's awesome, isn't he?"

He has hazel eyes, big and excited, filled with hopes and dreams. And death. I see it plain as day. This time it feels like a truck slammed into me. Seeing the death of a kid freaks me out.

"Yeah, he is," I mutter and almost leap back so he can scoot in closer.

I can't do this anymore.

"You okay, Leo?" J.C. stares at me with worry on his face. He grips my arm.

I don't even look his way. I pull back and scurry past the lines at the checkout stations. The glass doors slide open and I flee into the heat of the parking lot. Cars cruise past and a couple entering Pet Palace practically jog away from me, probably seeing my wide eyes and wild expression and thinking I'm crazy. Maybe I am.

I grip the row of shopping carts just outside the door and hold on tight. My head swims, I feel sick, and I wonder if I'm going to faint. J.C.'s arms surround me a moment later as I sag. He props me up against the carts and stands at my side while I fight to bring my ragged breathing under control.

"You okay?" His usual tart tone is gone. He sounds worried, even afraid.

I nod, without looking at his eyes. "Gotta catch my breath."

A couple of teen guys wearing board shorts and tank tops saunter past carrying large cups of coffee. They glance over with narrowed eyes and snigger. I realize that J.C. still has his arms wrapped around me.

"I'm okay, now. You can let go."

J.C. is glaring after the two guys as he releases me, and I regain my bearings. "Jerkwads," he mutters and turns back to me. "What did you see?"

I take a deep breath and expel it. My hands are trembling, so I thrust them into my pants pockets. "The old lady's gonna die in ten years, on January first."

His eyes widen to the size of ping-pong balls. "Really? She looks at least a hundred and twenty now."

I know he's trying to lighten my somber mood, but his joke doesn't help. "I think she just dies in her sleep, but I couldn't tell for sure."

"And the kid?" J.C. asks this as casually as if we were playing a game of Twenty Questions.

I shiver, both at his tone and at the memory of that boy. Those hazel eyes fill my mind's eye with their expectations of a long life. "He's gonna die when he's fifteen."

J.C. gasps and puts a hand over his mouth. He does that sometimes when he's really shocked. "How?"

I concentrate on what I saw in those eyes, but the details are hazy. "I think he gets run down by a car."

"Yeah?"

I nod. "While walking a dog. A German Shepherd."

"Holy crap! You really *can* see the future."

I'm torn up inside. The old lady doesn't worry me because it looks like she just dies from being old. But should I warn the kid, maybe tell him not to take that dog home? Would his parents think I'm crazy? Of course they would, and they'd probably get mad that I'm messing with their kid that way.

Make wise choices.

Would it be wise or foolish to warn that boy?

J.C. grips my arm again. "We've gotta find someone else who's gonna die sooner, so we can be sure."

I nod. He's right, even though he sounds callous. That's just how he's grown up, with a self-absorbed mother in a self-absorbed town. In La Costa, prestige is important, people aren't.

I wonder if maybe the old man gave me some crazy germ that's making me see things. Maybe Hank getting run down was just a fluke. Even though I dread it, I can't know for sure until something happens exactly the way I saw it.

J.C. leads me away from Pet Palace toward Coffee Cellar and hurries ahead to pull open the glass door. A couple of large umbrella tables with chairs around them adorn the left of the entrance, and several young people sit drinking from large colorful cups.

The pungent scent of brewing coffee assails my nostrils. I'm not a coffee fan. I find the smell intoxicatingly tempting, but the taste is just too bitter. A non-coffee Frappuccino on the other hand, is a different story.

J.C. is already at the counter as I enter. A guy stands behind the register taking his order. He's maybe high school or college age with wavy blond hair and picture-perfect features.

J.C. waves me forward with a sideways nod of his head. I purposely avoid the clerk's smiling face as he asks, "What can I get for you?"

I focus on the overhead menu. Selecting a caramel Frappuccino with whipped cream, I slip out my money to pay.

"That'll be five ninety-five," the guy says, his voice vibrant and pleasant.

I pull out a ten from my frayed wallet and hand it over. My hand shakes and I hope he doesn't notice. He reaches into the cash register for my change. I still haven't looked into his face, let alone his eyes. I focus on his nametag: Kyle. I feel a kick to the ankle and fight to keep my face neutral.

"Here's your change," the guy says with a smile. "Four dollars and five cents."

That's when I look up. His hand is outstretched with my change and he's smiling warmly. He has a beautiful smile. No question about that. I bet tons of girls have fallen for him. I shift my gaze upward and look straight into his pale blue eyes, and then stumble back in horror. I must look like I'm having a heart attack because his smile falters.

"Uh, you okay?"

I swallow hard and nod.

Glancing from me to J.C. and back, he reaches out farther with my money. "Your change."

My hand shakes so violently as I reach for the money that J.C. has to take it for me and place it into the palm of my hand. Kyle stares at us with wide eyes. A tip jar sits beside the register and, without taking my eyes off Kyle's confused face, I turn my hand over and hear the coins clink against glass as my change, bills included, drops in.

Still looking puzzled, Kyle says, "Uh, thanks, man. Appreciate the tip. I'll, uh, make your drinks." He hurries to the coffee machines and works on our order.

J.C. leans in to my ear. "What did you see?"

I shake my head. I can't say it. It's too horrible. I watch Kyle work. His bleach-blond hair makes me think he might be a surfer. Being so near the beach, that's likely. But his hands seem almost delicate, like maybe he plays piano. Does he? Does he have parents who love him? A girlfriend who'll be devastated when he's gone? I wonder what his career plans are, plans he'll never see come into being. I even think about what kind of music he's into. Cold envelopes me and I tremble like I'm inside a snowbank wearing only my underwear.

Light-headed, I stagger to a nearby table and sit down on a hard metal chair, dropping my head into my hands. I want to weep. I want to cry for this boy I don't even know. I sense movement as J.C. sits in the chair beside me and places one hand on my shoulder. I'm grateful he doesn't say anything.

I don't know how much time passes before I hear, "Hey guys, your order's ready."

J.C. slides out his chair and leaves the table. I keep my head down. I can't look at Kyle again. I just can't!

"Your friend okay?" I hear in Kyle's sonorous, but surprisingly gentle voice.

"Yeah," J.C. offers matter-of-factly. "Gets mean-ass migraine headaches."

I feel a hand on my shoulder and this time I look up. J.C. balances two cups in his other hand and looks down at me, lips twisted with worry. I take my drink with shaky fingers and rise unsteadily to my feet. I keep one hand on the table to maintain balance before glancing over at Kyle.

He's peering at me with what looks like genuine concern, as though we're best buds and he feels terrible that I'm unwell. "Hope you feel better, dude."

"Thanks, man." I turn and push my way through the glass door out into the hot afternoon sun.

J.C. follows, but doesn't say anything until we're back in my car sipping our drinks. My stomach feels queasy and I place my Frappuccino into the cup holder.

J.C. slurps his drink and waits till I'm ready. This is one of those moments I need a *lot* of time. Five minutes pass while I process everything I saw in Kyle's eyes. I know J.C. is about to jump out of his skin, so I finally whisper, "He's going to be shot."

"No way!" J.C. looks as shocked as I've ever seen him. "When?"

"Tuesday."

He gags on the sip he's taking. "You sure?"

I nod.

"Could you see where?"

I shake my head. "It was hazy. The gun went off and he was on the ground bleeding out."

"Oh, my God!" J.C. puts down his drink and we sit a moment in silence. He must know what I'm thinking because he says, "You can't warn him, Leo."

"Why not?"

He hesitates. "I don't know for sure, but maybe it's like he's supposed to die on Tuesday and if you warn him and he doesn't, then maybe you create some rift in time or something, like in X-Men comics."

J.C. is a major X-Men fan. Me, not so much.

"J.C., he's just a kid like us."

"I know." He pauses. "But what if you tell him now and on Tuesday he changes what he would normally do and because he changes his routine, that's why he gets shot."

Having had these geek conversations with him over the years about time travel and numerous "what if" scenarios, I understand what he's trying to tell me.

Make wise choices.

Was this what Mr. Franklin meant? That the choices I make to tell or not tell people what I see could be as significant as J.C. suggests?

"I'm serious, Leo," J.C. goes on, his voice tight with fear. "We need to leave it alone and see if anything happens to Kyle on Tuesday. If there's nothing on the news, we know you're not really Cyclops and maybe the old guy just messed with your head."

Cyclops is the X-Man who can shoot lasers from his eyes, but I'm not sure that's the most comforting analogy in this case.

Make wise choices.

How can I do that when I have no idea how this power works?

"Take me home, J.C.," I mutter, slumping back into the seat. I feel the weight of people's lives pressing in on my heart and soul and all I wanna do is sleep. If this is what being a mutant means, like in the X-Men comics, I understand why so many of them hate themselves.

We drive to my house in silence.

CHAPTER THREE

MOM, THIS IS REALLY IMPORTANT

LA Costa is a tiny beach town of narrow streets, large old houses, and maybe fifteen thousand people in the South Bay Area of Southern California. It goes way back to World War I and most of the original homes are Victorian style, like mine, or Queen Anne. Both styles are elaborate and ornate with gables and pitched roofs and latticework all around. Newer homes have sprung up over the years because I've seen a lot of style variations just in my neighborhood alone. Mrs. Santini, the school librarian, told me that this small town displays architectural styles representing almost every decade since 1918—when it was founded—up until the 1980s. No new homes have been built in the 21st Century because there's really no more room and the cliquey townspeople prefer to keep outsiders out.

I've lived here my whole life and I don't like it. Don't get me wrong—I'm grateful for everything I have—especially since I know first hand how poor people so many people are—and I want for nothing. I suppose I sound paranoid, like Holden Caulfield from *Catcher in the Rye*, but seriously, most people in this town are superficial. *Especially* my mom. She's a bigwig at one of the major film studios in L.A. and rakes in so much dough I can buy anything I want, including a boat or a plane. That's the truth. My mom always wants me to have "stuff," which I'm sure is just to keep me occupied so I won't bother her by like, you know, wanting to talk once in a while.

Mom's Jag is in the garage when J.C. slides my Prius in next to it. We get out and he eyes me with a furrowed brow. "You text me, Leo, if you start tripping out about the whole Kyle thing. K?"

I nod, still shaken and upset.

J.C. tosses me a supportive smile and saunters down my driveway to the sidewalk. He only lives on the next block over, so I don't feel bad about him having to walk home. I close the garage and enter the house.

My house has two floors, four bedrooms, a den, a living room, a family room, dining room, laundry room, kitchen, and five bathrooms, including one outside by the pool. All for just Mom and me. I never knew my dad. Mom says he took off after I was born because he wanted a girl, not a boy, and mom refused to have more kids. I guess it would have spoiled her ladder-climbing at the studio.

In any case, she's never let me get in the way of her success. I was always shunted off to daycare or parked with my nanny Estella when I was growing up. For a long time, I believed Estella was my real mom. In those days, Mom gave me video game systems to keep me out of her hair. Now it's iPads and smartphones and money to keep me busy. Most of the time she doesn't even realize I spend the money she gives me on the homeless people I work with. She's always texting me pictures of fancy, expensive cars and urges me to "junk" my Prius, but I just ignore her. With Mom, there's never any focus on me for more than five minutes, so I don't worry about her harping on anything for too long.

I step into our kitchen and hang my car keys on a peg next to the fridge. The kitchen is rectangular shaped, but seriously as long as a corridor at La Costa High. They could film one of those cooking shows in here. Plus, it's super high-tech with blue LED accent lights and everything voice or app activated. I'm not kidding. My mom *loves* to show off when she has Hollywood parties—during which I hide in my room and blast music through my headphones—by showing her actors and directors how she controls almost everything in the house from her phone. The recessed lights, the appliances, the air conditioning—you name it and it's controlled either by voice or an app on her phone.

Me, I just punch in the time on the microwave, but Mom will walk into the kitchen and tell the microwave how much time to cook while she messages people on her phone or scrolls through e-mails. Sylvia, our current housekeeper, knows Mom's routine to a tee and has the food already inside the microwave so my mother won't have to lower herself to actually take it out of the fridge and put it in there.

I confess that if this was someone else's kitchen, I'd probably think the gadgetry was cool and would want to play with it, which I did a lot when Mom first installed it. But since it's my house and my mother and she uses it to show off, I do my best to ignore it all.

My stomach roils with worry over Kyle and I open the fridge for a bottle of water (the fridge door, by the way, isn't voice activated yet, but Mom's working on that.) With only the slightest hum of the refrigerator for company, I gulp down the water in three swigs and toss the empty into the recycle bin, which we only have because I insisted. Mom talks "environmentalism" when it's needed to impress the Hollywood crowd, but otherwise couldn't be bothered recycling anything. I decide the best medicine for my unsettled mind is probably a strenuous workout.

I've taken both gymnastics and Aikido since I was little and have gotten really good at both. Mom put me in gymnastics so she'd have something to brag about, but she didn't count on having the shyest kid this side of a wallflower. The first time she put me in front of a crowd for a gymnastics competition, I froze and literally did nothing until the coach came out and escorted me off the floor. I still feel the embarrassment of that silent crowd just staring at me. And I still see the look on Mom's face as she glowered. It would've driven off a serial killer.

As I approach the stairs to go up to my room, Kyle's face keeps intruding, like, every few seconds, and I can't stop churning with anxiety. So I pause at the bottom of the stairs and then impulsively do something I'd long ago stopped doing—I go looking for Mom. I feel like I need her more now than at any other time in my life.

Naturally, I find her in the study, which sounds like a cozy room with books, but Mom's study is a den-sized chamber with a huge, sharp-cornered, oak desk parked in front of a wall adorned with framed movie posters, mostly rom-com stuff she produced. The desk takes up half the room and the LED computer monitor takes up half the desk. She's sitting in front of it, switching back and forth between typing on the keyboard and texting on her phone. My mom almost looks the same as she did before I was born. I've seen photos, so I know. Of course, she's had tons of work done (as they say in show business) and often jokes about it with friends.

"A nip here, a tuck there, and aging becomes a thing of the past."

She's forty-five, but looks twenty-five, with auburn hair down past her shoulders, a small nose, full lips and strikingly alert brown eyes. There's no way she can photograph poorly. Again, I've seen tons of pictures and no matter what she's doing, she looks beautiful.

Being that attractive, she's had all manner of boyfriends over the years, but never married any of them. I liked some of those guys. They talked to me more often than she did and some, I think, actually enjoyed playing with me.

Lots of her Hollywood friends say I look like her—same auburn hair, only mine just brushes my collar, same soft features and full lips—and insist that I should be modeling or in the movies because I'm "such a beautiful boy." For all I know, it was Mom's bragging about her "beautiful son" that turned me inward toward debilitating shyness. Most of the kids in La Costa are attention-seeking selfie fiends. Me, I want fame like I want cancer.

"Mom?"

She doesn't look up from her phone. "Have a nice day, Leonardo?"

Other than Mrs. Santini, Mom is the only person who calls me by my full name. "Yeah. I was downtown at the rescue mission."

She frowns at something. I hear the beep of an incoming text and her fingers and thumbs fly so fast in reply I almost can't see them. "You waste too much time down there, Leonardo. I've told you that before. You should be partying with your friends."

I nearly sigh. This is probably a mistake. But I really need an adult right now. I have to make her listen to me. "J.C. is my only friend and he doesn't party, either."

She sets down the phone as her computer beeps with an incoming Facebook message. She skitters her fingers across the keyboard in response. "You boys spend too much time together. People are talking."

I burn red and my anger starts to rise. I guess I'm considered passive because I almost never lose my temper. But these rumors about me and J.C. are getting out of hand. "He's my best friend, Mom. I have no one else to hang out with."

She grunts as the typing continues. The *clack clack clack* breaks the silence of the room.

"Mom, something happened to me this weekend."

Mom curses. She does that a lot. "You know I have this deal to lock in," she mutters while pounding the keys with her fingertips.

"Mom, this is really important." My voice comes out a raspy whisper.

"So is this deal. Damn!" She snatches up her phone and punches in a message of some kind.

I feel tears building up within me. I haven't cried since I was little. But everything that's happened to me this weekend is taking its toll and I feel like I'm breaking in two. "Mom, I really need you to be a mom right now."

She glances over at me, an exasperated look on her perfectly made-up face. "You need to talk about something, Leonardo?"

I nod.

She sighs loudly, as though me needing to talk is the height of rudeness. "Okay."

Relieved beyond measure, I'm about to plunge into my story when she scrolls through her phone and says, "How about Wednesday night, eight o'clock. Put it into your phone so we're synced. You'll have my undivided attention. How's that sound?" She offers one of her famous deal-closing smiles that are legendary within the industry.

My eyes well with tears and my entire body coils for flight. I nod because I can't trust myself to speak.

Wednesday.

Kyle will be dead by then.

She returns her attention to the computer screen and I spin around to leave. No way will I let her see me cry! I don't think I've ever felt as rejected as I do at that moment, and trust me, I've been rejected *plenty* of times. I flee the office and run upstairs to my bedroom.

I'm crying full on by the time I shuck off my clothes, throw on workout shorts and a tank top, then run down the stairs and into the training room Mom set up for me when she thought I'd be a gymnastics star. Like everything else in the house, the equipment is state of the art. I have parallel bars, rings, a large mat for floor routines, and multiple punching dummies. The UCLA gymnastics team could train here!

It takes me thirty minutes of pounding the punching dummy with my Aikido staff and another twenty doing multiple routines on the parallel bars before I feel at least some semblance of control. Dripping with sweat and drained of energy, I trudge upstairs to shower in my pristine, white-tiled bathroom, and then I crash onto my king-sized bed. I don't even eat dinner.

La Costa High was built in the 1920s, shortly after the town was founded. The buildings are pretty retro, obviously, but improvements have been made over the years, so some parts of the campus look ancient with art deco style buildings, like Wayne Tower in *Batman Begins*, one of J.C.'s favorite movies. Other parts of the school are very 21st Century with lots of glass and steel.

I slog my way through my morning classes with J.C. silently by my side. Like I said before, he knows me well enough to know when not to talk, and today is such a day. Last night's scene with my mom weighs me down more than it should. I don't know why I ever imagined she might actually listen, but her rejection knocked the wind out of me. I told J.C. about the incident and he nodded sympathetically. His mom is the same, so there's no need for details.

I also can't free my mind of Kyle's smiling face and concerned look. It makes me think he's the kind of guy I'd like if I got to know him. I have to fight the urge to leave campus, return to Coffee Cellar, and warn him. But what if he isn't on duty? More importantly, what if J.C. is right? Could I actually get him killed by warning him? Is that how this "gift" works?

Just before the bell rings for lunch, Principal Harris's deep voice bellows through the loudspeaker system, a painful everyday occurrence. I think he must be a huge fan of that movie, *Good Morning, Vietnam*, which I've seen in history class, because he comes on the loudspeaker multiple times daily to crack jokes or dispense what he calls "homespun wisdom." As everyone at Costa High knows, he grew up on a farm in Iowa and repeatedly says stuff like, "Education is like planting seeds to feed people in the future." He also regales us with endless tales of various farm animals he's cared for.

"Good morning, Costa High!" Harris's voice pounds through the wall speaker in my American Lit class at exactly 11:55 on the dot. You can tell the time by Principal Harris and that's no joke. "As you prepare to replenish your weary brains and empty stomachs in our award-winning cafeteria," he goes on as though announcing that the president is about to visit, "keep this bit of wisdom in mind—a pig in the hand is worth two in the stomach."

He laughs and my fellow students groan. J.C. glances over and rolls his eyes. I look away quickly.

"Just a little farm humor, girls and boys," Mr. Harris continues with a hearty laugh. "Seriously, don't forget there's a surf team meeting during lunch in Coach Wyler's room and an ASB meeting with Ms. Carter. You may bring your lunch to both meetings, but remember your manners and don't litter or mess up their rooms. A clean house is a happy house. Later, kiddos!"

The speaker clicks off with a kind of *thud* as kids shake their heads and roll their eyes. Even after three years as principal, Harris never ceases to amaze me with his soporific inanities. The bell rings and we are dismissed.

The cafeteria was remodeled before I came to Costa High and it's very modern with recessed lighting, fancy round tables made of high-tech metal that's pretty scratch resistant against wannabe taggers, and scads of windows to give it an almost open-air feel. We order our food at kiosks situated around the campus, so by the time we enter the actual cafeteria building the food will be ready and no one needs to wait in line. Despite being a small school, Costa is a rich one, so I guess they figured, why not?

J.C. is one of the few minority kids at this school and there's plenty of racism on display every day. Most kids, though they talk about J.C. behind his back, avoid pissing him off because of his mom being mayor and all. But not Chet Hamilton and his posse. They also punk me for being shy and for spending all my time with J.C. I guess every school has a Chet Hamilton, but not every Chet Hamilton has a mother who's the town chief-of-police.

As I enter the cafeteria to collect the chicken burrito I ordered, I spot Chet and his boys hovering around one of the tables as far from the cafeteria workers as you can get. Harris said something about a surf team meeting, but I guess Chet and crew don't care if they're late.

I nudge J.C. and point. He tosses me a grin and veers out of the short line toward Chet because he loves thwarting him whenever possible, I guess to make up for all the bullying Chet did to us in elementary. As always, I follow.

"Well, well, what have we here?" J.C. says, full on snark in his voice. "I didn't see pig on the menu today, so you must be here to bully someone, eh, Hamilton?"

White-blond hair practically glowing beneath the bright cafeteria lights, Chet's thin lips twist into an arrogant snarl. "Well if it isn't the resident Mexican and his Ninja Turtle boyfriend."

I stay calm, but J.C. flinches. I glance at the table to see today's victim and note it's the new girl. She's in my grade, but only transferred into Costa High this semester. Needless to say, I've never talked to her and haven't given her much of a looksee until now. With a short pixie-style blonde do and milky white skin, she's pretty, but not photo perfect. She's dressed kind of grunge, like she doesn't care if her clothes match or not, which I like since I'm the same way. Her pursed lips indicate her obvious annoyance at Chet's presence.

"Ordinarily," Chet goes on in his smarmy tone, "you queer boys wouldn't be interested in a girl, but since Laura, here, is a lesbo, you all have something in common." He chuckles. His two lackeys join him and one of them, another junior named Matt Wilson, offers a high five.

Chet is like a high school stereotype—built as hell from surfing and as narcissistic as they come. Even by Costa High standards, Chet's narcissism soars into the stratosphere. And he's a bully. It's almost like he's watched all the famous "bully" movies and decided to one-up them.

Wilson and Grady, the other spokes of the wheel, are almost as bad and almost as good looking. I have to admit, they're pretty badass surfers—Costa High always gives the larger beach cities a run for their money in the surfing department—but they are also supreme jerkwads.

"These guys giving you a hard time?" J.C. says to the girl in that very smooth Latino way he has. He keeps his thick, wavy black hair styled to the side and never dresses in anything but the latest fashionable styles.

She shrugs. "Nah. They're pretty boring."

Chet looks momentarily stung, but quickly regains his arrogant veneer. "She can't handle real men."

"Is that what you are?" Laura replies, her eyes wide with mock under-standing. "You act more like my brother's friends."

"How old are they?" Wilson asks with a smirk.

"Kindergarten."

J.C. busts up and offers Laura a high five. She slaps his hand and glowers at Chet.

Chet glowers right back. "Of course, a lesbo wouldn't be interested in men."

"She tell you she's a lesbian, Hamilton?" J.C. asks, his tone laced with derision.

He shrugs. "She's not interested in me, so she's gotta be."

Wilson and Grady chuckle and Chet flashes his killer grin.

J.C. smirks. "Wow. You come up with that line all by yourself, Hamilton, or did your homies help?"

Laura laughs and Chet turns to me. "What're you looking at, Ninja Turtle?"

I glance down, like I always do.

Chet lowers his voice to J.C., but I still hear every word. "Your mother might be mayor, Juan Carlos," he says, making sure the "Juan Carlos" sounds as Anglicized as possible. J.C. wants people to roll the R properly, but most never do, and Chet knows that. "But she can't protect you twenty-four seven. One of these days I'm gonna make you pay."

J.C. isn't cowed in the least. "Is that a threat? Maybe my mom will order your mom to arrest your ass. Wouldn't that be cozy?"

Chet smiles nastily. "Never happen, Mexican. You're just lucky your mom is mayor. For the moment. One day she'll be termed out and I'll be free to close your big mouth for good."

"I'm so scared," J.C. says, his voice an exaggerated warble. Then he gives a dramatic shiver.

Chet leans in so close I think he might kiss J.C. "The only reason your whore mother beat out mine for mayor was 'cause she screwed every guy in La Costa."

J.C.'s brown skin turns deathly pale, like all the color ran out of his face. He snatches up a plastic knife from the table beside Laura's food and plants it against Chet's throat.

Chet laughs. "Try it. I dare you. I want a reason to beat you senseless."

I release my breath and step closer. "Uh, J.C., back off, man."

He doesn't acknowledge me. Neither does Chet. They mad-dog each other something fierce.

"Kick his ass, Chet," Wilson goads, looking excited and pumped up for action.

"Get lost, Hamilton," Laura says as she stands beside J.C. and faces Chet.

Time seems to stand still. Silence has fallen over the entire cafeteria and I feel every set of eyes pinned to us. With my Aikido skills, I could easily stop both of them without anyone getting hurt and I'm reaching out to do just that when I hear, "I'll take the knife, J.C."

Mr. Harris!

I whirl as the principal strides forward like a linebacker and pushes his way between J.C. and Chet. He's a big man who, as he's told us kids a thousand times, played high school football, and he often uses the advantage of height and weight for incidents of this type. He sports his usual dark suit and loud tie. I'm vaguely aware that today's tie is a yellow so bright it could put the sun to shame.

A campus safety officer trails behind him as Harris extends his hand to J.C. My best friend tosses one more baleful glare at Chet before dropping the plastic knife into Harris's open hand with an exaggerated sigh. This isn't the first time the principal has intervened in a conflict between Chet and J.C. and I'm sure it won't be the last.

Harris shakes his head as though bemused. "My office, J.C."

J.C. points at Chet, standing beside the safety officer. "But he—"

"Save it for my office. I always find your stories amusing." Harris glances over at me and I make sure not to look him in the eye. "You too, Leo. You're a matched set."

He lifts one hand above his head and snaps his fingers. "Show's over, kiddies," he announces to the cafeteria at large. Everyone is sitting or standing in silence gawking at the scene. "Finish your lunch. Next period starts in twenty."

He waves a hand for us to lead the way. I glance at J.C., who looks furious, and then head toward the exit. J.C. follows and Principal Harris brings up the rear.

Chet's chuckle makes me burn with anger, but I don't dare turn around to confront him. And my rumbling stomach reminds me that I never even got my food.

CHAPTER FOUR

I FEEL LIKE A MURDERER

Mr. HARRIS'S OFFICE LOOKS LIKE A cross between that of a high school principal and a farmer. Certificates of accomplishment or praise adorn his walls alongside images of the countryside or animals grazing in a field. One photo depicts a huge barn with a curved roof surrounded by grass and he told me on previous visits it was on the farm in Iowa where he grew up.

J.C. slouches in one straight-backed chair and I'm in the other. Harris sits across his burnished desk from us, hands clasped together like he's praying. The impeccably neat desk is decorated with little animal figurines and a large collection of fancy pens in some kind of cup. He unclasps his hands to swig from a high-end metal water bottle as he regards us in silence. This is his standard tactic, to unnerve the kid with a stony silence before the boom falls. J.C. and me have been down this road so many times I could recite the coming script by heart.

Harris sets his bottle delicately onto a coaster and presses back into his leather chair, re-clasping his hands and steepling his fingers. "What am I going to do with you boys?"

J.C. glowers over the backpack planted in his lap. "He was messing with the new chick and he talked trash about my mom."

"It's common knowledge that you talk trash about your mom, too."

"Yeah, but I'm allowed to. Not that piece of—"

Harris holds up a well-manicured hand. I've never seen such perfect nails on a guy. "No cursing, J.C. You know that's not nice."

"You always take Hamilton's side."

Harris looks neutral. "Other than you two, no one ever accuses Chet Hamilton of bullying. Even the new girl you mentioned hasn't said a word."

"They're afraid to, sir," I offer, keeping my voice as steady as I can. My gaze is lowered, like always. I know every speck of dirt on my Nikes, that's for sure.

Harris sighs. "We've had this discussion many times before. If any adult witnesses Chet Hamilton bullying another student, Chet will be disciplined. But that hasn't happened."

"Because he doesn't do physical stuff anymore like he did when we were little," J.C. insists, and I hear the frustration in his voice. "Now it's all nasty taunts and insults."

"That may be true, J.C., but since his mother is police chief, I'd better have real evidence before suspending him."

"Our word isn't enough?" J.C. spits back. The derision in his voice is palpable.

"Sadly, no. Kids, as you well know, lie all too often, especially nowadays."

"And adults don't?" J.C. is almost trembling with rage.

I lean forward. "Mr. Harris, I don't lie, do I?"

Harris gives me a long look. I keep my eyes averted and only see him peripherally. "I don't know, Leo. Do you?"

I don't answer. He knows the truth. I have an excellent reputation among the teachers for honesty, but Harris doesn't want to make waves. He never does.

"You better not suspend me," J.C. pipes up. "You know my mom is beloved by the school board."

Harris chuckles. "I know that all too well, J.C. And you know I decry suspension as a punishment in almost all cases. Very ineffective. There are far better methods for dealing with arrogant, recalcitrant kids." J.C. sits up straight and opens his mouth to speak, but Harris raises a hand to cut him off. "However, I'm not going to employ them at this time."

J.C. pauses with his mouth open.

"Despite you threatening another student with a weapon, J.C., I'm going to let you off with a warning. Be nice to Chet Hamilton and he'll be nice to you. That's how the world works. Wouldn't you agree, Leo?"

J.C. looks like he's having a stroke.

I place one hand on his arm and squeeze. "Uh, sure. Whatever you say, Mr. Harris."

Harris grins. "There, you see, Leo? You do lie."

I burn with embarrassment.

Harris stands and ushers us to the door. "Let's all get along, shall we, boys? It makes life so much easier."

He opens the door and J.C. storms out. Harris pats me on the back and smiles. I hurry after J.C.

I let J.C. vent after school about what a "dweeb" Harris is and how "he just kisses ass to keep his job."

I remind him that's how the world works—rich people have all the power and a guy like Harris has to do whatever it takes to stay employed.

My mind remains fixated on what will happen the next day to Kyle, so to quell my fears and anxieties I engage in another hard routine in my workout room before dinner. Mom isn't home, as usual, but Sylvia has prepared some chicken, rice, and salad for me. An incredibly sweet, middle-aged lady, Sylvia lives in the city of Hawthorne when she isn't taking care of me and doing all the cooking and cleaning. She feels more like a mother than my real one, just like Estella did when I was little.

I troll the Internet until after midnight, searching with increasing desperation to any clues about this "gift" I supposedly have. The old man hinted that it's something passed on from one person to another. Depending on how long he had it, maybe there's someone else before him who was alive during the rise of the Internet and posted about it. I type in every key word I can think of, and tons of phrases like "ability to see when someone will die," but I only come up with fictional "what-if" scenarios, and none of those are helpful in the slightest. I'm still keyed up with worry when I log-off and climb into bed.

When I finally sleep, I'm plagued by images of guns firing and Kyle's handsome face twisted into a death mask. I wake up the next day so drained and on edge that I call J.C. to ask for a ride because I don't feel steady enough to drive.

"Like you gotta ask, bro?"

I thank him and get my stuff together.

To say that I can't concentrate would be an understatement. At every passing period, I check local news on my phone for anything about a young guy being gunned down, but nothing materializes. I'm both grateful and worried. What would it mean if Kyle survives this day? Do I really have that "gift" the old man said he gave me, or was he delusional? I know I felt something when he locked eyes with mine, but could it have been my imagination since I never lock eyes with anyone and don't know what it feels like?

J.C. hovers by my side like always. Chet Hamilton passes us in the hall and blows a kiss, generating laughter from other kids. J.C. turns to say something, but I grab his arm and drag him to our next class.

By the end of the day, I've managed to avoid any more run-ins with Chet and there's been no shooting story on the news. I begin to feel relieved until I recall exactly what I saw when I looked into Kyle's eyes—it was dark when he got shot. That means it won't happen until tonight.

J.C. insists on staying with me, which means he'll have to sleep over because of school tomorrow. His mom won't notice and neither will mine.

We have essays to write for American Lit, but I can't focus and, therefore, neither can he. We make dinner together, not because I'm hungry, but to give me something to do. I tell Sylvia she can go home early because she works so hard.

"Are you sure, Leo?" She looks concerned. "When my boy was your age, if I let him, he'd only eat junk food." She offers a smile, and that look of concern in her eyes is one I long for in my mother's.

I return the smile, even though it's the last thing I feel like doing. "It's cool, Sylvia. Me and J.C. will make something healthy. I promise." She thanks me for the early release and heads out the front door.

The kitchen looks like a hurricane hit by the time we finish making something that vaguely resembles my favorite food, lasagna, but Sylvia will forgive me, I know. We manage to get the place reasonably clean, which also helps my mood because it's physical labor and moving my body always calms me whenever I'm anxious or disheartened.

I put together some semblance of an essay on *The Great Gatsby* and J.C.

finishes his rough draft, as well. By then it's time for the eleven o'clock news, so we click on the flat screen in my bedroom and sit side-by-side on the edge of my bed to watch. The first story involves an earthquake that struck earlier in the evening out by Riverside. We didn't feel anything at my house, but the newscaster says people in San Diego got a good jolt.

I glance at J.C. and note him watching me, not the news. "Usually shootings are the lead stories, right?"

He shrugs. "The news isn't my thing."

We resume watching. Since J.C. is staying over, both of us have changed into workout shorts for sleeping, plus a tank top for me and a tee shirt for him. The news continues droning on in the background, but I mostly tune it out because my mind swirls with uncertainties. I hear an update on a missing teen from Hermosa Beach who vanished six months ago, but I can't really focus on that story. I seem to recall that several kids have vanished from South Bay high schools over the past few years, but it's old news and not on my radar. I hold a glass of water in my hand and am taking a swig when the newscaster intones gravely, "We have a breaking news story out of Manhatten Beach."

I freeze, the glass inches from my lips, and watch as the flat screen fills with images of flashing lights, police vehicles, and spectators behind yellow caution tape. A man with a microphone stands in front of the camera. Under him the caption reads, "Miguel Rosales, KTLA News."

"Here's what we know so far," he says in that dispassionate tone these guys always employ.

I feel J.C.'s eyes on me, but I can't pull my gaze from the screen.

"At approximately ten-forty-five tonight," Rosales drones on, "just prior to closing time at the Coffee Cellar, an unknown assailant confronted and shot the clerk before fleeing. The victim was pronounced dead at the scene. It appears the motive was robbery."

The camera zooms into the Coffee Cellar entrance. J.C. gasps, and the glass of water slides from my hand to bounce onto the plush carpet beside my bare feet. The water splashes my feet, but I pay no attention.

"Coffee Cellar owner, Mitch Vicenza, had left for the night, leaving the nineteen-year-old to close," Rosales continues. "The victim has been identified as Kyle Worthington of Redondo Beach."

A photo of Kyle's smiling, handsome face appears on screen. I gag and my breathing becomes ragged.

J.C. clicks off the TV and scoots to my side, wrapping an arm around my shoulders and reading my mind like always. "This isn't your fault."

Tears well in my eyes and I shake my head. "I should've warned him."

"I told you not to. If you wanna blame somebody, blame me."

I fight the tears, but can't stop them entirely. I feel like I pulled that trigger and ended Kyle's life. I guess that's crazy, but I can't help how I feel. "No. It was my call, my choice, like the old man said."

J.C. squeezes me closer and I have to confess it feels good to have someone hug me, even a side hug. I can't remember the last time my mother hugged me. Maybe I was three or four.

"You said that guy told you to make wise choices," J.C. goes on, his voice soothing for once. "You chose not to say anything because it might have made Kyle act differently."

I nod. "But it might also have made him decide to stay home from work today."

There's a moment of silence between us. Then J.C. says, "And then he might have gotten shot on the street by somebody wanting his wallet or something."

I look over at him in surprise, careful to avoid his eyes. "What are you saying? That he was going to get shot no matter what I did?"

He releases my shoulder and faces me. "It's possible, right?"

The tightness in my chest eases. "Yeah." I still feel guilty. Guess that's my nature. But now I know for sure. The power *is* real. I *can't* look anyone in the eyes ever again.

Fatigue overwhelms me and I want to fall asleep right where I am. I guess the stress of worrying all day has finally hit because I can't keep my eyes open. "I'm burnt, J.C. Gotta crash. Sorry, man."

"I get that. You've been freaking out for two days."

I nod and stand. The glass lies on its side and a dark stain spreads outward from my feet across the maroon carpet. Just water, my brain reminds me. It'll dry. But I don't even pick up the glass.

Feeling like I've been doing gymnastics for six hours straight, I drop onto my bed and throw myself face down on the pillow. "Thanks, J.C., for being here," I mutter into the clean-smelling pillowcase.

"Always," I hear, as though from far away because I'm gone and never even hear J.C. leave the room.

I wake up shaking. My eyelids feel like they've been sealed with superglue. I force them open to find J.C. pushing me hard.

"Time to get up for school, dude."

My overhead light is on. My backpack sits on the floor beside J.C. He's fully clothed in designer jeans, leather belt, a long-sleeved blue shirt with the cuffs rolled up, and dark blue loafers.

I sit up to get my bearings. Had I even dreamed? I don't think so. And then everything comes back. I sag back against my headboard. "It happened, didn't it?"

J.C. nods, biting his lip.

My stomach twists and churns. "I don't know if I can handle school, J.C."

"We gotta go. Harris'll call your mom for sure."

That wakes me up. Last thing I want now is to talk to my mother about all this, not after she blew me off when I really needed her. But I do need someone. An adult I can trust. And then it comes to me—Mrs. Santini! I spend so much time in the school library that she's almost another mom like Sylvia.

"Okay. I'm gonna talk to Mrs. Santini about… well, everything, and see what she says."

J.C. frowns. "Uh, not sure that's a good idea. What if she snitches?"

"She won't if I ask her not to. I hafta get some input from a grownup, you know?"

"I get that." He pauses and looks at me with wide eyes, which I avoid. "It's real, Leo. The power is real. You *are* an X-Man."

"I feel like a murderer, not a superhero."

He places one hand on my shoulder. "You're the biggest superhero I know."

I'm stunned and can't speak. I don't respond well to praise—it's another thing that goes along with being extremely shy. I know everything about shyness by now, except how to cure it.

"I got breakfast ready downstairs," J. C. adds with a grin. "Throw on some clothes and come on down."

I offer a grateful smile and he leaves the room.

We arrive at school forty-five minutes early, before the coastal fog has even begun to burn away. We've come early so I can catch Mrs. Santini before she gets too busy. I'm not sure if being shy drew me into reading, but I've always loved books and spent tons of time in all my school libraries. I'm probably Mrs. Santini's most frequent customer. She's an older lady who lives in a town just east of La Costa and has been head librarian for the La Costa Unified School District for, like, well, forever, I think. At least as long as I've been alive. She knew about me before I ever entered Costa High because the elementary and middle school librarians talked about me. I really hope she can help me with my problem.

"You're here early," Mrs. Santini says behind a big grin as I step into the library. J.C. hangs around in the outside quad area waiting for me. He isn't much into books unless they're fashion-related.

The La Costa library is like the school itself—equal parts retro and modern. There's a bank of computers used to locate specific titles, and for Internet access, of course. Half of the library still contains physical books, which I love, but the other half, to my dismay, is going "digital," which means a vast number of books can only be read in ebook form. Sadly, the school board plans to phase out all the physical books and make everything digital. I hope I'm long gone before that happens.

Mrs. Santini wears her hair in a kind of beehive do and favors dresses of pale hues. She's never worn pants as long as I've known her. Her tan face sports minimal makeup and her smile accentuates broad laugh lines around the eyes.

I make my way to the counter and glance at the books she's sorting. I've read all of them. The desk behind her is impeccably neat, with a plastic blotter covering the burnished wood top, a lamp that looks like it came from an old movie about a newspaper office, and a large wooden organizer filled with pens, pencils, paper clips, and other office stuff. There are also several chairs, including one for her computer station, set off to the side.

Now that I'm here, I hesitate. I honestly don't even know where to begin, not because I think she might snitch like J.C. said, but because I fear she just won't believe me.

"You look troubled, Leonardo. Anything I can help with?"

"I hope so."

She invites me to sit behind the counter with her and pulls two chairs over to the desk. Once we're seated, with her round, expectant face awaiting my story, I spill my guts, starting with the old man at the homeless shelter. She listens attentively and reacts with sympathy when I describe Kyle's murder.

"I heard about that young man on the news today," she offers sympathetically when I'm done. "So tragic."

I open my mouth and then pause. I can't go on.

"You blame yourself for not warning him."

I look up, but instantly avert my eyes. "You believe me about being able to see when people die?"

She tilts her head and regards me with intensity. "Have you ever lied to me, Leonardo?"

I shake my head.

"So why wouldn't I believe you?"

"Because it sounds crazy."

"There are more things in heaven and earth, Horatio, than are dreamt of in your philosophy."

"Hamlet," I mutter, recalling that line because it's always stuck with me.

"Written around 1600," Mrs. Santini goes on in her quiet voice. I guess being a librarian, she knows how to talk without ever raising her voice above a semi-loud whisper. "And just as true today."

"Why me? Why did that man give this to me? I didn't want it."

"Didn't you say he'd been watching you on the streets?"

"Yeah? So?"

She offers me the nicest smile I think I've ever seen on anyone. "So he obviously saw what I've seen for the past three years."

Confused, I make sure not to look directly into her face. "What's that?"

"That you are one of the most decent human beings on this planet, Leonardo Cantrell," she replies in a strong, sincere tone of voice.

I stiffen with shock.

"I mean that with every ounce of my being," she goes on. "I don't know why you're different from the others, why you don't have the self-absorption gene that permeates the very fabric of this town, but you don't. You're a giving person, someone who puts the needs of others first. Mr. Franklin saw that quality and that's why he chose you. He knew you would never abuse the power or use it to further your own ends. He knew you would use it wisely."

I sit rigid during her speech and only when she finishes do I realize I've been holding my breath. My eyes well with tears. Seriously, I get so choked up I think I'll start bawling right there in the library. I barely manage to choke out, "No one's ever said anything like that to me before." I'm trembling with emotion.

"That's why I said it. Because you need to hear it. You're such a good person, Leonardo. I wish you could see that."

I sit a long moment in silence, absorbing her words. I've never thought of myself as a good or bad person, just someone who's insanely shy and a misfit. "But what am I supposed to do about this, Mrs. Santini? I can't look at people anymore even if I want to."

"You'll find a way. That man made the right choice."

I choke up again. Damn! I don't want to cry like a baby in front of her or anyone else. Fortunately, J.C. enters at that moment and I use the sleeve of my hoodie to wipe away the dampness around my eyes.

Mrs. Santini stands to greet J.C. "Well, as I live and breathe. It's J.C. Rivera entering my library for what… the third time in three years?"

J.C. looks worried and I know it's about me. "Just checking on my boy." He looks my way. "You good?"

I nod.

"Uh, it's almost time for class."

I glance at Mrs. Santini.

"Scoot now." she says fondly, like we're back in elementary school. "But remember what I said, Leonardo."

"I will. Thanks." I hurry around the counter to join J.C.

As we turn to leave, Mrs. Santini says, "J.C.?"

We both turn back.

"Take good care of him."

J.C. looks confused, but nods. "I will." Then we push through the double doors into the crowded hallway.

J.C. leans in and whispers, "What did she say about, well, everything?"

Students brush past us on their way to class and the chattering voices make it hard to hear.

"I'll tell you later," I reply and we head to our first class.

I keep Mrs. Santini's words in my mind and heart as I suffer through Algebra 2, Chemistry, and Art History, but I still feel guilty about Kyle, and his murder weighs me down. I don't think I hear a word my teachers say in any class. J.C. isn't the best note-taker, but I know he'll share whatever he has with me.

By the time lunch rolls around, I've made a decision, what I consider a very wise decision: I will never look into anyone's eyes again. Ever. I'm shy anyway and no one expects me to look at them, so this plan should work.

But then Chet Hamilton makes me look into J.C.'s eyes and my world turns upside down.

CHAPTER FIVE

WHY DID YOU MAKE ME LOOK?

J.C. AND I TAKE OUR USUAL lunch table all the way at the back of the cafeteria where we can avoid the Chet Pack. After what Harris said, I don't want any more trouble. At first, it looks like my strategy has worked. I manage to tell J.C. what Mrs. Santini said, but I don't use all the huge complimentary words she did to describe me because, well, I don't feel special in the least.

But J.C. shocks me when he says, "She's right about you, Leo."

Just about to take a bite of my burrito, I freeze, my mouth open, the burrito hovering in midair like a plane coming in for a landing. Then I hear, "Hi, guys."

Startled, I look up to see Laura, the new girl, standing there with a tray of food in her hands.

J.C. breaks into a huge grin. "Hey, new girl, welcome. Have a seat."

She cracks a smile and sets down her tray before sitting. J.C. can be equally charming and annoying. Right now, he's going for charming.

"Hi," I mutter because I don't want to seem impolite.

She offers me a smile that I like. It seems genuine. "I never got to thank you for helping me the other day."

"No sweat," J.C. says with a wave of his hand.

She glances at me. "Did, uh, you guys get in trouble with the principal?"

J.C. chuckles. "No way. My mom's mayor of this crappy little town. I can do whatever I want."

She frowns. "Another cocky rich boy. I thought you guys were different." She grabs her tray and stands.

"Wait." That's me. Did I just speak up? "Uh, J.C.'s really not that bad."

She gives me a long, appraising look that makes me squirm. "You're not like him. Or the others." She resumes her seat and replaces her tray on the table. "Why do you hang around him?" She tosses a thumb at J.C. who, even from the corner of my eye, looks really offended.

I set down my burrito and look at her as directly as I can, which means at her nose. It's a nice-shaped nose, by the way, if, you know, noses are your thing. "J.C. is my only friend. He lets me be me. The snark is for all the jerk-wads in town."

She considers my answer and then turns to J.C. "That true, rich boy?"

He shrugs. "Pretty much. I hang with Leo and don't play their games." He indicates the rest of the kids around us eating and gossiping. "Plus, being Mexican, I get a lot of crap from these kids."

She nods and takes a bite of her salad.

J.C. gazes at her appraisingly. "So, what's *your* story?"

She shrugs. "My parents are rich, too, but to me, it's a whatever. I was going to school in San Diego, but my dad wanted to make more money in L.A., so we moved. He's an entertainment lawyer." She says that last part with her nose in the air and in an exaggerated tone of voice. Then she scrunches her face into one of disgust. "And they wanted to get me away from my girl-friend."

J.C. spits out his orange juice, right onto the table. I'm serious. Just like in the movies. Laura scoots away in disgust and I actually smile at the look of shock on my friend's face.

"For real?" J.C. has his mouth open like he expects someone to shove a donut into it. "How did Hamilton know?"

"He doesn't. With idiots like that, throwing out the 'queer' label is always their first line of attack."

"Speaking of which," I mumble under my breath as I spot the Chet Pack heading our way.

"Oh, crap," J.C. mutters.

"Don't let him get to you," I say, hoping my urgent tone comes across.

"He's right," Laura says quietly, pointedly ignoring Chet and his crew as they sit one table over.

Their choice of table isn't by accident or out of necessity. There are at least fifteen empty tables. They're here to start trouble.

I eat my food while watching them from the corner of my eye. They sport surf team letter jackets, unbuttoned to reveal tight compression shirts that accentuate their muscular chests and abs. Chet drops his tray onto the table. Hard. The *slam* draws the eyes of other kids in the surrounding area, but we ignore it.

I'm finishing my burrito and reaching for my bottle of juice when I hear Chet say quietly, "Isn't it cool that the queers stick together? I think we should ask Principal Harris to name that table "the queer table." What'chu guys think?"

J.C. sucks in a loud breath as Wilson and Grady high-five Chet. I shake my head at J.C. just as he's about to say something. Laura does the same. J.C. gets the message and closes his mouth. I slide my French fries over so he'll have something to keep him busy. J.C. eats his food amazingly fast and his beef burrito is already history. He simmers like a teapot while shoveling fries into his mouth one after the other. Laura glances at me and I shrug as I eat my food with great deliberation.

Chet says to his buddies in a low tone, "I wonder if Ninja Turtle knows his boyfriend's been hitting the club scene."

That catches me by surprise and I involuntarily look up at J.C. He's frozen in the midst of grabbing a fry.

"Yeah?" Wilson asks. "Where?"

"Where else?" Chet answers, his smarminess in full force. "West Hollywood. Queer Town."

Now I freeze. I hear high-fives from Chet's table, but keep my head tilted toward J.C. His anger meter has risen a few notches and I know he'll go off any minute.

"You guys figure he hooks up with girls at those clubs," Chet goes on tauntingly. "Or boys?"

"Boys, for sure," Grady opines in his usual kiss-ass tone.

"Way for sure," Wilson adds with a chuckle.

They high five again and J.C. starts to rise.

"J.C.!"

He stops and looks across the table at me. I forget in that heated moment and meet his gaze straight on. "It's not worth it." And then I see it. The worst thing I'll ever see. I drop my juice and leap to my feet like I've been electrocuted. "No!"

Laura stands, looking concerned. "Leo, what's wrong?"

But my eyes remain fixed on those of my best friend.

His anger turns to fear. "What?"

My body stiffens and I can barely breathe. My pounding heart feels like it'll explode. "Why did you make me look?" I spin around and run.

"Leo!"

"Uh, oh," I hear Chet say. "I think they just broke up." Laughter follows, but I'm too far across the cafeteria by then for it to matter.

J.C. keeps calling my name and I hear footsteps in pursuit as I dodge tables and bolt through the double doors onto the fancy paving stones of the outside quad. Students sitting around eating or talking stop to stare as I pelt past them toward the parking lot. J.C. keeps begging me to stop, but I can't. I dash through and around the parked cars—ignoring the heat that assaults me as soon as I hit the pavement—and then bolt into the street. I run and I run, not even sure where I'm running to. In my frozen mind, if I keep running I might forget what I saw, or maybe what I saw won't come to pass because I'm moving too fast to let it.

By the time I reach the beach, I've long since left J.C. in the dust. But even with me training almost every day, I've never been a long-distance runner and after that mile-long run in unforgiving heat, my lungs feel like a nuclear reactor. Gasping for air, I collapse onto the sand and weep. I lie there, tears streaming from my eyes as my mind plays over and over again the horrific images I just witnessed.

It can't be true. It can't!

Ignoring the rough sand sticking to my sweat-soaked clothes, I curl up into a fetal position and bawl like a baby. I don't even care if anyone sees me. I just want to forget everything and go someplace else for a while. But I can't escape my thoughts.

I guess this is why so many kids use drugs, to try and do just that. Problem is, the thoughts and feelings and problems are still there when the drugs wear off. Same with me, trying to run from what I saw. I could lie here for days, but every one of those days would still bring me one step closer to the death of my best friend. Crying isn't going to change that, but I cry anyway, because my body won't let me do anything else.

I'm not sure how long I lay curled up on that beach before I hear someone huffing and puffing above me.

J.C.

I crack open my eyes. He's doubled over, clutching at his sides and fighting for breath. Sweat streams from his wavy black hair down onto his face. "What…" he wheezes, struggling to breathe, "did… you… see?"

I unravel myself and sit up, pulling my knees in and clutching my legs tightly. I don't look at him, instead scanning the surrounding beach. It's a weekday and there's nobody around except the lifeguard in his station, and he isn't very close.

"Leo!"

I look up as he collapses to the sand and gazes at me with wide, terrified eyes.

Still, I can't bring myself to say it.

He grabs me by both shoulders. His grip feels like iron. His panting has lessened, but not the fear on his face. "Tell me. *Please.*"

I lower my eyes again. "You're…" I force myself to breathe. "You're going to be…" I can't say it.

"What?"

"Murdered!" I blurt, glancing at the stunned look on his face.

His mouth opens, but nothing comes out for a long moment. "When?" His voice is a choked whisper.

I don't want to say it, but I have to. "A week from Friday."

He gags, like he's gonna throw up all over me. I've never seen him so vulnerable, so small and afraid, and that scares me more than what I saw in his eyes. He collapses onto the sand and cries.

I'm so stunned to see my smart-ass, snarky, fearless friend crying like a little kid, I momentarily forget my own despair. I grab him and pull him in close, resting his head against my shoulder.

"It's not gonna happen, okay?" I assure him, trying to keep my voice steady. "We're gonna stop it. You won't end up like Kyle. I won't let that happen."

He pulls away and gazes at me with desperation in his eyes. I flinch because once again I see his death reflected back at me.

"How can we stop it?" he spits out, fighting to regain control of his emotions.

I pause to consider what I saw. My body has ceased its trembling, but J.C. still thrums like a tuning fork.

"How do I die?"

I glance at my friend's wide-eyed expression of hopelessness, then lower my gaze. "Stabbed," I say quietly. "There was blood everywhere and…" I trail off, running the images through my mind's eye.

"And what?"

"The killer is wearing a jacket and black pants."

"What kind of jacket?"

I shake my head. The images are fragmented, like pieces of a puzzle that aren't all there. "Not sure. But it has a snake on the back."

J.C. leans in and I see he's trembling, but his voice rises with excitement. "A snake? What kind of snake?"

I hug my knees again and bite my lip in concentration. "A cobra, I think, with its hood spread open. And the body looks like it wraps around to the front of the jacket."

"Can you see anything else?"

I shake my head. "No. It's too dark."

"Dark, like nighttime?"

"Yeah."

"Any idea where it happens?" His wide eyes make me feel guilty for telling him, but what choice did I have? Let him die like Kyle?

"No. But I won't leave you alone that Friday," I affirm, my voice steadier than it has any right to be. "I will *not* let anything happen to you."

It's weird. Guys like Chet Hamilton talk smack about me and I don't do anything, but my shyness just went out the window now that someone I care about is threatened. Anyone out to get J.C. will have to go through me. I hate fighting, despite my martial arts skills, but sometimes there's no choice.

Gratitude floods his face, but his eyes remain dark with despair. "Who would want to kill me? What have I ever done to people?"

I could say he's snarky and nasty to just about everyone in town, but I don't want to make him feel bad, or scare him even more. "Could be somebody out to get revenge on your mom," I offer, though I don't really believe it. "She's in politics, after all."

He shrugs. "Maybe." He sounds dubious.

"Can you ask her?"

"I'll e-mail her."

I consider other options. The hot sun has dried the sweat on my face and the gentle ocean breeze, coupled with the salt smell, has calmed my pounding heart. "I say we start with an Internet search for that cobra jacket I saw. Maybe we can find out who sells them."

"What if no one does?"

"We'll worry about that later." I untangle my legs and stand to stretch. "C'mon, let's get back. We're already in trouble for ditching. Let's just get the car and head home. We can start searching the Net."

I reach out with one hand. He clasps it and I pull him to his feet. He ducks his head, suddenly bashful, and hesitates as if he's unsure what to say. "Uh, thanks, Leo, for helping me."

"Best friends, right?"

"Hell, yeah."

We trek back across the beach, kicking sand up into the breeze. We brush the sand off when we enter the beach parking lot and when we get to the sidewalk, we head for school.

I'm surprised to find Laura hanging out by the entrance to the student parking lot. She sits up against the low brick wall so she won't be seen from the administration building. She leaps to her feet and hurries over as we approach.

"You guys all right?" She sounds concerned, something I'm not used to.

Neither is J.C.

We exchange a look of surprise before I say, "You been waiting for us?"

She pulls the bud from her right ear and wraps the cord around her phone. "Well, yeah. I mean, we're kind of a team, now, right? I was worried about you."

I feel a weird sensation wash over me that I can't quite pinpoint. "Thanks. I, well, we, have a problem."

She nods. "I figured. Harris is looking for you. Heard about the cafeteria incident."

I shrug. Harris is the last thing on my mind.

"Can I help?" She looks from one of us to the other.

J.C. and I exchange another—in my case, quick—look. We've always been together, just the two of us. No other kids have ever wanted to be in our tiny circle. But Laura does. I hear the sincerity in her voice, even if I don't dare search for it in her eyes. J.C. nods.

I wave her back to the wall and we all drop down to the pavement, pressing our backs up against the bricks. I still have to get my car before Harris finds us, so hiding in plain sight might work best. I tell her everything. She listens, I know, because she doesn't ask any questions. J.C. fills in some parts about how much I always help homeless people, which embarrasses me. When we finish, she stays quiet for a long moment, fingers silently drumming on the blacktop.

Unnerved by her silence, I glance over. "Do you believe me?"

"I have good instincts about people," she replies without pause. "I also asked a couple of teachers about you yesterday afternoon. They said good things."

"What do they say about me?" J.C. asks, leaning forward onto his up-raised knees.

She grins. "Cocky and snarky with an attitude the size of North America, to quote Mr. Morton. But I'd already figured that out."

J.C. frowns. "I don't feel so cocky now that someone's out to kill me."

"How can I help?"

She leans forward to look into my eyes.

I quickly look away. "Don't do that, please."

"Sorry, I forgot. I don't wanna know when I'll die, anyway."

I look up, but keep my gaze on her face, not her eyes. Her mouth is crinkled slightly, like she's thinking. "Why not?"

She considers a moment. "I think if I knew, I'd stop being me."

"Huh?" That's J.C., but it might as well have been me.

"It's just that, I think I'd act differently, make different choices that wouldn't necessarily be the real me," she answers soberly. "I think there are some things we just shouldn't know."

"Not me," J.C. pipes up, his voice stiff with fear. "If Hamilton hadn't caused Leo to look me in the eye, I'd be dead next Friday. Now we have a chance to stop it."

"How?"

I explain about searching for the cobra jacket.

"Can I help you with that?"

This time I don't hesitate. She said it before—we're a team. "Sure. Wanna come over to my house? That's where we're headed soon as I can get my car from the lot."

She nods and offers a wry smile. "That'll work. My dad won't care. He'll be happy I'm hanging out with boys." She chuckles.

The way her pixie hair sparkles in the sunlight coupled with her little laugh draws a genuine smile from me, a rarity.

We talk about various ways to keep J.C. alive past April twenty-eighth, which is a week from Friday, until we hear the bell ring in the distance, signaling the end of the school day. My hope is to sneak over to my car while the other students rush to theirs, so they can provide cover. I tell the others to wait for me down the street by the CVS pharmacy and I'll pick them up on my way. Then I slink around the wall and enter the parking lot.

Kids mill about and a fair number give me smirking looks or mocking laughter. Obviously, my meltdown in the cafeteria has become fodder for their petty little minds. A few shout derisive comments, but I ignore them and keep my head down as I walk, glancing up only enough to stay out of the way of cliques and moving cars. I've nearly reached my Prius when I bump into someone. Startled, I glance up.

"I'm sorry, I—"

It's Mr. Harris.

Crap!

"Hello, Leo." The light breeze should be blowing his hair every which way, like it's doing to mine, but he uses so much gel his hair looks like a wig.

I avoid eye contact. "Hi, Mr. Harris."

"I heard about your, how shall we put it, 'performance' in the cafeteria. Care to illuminate me on why you ditched your afternoon classes?"

I say nothing. I'm not a liar by nature and he knows that, despite what he said in his office yesterday. But what can I say now that won't be a lie? "No, sir. It's… personal."

"Boyfriend troubles, perhaps?"

I look up in shock, but avoid locking eyes with him. "No." I keep my voice low because I don't want passing kids to overhear us. "J.C. is just my friend, okay?"

He nods, but I can tell he doesn't believe me. Jeez! Can't guys be best friends anymore without everyone calling them gay?

"You know, Leo, even back in my high school days," he goes on in that reminiscing tone he always has when he talks about "the good old days," "Boys your age who didn't have girlfriends were assumed to be, well, you get my drift. Maybe you'd fit in better here if you and J.C. worked on that instead of spending all your time with each other."

I can't believe what I'm hearing! Since when is it a rule that at a certain age a guy has to have a girlfriend? Doesn't love happen by accident—you meet the right person and click? This whole obsession with having to be in a relationship every minute is disturbing to me. And why is everybody so fixated on fitting in all the time anyway?

I could argue with him, but it wouldn't do any good.

"I'll keep that in mind. Thanks for the suggestion." I try not to sound like J.C.

"Just doing my job," he replies smugly. "I like to see my kids happy."

I'm not your kid.

I fidget with my key fob for a few seconds before I get up the nerve to ask, "Are you going to suspend me for ditching?"

He chuckles. "Of course not. Your mother has been a good friend to this school."

You mean she donates a crapload of money, I think, but don't say it.

"You will need to make up all your missed work, naturally, and I'd like you and J.C. to avoid the cafeteria for the time being. Eat your lunch outside. That sounds equitable, doesn't it?"

Once again Chet Hamilton creates a problem and J.C. and me have to pay for it. But, at least Chet's goading revealed what's going to happen, so in a weird way I'm grateful to him.

"Yes, sir. May I go now?

He steps back and extends a hand toward my car. "Enjoy the rest of your day, Leo."

I nod and press the button to unlock the car. Harris actually waves as I drive off, a huge grin on his stupid face. Incredible!

I put Harris out of my mind as I pick up J.C. and Laura and head for home. We have much bigger problems than Principal Harris or Chet Hamilton. We have a murder to prevent.

CHAPTER SIX

I'M AS GOOD AS DEAD

I GIVE LAURA THE SHORT TOUR of my house because, well, like everyone else, she's fascinated by the movie business. My mother has put up framed posters from every film she ever worked on in any capacity, except for the ones that embarrass her, of course. These posters adorn the living room, family room, and entry hall and Laura nods approvingly. Most are lame comedies that I don't like, but Laura mentions that a few are personal favorites of hers.

She points out a teen actress on one of the posters and says, "I had a major crush on her in ninth grade."

J.C. and I don't quite know how to respond to that comment, so we ignore it. Well, until J.C., to keep himself in the attention loop says, "Yeah, me, too," even though it isn't true. I glance his way, but say nothing.

Once Laura scopes out the entire house and ogles all the props my mother kept from film sets and production houses, we settle into my spacious bedroom to get on my three computers. I have a laptop, which Laura takes and sprawls out on my (fortunately) made bed, a tablet that J.C. favors because he has one just like it at home, and a desktop model. J.C. plops into my beanbag chair and I sit at the massive rolltop desk and fire up my Mac. I use Google, Laura tries Yahoo, and J.C. goes on Bing. We all type in variations of "jacket with cobra on the back."

I find a few images, but the snake isn't like the one I saw. Lots of them relate to the Mustang Shelby car and aren't even similar to the one in my vision.

Laura comes up with one that's a decent match. The cobra is looking straight ahead, but the body isn't wrapped around the front and this image is more cartoony than what I saw.

J.C. retrieves lots of cobra racing images on jackets, but they're all car-related and none look exactly right.

We try variations on search words and spend a good hour scouring the Internet, but come up empty.

Laura finally rolls over and sits up. "This is getting us nowhere."

"Agreed," J.C. says with an exasperated sigh.

"Any other ideas?" I ask, turning away from my screen to face them.

Laura plays with her short hair as she thinks, and I watch her fingers. They look hard, like those of an athlete, and I wonder if she played any sports at her old school. "It might help if we knew what kind of jacket."

"Why's that important?" J.C. sets aside the tablet and leans forward.

"It's just, some material is hard to put images on," she explains, her fingers still dancing. "Denim is its own animal. So is leather. You can't just iron on stuff, and coloring leather is a special process."

I see where's she's going with this. "So if I can narrow down the material, we might be able to search only places that make those kinds of jackets."

"Exactly."

J.C. glances over at me, but I keep my eyes averted from his. "Can you tell, Leo?"

I replay the images in my mind, gripping the arms of my chair to keep from freaking out again. I see J.C. torn up and bloodied; a knife dripping something red; the cobra. But nothing else. I shake my head.

Laura sits up so fast I recoil. "Look again."

"Huh?"

"I bet if you look into his eyes again, longer this time, you might get more details. You freaked out the first time and ran, so you barely saw anything."

I press myself back against my desk in horror. Look again? See J.C. bloody and dead? My heart leaps into overdrive just at the thought. "I can't."

J.C. slides off the beanbag and scuttles over on his knees. "She's right, Leo. You might learn something more. Please?"

He stops in front of me, almost like a dog begging for a treat or a pat on the head. I stare at his hands dangling at either side. They tremble. He's just as scared as me. But he needs to know. *We* need to know. I swallow hard and nod.

I see in my peripheral vision J.C. lift his chin so his eyes are tilted upward. I take a deep breath and expel it. Laura leans forward off the edge of the bed, gazing at me with such intensity I squirm. I turn my head and look down at J.C. I slowly bring my gaze upward from his chin to his nose to… I lock eyes with him, and freeze.

Blood. Pools of blood. J.C.'s face is sliced up like a Thanksgiving turkey. Trails of thick redness seep down his cheeks and add to the growing pool beneath his head. He's on the ground or maybe it's a dirty floor. There's a smell this time—musty, rotting. The knife blade glints and it's like now the movie director in my head has called for a medium shot, because I see the back of the jacket. The cobra leers at me, its eyes blazing, its huge mouth open, the enormous fangs dripping venom. I try to focus on the jacket itself. Black. It's black, but the darkness surrounding it makes the material hard to discern. The jacket moves, like the killer is standing up into the shot.

Leather! It's definitely leather. I can see the creases and the way the snake has been painted right into the material. The jacket turns slightly. I can almost discern a hand holding something. Looks like a phone, maybe? I try to make out more of the location, but I can't. It's too dark.

I lean away from J.C. and expel the breath I've been holding. I nearly gag as the images begin to fade.

"What?" J.C. stands and looks at me.

Laura scoots off the bed to stand by his side. "You saw more this time, didn't you?"

I nod, but don't speak just yet. I focus on those images. I don't want to lose them. As horrifying as they are, I need to recall every detail. Slowly, with the slasher film unspooling in my mind's eye, I describe what I see and smell. J.C. and Laura listen attentively. The fear returns to J.C.'s brown eyes and I feel bad for increasing it.

Laura sits back onto the bed when I finish and says, "So we know the jacket is leather. That helps a lot. We can check clothing manufacturers who specialize in leather."

I nod.

J.C. doesn't look relieved. "What about that smell you said? Can you tell what it was?"

I consider a moment. "No."

"Okay, we table that for now," Laura says, reaching around to grab the laptop. She rests it on her thighs and begins typing. "Let's find places that make leather jackets."

J.C. stares at me.

I avoid his eyes, but offer the most reassuring look I have. "It's a start."

He nods and plops back onto the beanbag chair, swooping up the tablet and getting to work.

We search for another hour bookmarking leather manufacturers before Laura announces she has to get home. "Or else my dad'll send the cops out looking for me."

"He gets that worried?" J.C. asks as he shuts down the tablet.

She laughs, but it's bittersweet and tugs at my heart. "Are you kidding? He just thinks I'll run off to San Diego to be with Tara. That's my girl."

J.C. nods as he stands, but I say nothing, as usual.

"I'll keep searching for places from home," Laura promises. Then she does something that surprises J.C. She pulls him into a hug and holds him for a few moments. Outgoing as he is, J.C. isn't accustomed to affection from anyone, so he just stands there, unsure what to do. "Don't give up. Leo will save you." She releases him and looks my way. "Won't you?"

I'm always the follower, not the leader. But she's right. I *will* save J.C., somehow. I nod.

I drop her off at the palatial-looking home she directs me to and then drive J.C. to his house. He sent his mother an e-mail earlier, but she hasn't responded. He's determined to pick her brain about any death threats that might have come her way.

"I think I can squeeze five minutes out of her schedule," he says with quiet sadness.

We say our good-byes and I head on home. The image of blood pooling around J.C.'s lifeless face fills my mind the entire journey.

I don't see Mom at all that night, so I grab the tuna casserole Sylvia made for me and eat alone, like always, at the huge dining room table that's made for parties, but usually just seats me, kind of like the banquet table in *Beauty and the Beast* before Belle sat down to eat with the Beast. In my experience, most kids hate being alone, but I don't mind it. I think people don't like looking into themselves too much because they're afraid of what they'll see. Me, I think I probably know myself better than most people do because I spend so much time alone *with* myself. Do I always like what I see? Hell, no. I wish I could be more outgoing and social, but then I think about how I hate crowds and parties and the stuff "social" kids do, so maybe I don't want to be like that, after all. Knowing yourself doesn't mean you have all the answers. It *does* mean you can choose not to follow others blindly or go with the latest "trend." But it *can* be lonely sometimes. I'm lucky to have J.C. He's all I need.

The following day, I swing by and pick up J.C. on my way to school. I've done that a lot this year, even though he has a swanky new BMW coup his mother bought him when he turned sixteen. I mention it to him once in a while, like how come he doesn't drive the new car so much, and he just shrugs. The J.C. I grew up with shouldn't want to be caught dead in a low-end Prius like mine, but he still prefers riding with me over driving his own. Truth be told, I am a better driver. He tends to have a lead foot and maybe rides with me to avoid problems with Chet's mom, who'd like nothing better than to slap a ticket on the uppity Mexican son of the uppity Mexican mayor who beat her in the election. Yeah, small towns can be pretty crazy, especially for us kids.

As we make our way from the parking lot onto the main campus, I see Mr. Mendez, the janitor, mopping up something in the quad area. Probably some kid dropped his breakfast. But what catches my eye is the Chet Pack heading straight for him. Most of the kids think Mendez is creepy because he's an old Mexican dude who never smiles and always seems to stare at people. I've talked to him a few times and he seems okay to me, just shy and anti-social. I can relate.

J.C. and I stop before entering the quad because we don't want Chet to see us. Mr. Mendez is swooshing the mop back and forth when Chet walks up from behind and makes sure Mendez hits his foot with the wet mop head. The old man recoils, looking mortified.

Chet sticks a finger into his chest. "Look what you did to my shoe, you idiot!" He points down at his Jordan's. I can't quite see, but figure there must be dirty water on them from the mop. "I could have your old ass deported. That what you want?"

Mendez shakes with fear. Even from a distance I see the terror on his face. "I'm… I'm… sorry," he stammers. "I didn't see you."

Chet turns to his lackeys. I notice another of his jock pals is with them today, a beefy football player named Cranston. "He didn't see me." His tone reeks of derision and self-importance.

My stomach clenches at his treatment of the older man.

Chet leans into Mr. Mendez so quickly the man stumbles back and nearly trips over his bucket. His foot hits the side and water sloshes over his shoe.

"Now we're even," Chet remarks, smirking at the old man. He and the others turn to head toward the cafeteria. Chet stops and spins around, giving the bucket a swift kick that upends it. The dirty water splashes Mr. Mendez's pants, and the bottles of cleaning solution hanging around the rim roll away in different directions.

Wilson and Grady offer Chet hearty high-fives, Cranston slaps him on the back, and the four chortling bullies push their way into the cafeteria. As usual, no one but a few kids saw the altercation, so Chet will not be punished.

I jog over and right the bucket, setting it down near the visibly shaking Mendez. Then I retrieve all of his cleaning bottles and place them beside the bucket. He eyes me with a stunned expression.

"Are you okay, Mr. Mendez?" I avoid his eyes.

"Thank you for your help," he croaks, his voice raspy with age. He reeks of cigarette smoke, which likely adds to his vocal hoarseness. "But you didn't have to."

I eye the splashed water and picture Chet's haughty face, and my anger rises. "I wanted to. You have a good day, sir."

I turn and find J.C. gawking at me. He moves to my side, giving Mr. Mendez a disdainful look as we head past the cafeteria toward the main building where our lockers are housed.

"Why'd you help that old *paisa*?" he says loudly.

I turn back and see Mr. Mendez watching us. He obviously heard J.C. call him a *paisa* because he looks angry. It's a derisive term for Mexicans in the U.S. with limited English. I glare at J.C., briefly making eye contact so he understands I'm mad. "He's a human being, not a servant. You keep telling me you don't wanna be like Chet or your mother, and here you are acting like you're better than a man who wasn't born rich. What's wrong with you?" I stop, stunned that I said so much at one time.

J.C.'s mouth hangs open in surprise and then his face clouds over with shame. "You're right." He pauses long and hard, looking back at the old man picking up his scattered materials. "I keep thinking that could be me, if things were different and my mom didn't marry a rich guy who ditched her and left us all that money. I could be just another Mexican gardener or janitor."

"There's no such thing as just another anything," I say quietly. J.C. and I have had this discussion before about the homeless people I help. "Every job is important and so is every person. You know Maria is more like your mom than your real one, same as Sylvia is for me." Maria is J.C.'s housekeeper who's been with his family since J.C. was a toddler.

"You're right." He pauses and takes a deep breath. I've never seen him so uncertain before. "But if my mom wasn't mayor, I'd be nobody, Leo."

"That's not true. You'd always be somebody."

J.C.'s face twists into his characteristically cynical mode. "Yeah? Who?" The tone is pure snark.

"My best friend." I see his eyes go wide as golf balls before I look away.

I hear a slight gagging sound, like he's got something caught in his throat, but I don't look up because I don't want to embarrass him. I slap him on the back. "C'mon, we're gonna be late."

Without another word, we pull open the wide double doors and enter La Costa High.

We get through the day, hanging with Laura whenever possible. After school we head off to the garment district in downtown L.A. to check out jacket makers since Laura printed out the names and addresses of every leather shop in Los Angeles. It will take us days to check them all, since we can only look after school hours, but hopefully one of them sells the jacket I saw.

Laura sits in my backseat with the window cranked all the way down. "I like wind in my face," she says as she does it.

It's another hot day, so J.C. and me keep ours rolled up and use the AC. We move slowly along the 105 Freeway towards L.A. amidst pockets of heavy congestion interspersed with hundreds of feet of near empty roadway.

Laura asks from in back, "So, J.C., have you thought of anyone who might have it in for you?"

J.C. whips his head around and goes pale again. "My mom answered my e-mail. She thought it funny that anyone would be out to hurt her or me. Said I was being a drama queen. I hate when she calls me that, even in an e-mail."

Laura pushes hair from in front of her face and shrugs. "Okay, so your mom laughs it off. Do *you* have any enemies?"

"Of course not," J.C. insists, sounding wounded that Laura could even suggest such a possibility.

I clear my throat. "Uh, J.C., truth here?"

"Yeah?"

I sigh. Is he really this clueless? "Bro, the whole school hates you and so do their parents."

"Huh?"

I nod. "And not just 'cause you're the mayor's son."

"Why does everyone hate him, 'cause he's snarky?" Laura asks from the rear.

I accelerate to pull ahead of a big open bed truck. I'm not superstitious or anything, but ever since I saw *Final Destination 2* with the logs flying off a flatbed and causing a major pileup, I never stay behind open bed trucks.

"Every kid is snarky," J.C. protests indignantly.

"Leo isn't," Laura says casually. "Me, either, at least not very often."

"It's not just 'cause you're snarky, J.C.," I say while hitting the gas to flow with traffic. "It's 'cause you treat people like you're better than them."

"I do not!" He sounds mad, but he knows I'm right.

"Like you didn't insult Mr. Mendez this morning so he could hear you?"

J.C. deflates in his seat and lowers his head. "You know why I did that. I told you."

"Yeah, but that doesn't change anything," I say, keeping my voice steady and my eyes on the road. "You could have made somebody really mad."

"Mad enough to kill me?"

"Happens all the time, J.C.," Laura says, leaning forward as far as her seatbelt will allow. "Watch the news sometime."

"In that case, I'm as good as dead," J.C. mumbles, almost to himself. "You're right, Leo. Everybody hates me almost as much as they hate Chet Hamilton."

"They don't hate you *that* much." I offer a grin, trying to lighten his mood.

He returns my grin. "At least I have you."

"And me," Laura pipes up from the rear. "We're a team, remember?"

J.C. twists his head around to face her. "Thanks."

We drive the rest of the way in silence.

I swear we must've looked at two hundred leather jackets that first afternoon. Not only do I not see anything even close to the one in my vision, but the guys who run these stores all indicate they haven't seen any design like what I described, except for the Mustang Shelby stuff I found on the Internet.

I'm tired and hungry and frustrated. If you've ever tried parking in downtown L.A., you know what I mean. It's easier to find a needle in a haystack, as Principal Harris might say, than a parking space in Los Angeles. So once I find one, we spend a couple of hours walking everywhere and by the time we return to the car, I'm cranky and J.C. is stressing big time because our search turned up nothing. But Laura remains positive and upbeat.

"Just our first day, guys," she says calmly as she slides into my backseat and J.C. plops down in the shotgun. "We still have time."

"Easy for you to say," J.C. shoots back with snarl.

I start the car and hear Laura say from behind me, "Chill, snarky boy. I'm not the one who wants to kill you."

"She's right," I add as I pull into the heavy street traffic. Late afternoons in L.A. are the worst time to be on the road. We'll be lucky to get back to La Costa within an hour.

J.C. grunts and mumbles, "Sorry," which is pretty impressive for him. Other than me, I've never heard him apologize to anyone.

I decide the freeway will be a parking lot, so I stick to surface streets. I really need to focus on my driving because there are as many idiots on the road in L.A. as there are grains of sand at the beach.

"Hey, Leo," Laura pipes up from the back after about fifteen minutes of what could best be described as a sulky silence.

"Yeah?" I'm keeping a close eye on this one knucklehead to my right who I just know is going to cut in front of me the first chance he gets, even if there isn't any room to do so. He has "the look."

"If you can describe that cobra in detail, I can draw it."

I don't turn my head, but J.C. says, "You can draw?"

"Oh, yeah," she replies. "Art's my thing. Always wanted to be a police sketch artist when I was younger, you know, from watching those cop shows."

"What would we do with the drawing?" I ask, and then slam on the brakes as Mr. Knucklehead swerves directly in front of me so he can weave around an SUV and then whip back into the lane he started from. Jeez!

J.C. curses and lowers the window to cuss the guy out, but he's long gone. The creepy part is, the guy was driving a Mustang Shelby.

"I love L.A. – Not!" I mutter.

"We can share the drawing on social media," Laura goes on as though we didn't almost just crash. "Ask if anyone has seen a jacket with that image. Can't hurt, right?"

My adrenaline rush from slamming on the brakes begins to subside and I consider her proposal. "Not a bad idea. What do you think, J.C.?"

"I don't have any local followers on Facebook or Instagram," he replies to her, "But I do have a lot of people who like my dance videos."

"And I have no followers except J.C." Yep, I'm even shy within the anonymous barriers of cyber space.

"I have tons," she says, and somehow I'm not surprised. She's pretty outgoing. "But it's not the followers we have, it's the hashtags we choose. Those will draw in all kinds of people we never heard of. We might get lucky."

"Can't hurt," I say as I swing a cautious right turn onto Slauson Avenue. That will take us back to the Westside and I can get us home from there.

"Sounds like a plan," J.C. adds quietly.

Then the talking stops and I focus on driving.

CHAPTER SEVEN

YOU CAN'T HIDE FROM ME

B Y THE TIME WE GET back to my house, I'm starving, but J.C. wants Laura to do the drawing right away. I guess I can't blame him.

We go into the kitchen and Laura calls her mom. "I'm having dinner with two boys from school." There's a pause as J.C. and I wait. "No, Mom, they're just friends." She rolls her eyes and I smile at her exasperation. I know all too well about parents who don't accept their kids as they are. "We're working on an art project together. Don't worry, I'll be home in time to finish my homework." She ends the call.

"Is she always that way?"

Laura nods. "She keeps thinking I just need to find the *right* boy." She does the air quotes with "right" boy and laughs, but it's bittersweet.

Principal Harris's "recommendation" that J.C. and me find girlfriends to quell all the rumors flashes through my mind and I grimace. When will adults stop messing up kids' lives?

J.C. lunges for the fridge door. Naturally, my mother never puts up any of my school work with little magnets the way most parents do, nor even any family photos. She collects magnets of, can you guess? Yup, movie posters. My fridge door overflows with them. You almost can't open the door without three or four falling to the tile floor, which is what happens now as J.C. flings it open.

"Oh, sorry," he says. "Forgot."

I reach down and pick up *Casablanca, Citizen Kane,* and *Wings,* three really old movies that are in black and white, for crying out loud. I've never seen any of them.

I re-attach them to the open door and then look inside for the meal I know Sylvia has prepared. My stomach rumbles when I spot the rectangular casserole dish filled to the brim with freshly made lasagna (much better, I already know, then the plastic-like stuff J.C. and I made on Tuesday.)

Thank you, Sylvia!

And almost as though she knew I would have company, there's more than enough for all three of us.

I turn on the oven and pop in the casserole dish to warm it up. I refuse to show off and use the voice-activation. My fingers work well enough to push the buttons. Tossing J.C. and Laura a Coke each, I run upstairs to my room to bring down my art supplies. I enjoy drawing—hey, it's a solitary activity, so of course I like it—but I'm not good enough to win any awards or anything.

While the lasagna warms up, Laura sits at the dining room table with my sketchpad and colored pencils and looks at me expectantly. J.C. plants a hand on my shoulder. It seems like a friendly gesture, but I know it means much more. I feel the tension in his fingers as they squeeze my trap muscle. He's desperately hoping this idea will work. He also knows how hard it is for me to keep reliving his death and wants to assure me he's grateful. Us guys can say a lot with just a hand to the shoulder.

I take a deep breath and hold it a long moment. Letting the air slowly exit through my nose, I call up in my mind's eye the image on that jacket. The snake head rearing; the fangs dripping, the hood spread wide, the scaled, shiny body extending down and disappearing around toward the front; the tail appearing on the opposite side and sticking upward as though pointing to the head; the colors of the scales themselves—yellowish-cream along the belly, olive green around the hood, brown everywhere else.

I describe the snake as best I can, and in no time Laura holds up her sketch.

"Does it look like this?"

Damn if she hasn't plucked the image right from my mind and create an exact duplicate. She could be a police sketch artist on steroids with her talent.

Stupefied, I nod dumbly. "Exactly." I glance at J.C. in astonishment, but he just shrugs. I guess he doesn't care how she did it; he's just glad she did.

The oven timer *beeps*, and that unfreezes me. I pull my gaze from her amazing work of art and hurry into the kitchen to yank open the oven door. Using mitts big enough to fit Mickey Mouse, I slide the bubbling hot lasagna from the shelf and set it onto the stove.

I switch off the oven while J.C. pulls open the cupboard for plates, which he sets onto the table. Laura enters and I indicate the utensils drawer. She shakes her head in amusement at the blue LED lights illuminating the cupboards and counters before sliding open the drawer and pulling out knives and forks for each of us.

Once the lasagna is situated in the center of the dining room table, we dig right in. We're all so hungry we don't even talk about the drawing until our third helping. And only then do I realize that I have someone at this table other than J.C. Despite our current dilemma, I understand how the Beast felt when Belle joined him for dinner that first time because I finally feel like I matter to other people. And I like that feeling.

"Do you think anyone will comment on the drawing?" J.C. asks around a chewy mouthful. A thin string of melted cheese hangs from his lower lip, but he's too intent on Laura to notice.

"Oh, they'll comment all right," she replies, pointing at her lower lip with a smile.

J.C. gets the message and uses his index finger to remove the offending dribble of cheese.

"My Instagram gets lots of traffic whenever I put up a new art piece," she goes on, swigging from her can of Coke. "We'll upload it after dinner and see what we get."

J.C. is eyeing her in a way I haven't seen him look at a girl before. Usually, he just acts like he's "all that" and flirts with pretty girls because he thinks they should like him just because he's him. But this look is different. He looks interested in her, which would be crazy because she likes girls, not boys. Maybe he just admires her talent. Or maybe he feels like the Beast, too.

Feeling suitably gorged on lasagna—we ate the entire casserole—I put the dishes into the sink for later cleanup and we hike upstairs to my room where Laura gets to work. She snaps some pictures of the cobra drawing with her iPhone and uploads them to her Instagram, Facebook, and Pinterest accounts right from the phone. She friends me on Facebook and messages the pix over. She does the same for J.C. and she gives us a list of hashtags that she thinks will bring the most traffic to the image, ones like #cooljacketdesign and #cobrajacket.

She does all of this in, like, fifteen minutes, while J.C. and I stand behind her gawking like idiots. I'm pretty good with computers, but lousy with social media because, well, it's "social." J.C. posts all kinds of stuff on social media, but most of his "friends" are people who don't know him personally. He has no online friends who attend Costa High except me. Unlike him, I keep my Facebook account set to private. He doesn't because he practices dance moves and posts up the vids to try and get followers, and he's got quite a few last time I checked. But neither of us use the Messenger feature.

Laura finishes and sits back with a satisfied smirk. "We should get plenty of hits. Hopefully, someone will have seen this design somewhere."

I point to her caption beneath the image "You didn't mention black leather in the description."

She chuckles. "People steal stuff all the time off the Net, artwork and such. This way, we don't encourage anyone to put the design on a black leather jacket. We're just asking if anyone has seen *any* jacket with that design."

I grin. "That's very slick."

She returns the grin. "I like to think ahead."

J.C. gushes, "Thanks, Laura. I mean, you're smart and really awesome."

She rises, stretching her arms to restore circulation. "Just doing my part for the team." Then she gives J.C. a long look. "So, what's up with some of the stuff I saw on your wall, J.C.? Do you really care that much if random people like your dancing or your clothes or your hair?"

J.C. turns a little red and glances over at me. I remain poker-faced. He knows I've been asking him about that for years.

He doesn't reply and that forces me to say, "Thanks for everything, Laura."

She smiles. "What are friends for, right?"

It amazes me how in a matter of days, Laura has become the best friend I've ever had besides J.C. Life is crazy.

"I better head on home," she says, shrugging.

"I'll drive you." I start for the bedroom door.

"It's okay," she says, catching up with me. "After all that food, I need the walk. It's only a few blocks. See ya tomorrow."

"Okay."

"See ya, J.C." She tosses him a head nod and vanishes into the hall.

J.C. doesn't respond. He just stands there staring after her. I hear the front door open and close. I'm pretty sure I know what's bugging him, so I just wait.

"I know, I know," he finally blurts out. "You tell me all the time not to worry about what other people think of me."

"So why do you still do it?"

He plops down onto my bed and lowers his eyes to the floor. "Don't you think I hear the nasty little comments as I walk down the hall? The slurs like "wetback" and "beaner"? I let 'em roll off most of the time, but I never forget I hear 'em. How can I?"

I move to the bed and stand before him. "People like that aren't worth impressing."

"I know. They just make me feel so… different."

"Different is okay," I remind him again, for probably the hundredth time. "That's why you and me are friends."

He looks up with relief, but I have to avoid his eyes. Ordinarily, this would be the time for eye contact. It's one of those human moments too many kids don't have anymore because they spend all their time staring at screens. But I don't want to see the murder again, so I focus on his long, feathery eyelashes.

"Thanks, Leo. You're the best."

I nod and turn away quickly. "C'mon, let's post that cobra pic to our pages."

He rises and pulls my extra chair over next to the one at the computer and we sit before the monitor.

I scoot aside so J.C. can work the keyboard. I watch as he follows Laura's instructions for posting the drawing.

"I'll put it on Instagram from my phone," he says.

I nod. Not having an Instagram account, I've never seen what he posts there, but I'm sure it's all stuff about himself. I stare at his Facebook Messenger screen and an odd feeling comes over me. Call it a premonition, but I ask, "Have you ever checked for hidden messages?"

"What are those?"

"Messages from people you don't know," I reply, tapping a few keys. I select "Messenger" on the left side his screen under News Feed. "I heard about them on this tech guy show I listen to on the radio." I click on the Settings cog at the top and a dropdown menu appears. I click Message Requests. "Those end up in this folder."

The folder opens, and J.C. gasps. The left side of his screen is filled with messages. Most look like spam. But there's a series of recent ones with no picture and the same name: Yury Muerte.

My mouth goes dry. I try to swallow, but there's nothing there. "Isn't *'muerte'* Spanish for 'death'?"

He nods. Once again, he's gone so pale he could be my twin. He clicks on the latest message.

> 'Think you can avoid me by ignoring my messages? Think again, queer boy.'

There are eight messages delivered over the past two weeks. J.C.'s hands shake and I take the mouse from him. Scrolling down, I open the first one, sent on March thirtieth. It reads:

> 'You better watch your back.'

I glance at J.C. He's practically hyperventilating. He nods, and I open each of the next six messages.

> April 1: 'I'm coming for you.'

> April 7: 'You can't hide from me.'

> April 10: 'Your big mouth is gonna be closed soon.'

> April 13: 'Too afraid to reply? Good.'

> April 16: 'I will love hearing you squeal like a pig.'

> April 17: 'Your time is almost here. Ready for it?'

The first one we looked at, actually the latest one, was sent yesterday. My hand trembles as I abandon the mouse and give J.C. a sideways look. He's shaking like it's the middle of winter in Alaska and looks so ashen I wrap one arm around his shoulders, allowing him to rest his head against me.

He tries to speak, but it comes out choked, like he's fighting back tears. I don't look at him. I just hold him. Finally, he manages to whisper, "Somebody *does* hate me that much."

"I'll keep you safe."

"How can you be sure?"

I wasn't sure before, but now I am. "I wasn't given this power last week just because."

He sits up and I let him go. Embarrassed, he wipes away what looks like a tear, but I pretend not to notice. "Whaddaya mean?"

"That man didn't give me this power by accident two weeks before you're supposed to die," I say with conviction, because I've come to believe it "I don't know if it was from God or something else, but he gave it to me so I'd have time to save you."

His eyes become saucers. "I never thought about it like that."

"I've thought about nothing else," I say with a heaviness in my voice. "I kept wondering why me. And now I know."

"It's crazy, fool," he says with a half grin. "You always seem to know what to say, but you hardly ever say anything."

I shrug and return the grin. "Maybe I spend so much time thinking that when I do finally say something, it comes out okay."

He glances anxiously back at the computer screen displaying the ominous messages. "Any way to track this guy?"

I click on the empty ID pic, but nothing comes up except *'This user is private. Send a friend request if you want to make contact.'* There isn't a 'Request' option available, however. Whoever this is, he's covered his tracks.

"Let's see what happens if I reply."

I start to type and he grabs my arm. "Wait. What if that pisses him off?"

I offer my best version of his snarky expression. "Dude, he's already going to kill you. How much more pissed can we make him?"

He actually chuckles.

"Besides, maybe we can get him to say something that will give away his identity."

He brightens at that. "Good thinking."

I respond to the last message, the one sent yesterday.

> **'I haven't been ignoring you. Couldn't be bothered responding to a wuss who hides in the shadows and won't face me man to man.' I hit send.**

"That should get his attention."

"He might get so mad he'll wanna kill me twice," J.C. says, and then we both bust up. The laughter feels good, helping to relieve the pent-up tension in my gut. Despite my assurances to J.C., there's no way I can guarantee to protect him. I can only do my best.

A few moments pass while we stare at the screen. Then Yury Muerte replies.

'Nice try, queer boy, but you're not a real man so it's a moot point.'

I glance at J.C. for inspiration since he's the one who dishes out all the insults. "Tell him he's as dumb as Principal Harris. That way we might see if he goes to Costa."

I type in what J.C. said and we wait. Barely a moment passes before this response comes through:

'Who?'

"Could be a trick to throw us off track," I say to the computer as much as to J.C. and pause to think. "I know." I type in 'You wanna kill me just 'cause I'm gay?'

I'm about to hit 'send' when J.C. grabs the mouse away. "Why are you writing that?"

The intensity of his reaction surprises me. "I wanna see how he responds. Might give us a clue."

He doesn't look happy, but nods and gives me back the mouse. I slide the cursor to 'send' and click.

We wait. The seconds tick by.

'So you finally admit it' enters the little message bubble.

J.C. and I look at each other and I know he's thinking the same thing I am. Someone from school.

I type 'Just copying what you say. I admit nothing.'

'I saw you going into'

The message cuts off, as though the sender hit "Enter" before finishing.

I glance at J.C. He looks even more surprised… and maybe a little guilty? That might be my imagination because I'm so stressed, but he says nothing and I wait for the rest of the message. Nothing appears.

I type 'Still there, loser' I want to make him mad so he'll give something away about his identity. He might have already done that with the unfinished message. A memory tickles the back of my mind, but I can't quite grasp it at the moment.

'Your day is coming' pops into the message box.

We wait, but nothing more appears. I type 'why are you doing this?'

Another few moments pass and I think maybe he's gone. Then one final message shows up:

'You think you're all that but you're nothing and I'm gonna prove it.'

I don't look at J.C. We both know that his uppity attitude pretty much angers everyone he meets. This could, sadly, be almost anybody.

Nothing more appears and I can't think of any other questions that might trigger a useful response, so I sit back from the keyboard and study the messages. I guess J.C. does the same, because his chair squeaks a little with movement, but he says nothing and I don't look over at him.

"I think it's Hamilton." J.C. finally breaks the heavy silence between us.

I hear the air conditioner kick on as I consider his suggestion. Watching the messages appear on screen, I had the same thought. But now I'm not so sure. "I think that's unlikely."

He's squinting and looking both scared and mad as hell. "Why not? The gay thing is all him. He started those rumors."

I glance down at the plush maroon carpet beneath my feet. "I know. But he used the word 'moot,' for one thing. Chet doesn't talk like that. I doubt he even knows what it means."

"He hates me enough to wanna kill me, I know that much. I make him look like a fool all the time and he can't do crap about it."

Most kids just say whatever comes into their heads to everything that happens. But I never do. My shyness has created an innate need to pause before speaking, and I do that now.

I think back to first grade when Chet Hamilton was the biggest kid in our class. Most of us were maybe three and a half feet tall, but Chet was almost a foot taller and he never let us forget it, either. That's when he started taking command. One by one, he cornered all of us boys in the bathroom and did a swirly on us—forcing our heads into a toilet and then flushing it. He was strong, too. Had a big brother who worked him out with weights from a young age.

My swirly came just before Christmas vacation, but unlike the other boys who kissed up to Chet after he became alpha dog, I vowed he would never touch me again. I'd already started gymnastics, which had gotten my upper body decently strong for a six-year-old, but I didn't know how to fight or defend myself so I convinced my mom to let me take Aikido. I wasn't into the idea of hurting people, but I *did* want to make sure no one could ever hurt *me* again. Mom didn't care what I did so long as I stayed out of her hair, and Sylvia drove me everywhere, anyway.

I continued with gymnastics and added in Aikido three times per week. This was before J.C. and me became friends. By the time second grade rolled around, I had gotten pretty decent at deflecting kids much bigger than me and could take down most of those in my Aikido class with ease. Chet continued his reign of swirly terror, I guess to reassert his alpha male status among the now-seven-year-olds. I know he swirlied J.C. again because I found him hiding in the bushes behind the gym, his head and torso dripping with water, bawling his eyes out. I sat with him until he calmed down. I didn't say anything; just being there was enough. We've been inseparable ever since.

Anyway, the next day Chet managed to corner me alone in the bathroom, despite my best efforts to avoid him. I had peed in a stall and just stepped out when he entered. Already, Wilson and Grady followed him around like puppies. They'd been cowed into submission. Rumor had it that Wilson's dad was beyond furious that his son had caved in to a bully. I remember seeing his dad in the parking lot beside their Lincoln Town Car glowering at all of us kids and berating Wilson under his breath, demanding to know who the bully was. I almost felt sorry for Wilson, especially when his dad died of a heart attack at the beginning of freshman year. I guess being mad all the time isn't good for your heart.

Chet grinned when he saw me exit the stall.

"Well, look who's here. Ninja Turtle." Yeah, he'd already started that nickname going around school. "Heard you hung around that wetback yesterday after I dunked him. Bad mistake, Ninja Turtle."

He stepped forward menacingly. All the while, my gaze focused on the small green tiles of the floor. But as I sensed movement, I stiffened into a defensive stance and looked right into his eyes. I mad-dogged that little jerk something fierce and never broke eye contact. I must've looked scary because he stopped and the smile faltered. I wasn't afraid of him anymore and I think he figured that out.

He stood there staring at me with a kind of disbelief on his handsome face. The bell chimed in the distance, signaling the end of lunch. Chet gave a sort of nervous smirk and brushed blond hair off his forehead.

"Your lucky day, loser." He snapped his fingers and turned to exit the bathroom, the other two trailing dutifully behind.

But every day thereafter was my lucky day because he never tried to swirl me again. Or J.C., for that matter. Sure, he talked crap about us when the teachers weren't within earshot, but he never again made a move.

Sitting by J.C. on my bed, I think back on this incident and how it changed the relationship I had with Chet Hamilton. Of course, once J.C.'s mom became mayor back in middle school, Chet really couldn't do anything to him except spew his quiet, insinuating BS when adults weren't looking. I consider the possibility of Chet Hamilton having the nerve to kill another human being and I just don't see it. I don't think he's even been in a real fight. He cowed all the boys at such a young age that no one ever considered standing up to him when they got bigger.

I remind J.C. of this incident from second grade and share my belief that Chet is too cowardly to do something so extreme as murder.

J.C. digests what I say like he's swallowed an onion. Clearly, he wants Chet to be the culprit. Everything is neat and tidy that way. "He might hire someone."

I consider that possibility with care. This time, even J.C. becomes exasperated with my long pause.

"Well? Isn't it possible?"

"Yeah, I guess it is possible, but I don't think so."

"I say we follow him after school to see where he goes."

"What if he spots us? His mom is still police chief."

"If he's hiring someone to kill me, he won't do it in Costa," J.C. asserts with conviction and I know he's right.

"Okay," I finally say after pausing again. "But let's see what happens with the drawing first, and we'll watch Chet at school before we follow him around. He might show some sign that he's the one we just messaged."

J.C. looks disappointed that I didn't jump all over his plan, but he knows I'm the more sensible one. And I think he sees me in a different light since I acquired this new "power." I think I scare him now, though he'll never admit that. Truth be told, I scare myself.

CHAPTER EIGHT

WE'RE TRAPPED

T HE NEXT DAY IS FRIDAY and won't give us too much time to scope out Chet Hamilton, but I hope to see some reaction from him that might indicate he's the one messaging J.C. We don't have him in a class until second period, but J.C. and I practically sprint down the corridor past chatting, aimless kids to room twenty-three so we can be in our seats when he arrives. This being history class, the walls are decorated with posters of famous people like Martin Luther King, Cesar Chavez, and JFK, interspersed with maps and bulletin boards displaying some of the essays we've written. I'm a solid writer and a good thinker and Mr. Morton always puts up my work (not that my mom sees it, of course. She hasn't been to a single Back-To-School Night *ever*. Estella accompanied me in the early grades and then Sylvia in middle school.)

Understandably, J.C. looks really stressed out, his forehead furrowed with worry and his face a little pale. I don't blame him. Our classmates trickle into the room. The heat spell is still in force, so the girls wear as little clothing as they can get away with. Yeah, there's a dress code, but it's hardly ever enforced. Principal Harris never makes waves if he doesn't have to. Most of the boys sport tank tops or muscle shirts so they can show off their arms to the girls.

Me, I throw on whatever, run the brush through my curly hair a couple of times, and leave the house. Today I wear a plain brown tee, cargo shorts and the Jordan's I got from my aunt for Christmas. J.C. always wears a short or long-sleeved shirt with a collar and some stylish designer jeans or slacks and, of course, his hair is perfect.

I know what you're thinking—J.C.'s just as self-absorbed as everyone else in La Costa, which is sort of true. But—and here's the *big* but—he's the only kid who's willing to hang out with me and, by extension, go downtown with me to help the homeless. I know J.C. frets over getting dirty or picking up germs from somebody down there, but he still goes and that counts for a ton in my book.

As they enter the classroom, the girls flirt with the boys and the boys flirt with the girls and it's all the height of superficiality, and none of them give J.C. or me a second glance. We're both focused on that open door and I'm holding my breath as the Chet Pack saunters in like they own the place. Girls fawn over Chet like he's the biggest rock star ever. Of course, most of those girls really think he's a jerkwad. I know because I'm so invisible around here I can eavesdrop at will (not that I try to, by the way.) They play the flirting game, but almost all the girls hate Chet because he thinks he's prettier than they are.

Chet glances over and I focus on his face as he spots us. He smirks like he always does, but doesn't display any other reaction that might indicate he's the mysterious Yury Muerte.

Wilson kisses air in our direction and gets a high five from Grady, but that's an everyday occurrence.

I glance at J.C. He looks disappointed. "We'll track down whoever it is," I whisper. "That's a promise."

He nods, but watches as Chet seats himself at the very back of the room like usual.

The tardy bell rings and I reach into my backpack for a notebook and pen as Mr. Morton greets us with a hearty, "Happy Friday, class!"

Some kids reply with a sing-songy, "Happy Friday to you, Mr. Morton."

This a regular Friday routine and Morton grins before beginning his opening monologue.

J.C. and I don't see Laura until lunch, so that's when we meet. To comply with Principal Harris's "request," we sit at one of the outside tables planted beneath large shade trees and talk over the newest developments. I'd already sent her screen shots of the back and forth messages between J.C. and his stalker, but being new to town she doesn't have much to offer.

"But I'm getting tons of hits on that image," she says around a bite of turkey sandwich.

"Yeah?" J.C. pipes up, looking hopeful. "Anybody seen it before?"

"No. But they all love it and think it would look badass on a jacket." She shrugs.

"That doesn't help," he mumbles sullenly.

She reaches across the metal picnic table and gently takes J.C.'s hand in hers. He looks surprised. "We'll find out who's after you and we'll stop him."

"You sound so sure."

I can tell by his voice that he's anything but sure.

She offers a pretty smile. "Call it woman's intuition, but I have faith in Shy Boy over here."

I involuntarily look up from my food and gaze at her with my mouth hanging open, not for her use of my nickname, but because of her solid affirmation. Then to avoid seeing anything in her eyes, I avert mine. "Why?"

She shrugs again. "Just do." She squeezes J.C.'s hand and then lets go.

I can tell he wishes she was still holding it. But as I study the set of his face and notice the faraway look in his eyes, I decide he's not crushing, just feeling appreciated for once, rather than scorned.

Eating outside in the soft breeze and warm sunshine is amazing, really, and I wonder why I haven't thought of it before. Prior to afternoon classes, we agree to eat out here every day and avoid Chet and the other hecklers who populate the cafeteria. Laura offers a fist and we bump, sealing the pact.

Friday ends with no more Chet sightings, for which I'm pleased. But as J.C., Laura, and me clamber into my Prius to show the cobra drawing to clothing establishments in neighboring cities, I find myself shivering, despite the hot afternoon sun. If we can't come up with a solid plan of action, my best friend has only one week left to live. I shove that thought aside and navigate my way out of the jam-packed parking lot.

By the time I drop Laura at her house, we'd spent three hours searching through tiny air-conditioned boutiques featuring racks of aromatic leather all up and down the coast: Redondo, Manhattan, Hermosa, even Lawndale. Since leather jackets are expensive and custom jobs more expensive still, our thinking was that the perpetrator must be someone with money. Plus, the messages sent to J.C. indicate somebody who knows him well, likely a local, and that means rich. But we come up empty. Lots of the jacket designers praise the image and say they'd love to create one for us, but no one has ever seen it before.

The three of us engage in more store-hopping over the weekend and I don't even help out at the homeless shelters like I normally do. One of the regular volunteers calls my cell to make sure I'm okay—yes, that's how consistent I am. I feel bad for missing an opportunity to help the people down there and explain to the volunteer that something urgent came up and I'm helping a friend. I think an impending murder counts as "urgent," right?

By Sunday, I can tell that J.C. is getting super stressed out because he hasn't styled his hair and his clothes don't quite match up. Today he wears red Jordan's, washed out jeans, and a dark blue polo with flowers across the chest that he bought from Hollister. And his black hair sticks out in all directions like an anime character.

I feel badly for him and, even though I'm pretty sure I can protect him from some knife-wielding psycho, what if I can't? Laura insists on being with us on Friday because "two lookouts are better than one," but what if the killer knocks me, or both of us, out?

The three of us sit around my room late Sunday afternoon and stew over our collective failure to find even a hint that the jacket I saw in my vision exists.

"We need a Plan B," Laura finally says. She's plopped in my beanbag chair staring up at me as she does.

I'm sitting in my desk chair and J.C. is sprawled out on my freshly made bed. I always tell Sylvia she doesn't have to make it up every day, but she says Mom will get mad if she doesn't. The bedcover is a pattern of dark reds and greens that I picked out myself because it "felt" like me.

J.C. sits up wearily and looks more afraid than I've ever seen him. "What kind of Plan B?"

She faces him. "A place to hide where no one can find us."

"J.C.'s place has more alarms than the White House," I say, not joking in the least. His mom is pretty paranoid.

"Are you crazy?" J.C. blurts across at me, shoving his errant bangs out of his eyes. "You saw *The Purge*."

Laura says, "Huh?"

"It's a movie," I tell her. "This family gets held hostage for trying to help someone who's supposed to get murdered on national purge night—"

"I saw it," she interrupts. "I just meant I don't get why you said that, J.C. This is different."

J.C. sits, eyes narrowed in a stubborn look, and says nothing.

I give him a long look. "She's right, no one's gonna *purge* your house. This is just one guy who's after you."

Everyone's quiet for a moment, and then Laura asks, "How do you know that for sure?"

"I saw it in his eyes, remember?"

She chews her lower lip. "You saw one guy *doing* the killing," she reminds me. "Doesn't mean others aren't involved."

"Holy crap!" J.C.'s eyes go round in stunned surprise. "She's right, Leo."

I consider Laura's idea, shuddering as I replay the scene in my mind. The jacket. The hand with the knife. J.C. bleeding out. "I don't think so."

"Why not?" Laura looks at me with her big, inquisitive blue eyes.

I shake my head to clear out the vision. "I only sense one person."

"My life depends on you sensing things, now?"

His angry tone causes me to recoil and I feel like I did something wrong, so I lower my gaze to the floor. "I'm sorry. I wish I could do more."

"J.C., Leo's busting his butt to keep you alive!" Laura snaps, her tone angrier than I've ever heard from her. "Least you can do is be grateful."

There's a long pause and then I hear "Sorry, Leo" in a grudging mumble.

Then I get an idea. I lift my head, excitement filling me. "The haunted house."

"Huh?" Laura gives me a look.

"What about it?" J.C. asks, not looking straight at me. I know he feels bad about disrespecting me, but I shrug it off.

"We can hide there," I say, my heart racing with the possibilities. "No one ever goes near that place except on Halloween. We'll be safe till morning."

Laura taps one hand atop the other in a time-out motion and says, "What are you guys talking about?" She points to herself. "New in town, remember?"

I nod at J.C. since he's the talker in this group.

"The haunted house is, like, the oldest one in Costa," he explains. "The guy who founded this town built it and lived there until he died. I guess he was, like, a hundred something when he finally kicked it."

Laura shrugs. "So? Why is it haunted?"

"It isn't," I mumble, but she's too focused on J.C. to turn my way.

"Well," J.C. goes on, ignoring my comment, "the house stayed in his family for generations until the last of his kids died. Then it got rented out by whoever owned the place at that point. Anyway, back in the day—"

"It was only eight years ago, J.C.," I mutter, but again I'm ignored.

"—the family who lived there had a grown son and teenage daughter and the son went all Amityville Horror on his family one night. Sliced them up with a big-ass butcher knife and then slit his own throat."

Laura pulls a disgusted face. "Oh, gross!"

As though J.C. suddenly recalls that this event was both horrific and involved a knife, he turns to me aghast. "Why the hell would we hide there? We scared the crap out of each other when we tried staying all night, remember?"

"Yeah, and we were nine years old."

"I heard weird noises that night," J.C. insisted. "So did you."

I turn to Laura, who looks annoyed that we're ignoring her. "It's a really old house and creaks and groans a lot," I explain. "There are no ghosts there."

She grins. "Even if there are, sounds like a dope place to hide out. Can I see it?"

J.C.'s face falls. "You mean right now?"

"Sure. Why not?" She turns from him to me, since I'm the designated driver.

"We can cruise by, but we can't get out of the car," I say.

"Why not?" That's J.C.

I look his way without making eye contact. "If neighbors see us creeping around the place tonight, it might give away our plan to hide there on Friday. We still don't know who has it in for you, remember?"

His eyes widen with fear and then he offers a congratulatory chin raise. "Smart thinking, Leo."

I stand up. "Let's go.

The haunted house, formally known in town as the Bresdin House after the guy who built it, sits almost alone at the very end of Main Street, right where the street curves away from the beach and becomes Beachfront Road, and the house has a great view of the ocean. Or so I've heard. Other than that one

Halloween when I was nine, I haven't been inside. And that time was at night and too dark to see the ocean. I heard it, though, loud and clear. That place was so creepy, and the mournful sound of the ocean so intense that, ghosts or no ghosts, I almost avoided going to the beach the following summer.

The house is a Victorian like mine and I like that style better than most of the newer homes in Costa. Despite having been built in 1918, it's in pretty decent shape, if you ask me, especially with no one taking care of it and all. Sure, the light blue paint is faded almost to white, but all the windows and doors are intact and, from the outside anyway, the place looks livable.

It has three floors because there's an attic. Well, four, if you count the basement. Most houses in SoCal don't have basements because of earthquakes, but I guess George Bresdin didn't think a quake was likely to strike near the beach. We haven't had any, either, though I've heard rumors that the Inglewood fault runs close enough to give us a hella good shake if it ever cuts loose.

The haunted house sits on a rise so there are wooden steps leading up to the porch and a heavy, brown-colored front door. The porch is set back from the rest and has a peaked roof above the door. A lot of the exterior paint has been eaten away, probably by the salty air. The windows are the slide-up kind and still in their original frames, from the look of them.

That Halloween when J.C. dared me to stay in the house with him, we'd snuck in through the backyard. Two concrete steps lead to a small, covered back porch that still has an old rocking chair resting by the door. Stairs ascend to the second-floor balcony which must jut out from a bedroom. I'm just guessing about that—J.C. and me never got that far. The house is locked up tight because the cops know us kids love to scare each other on Halloween. But we all know a way in through the basement crawlspace. From the basement, we can make our way up to the first floor, which is as far as J.C. and me got on that long-ago night.

I park half a block away and gaze through the windshield at the haunted house while J.C. regales Laura with our less than stellar adventures within its ancient walls. An old Chevy with faded black paint catches my eye in the rearview as it cruises up the otherwise empty street. It looks familiar, but I can't quite place it. As the car cruises past, the driver glances over and I hold my breath in surprise. It's Mr. Mendez, the janitor from school. He sees me and his facial expression instantly shifts. Seriously, he looks like the kid who got caught red-handed doing something wrong in every movie ever made.

I nudge J.C., who's telling Laura how we both hid underneath a big sofa when we heard rustling in the walls. He stops and looks at me. I point and he turns to stare out the windshield. By now, the car has slid on past and I watch as it slows slightly in front of the haunted house, as though Mr. Mendez plans to stop. Then, with a roar of the old engine, the car picks up speed and turns left onto Beachfront Road, vanishing from sight.

"What?" J.C. asks, his brows furrowed with confusion.

I don't answer. Instead, I shift into 'Drive' and pull away from the curb, heading in the same direction as Mendez. Beachfront Road eventually loops around to the back of Costa High. Why would Mendez be going there on a Sunday night when the school is closed? It makes no sense.

"Uh, Leo, talk to me here." J.C. sounds irked, like usual.

"Yeah, Leo," I hear from the backseat. "Clue us in. Who was that?"

I tell them who's in the car I'm following as I navigate the empty road alongside the beach. It is nearly dark now and I see a few stragglers walking to their cars carrying surfboards. Thankfully, none of them are Chet or his posse.

Laura has no opinion except that it's strange for the janitor to be around this neighborhood at night. J.C. agrees, but being J.C. proclaims, "He's up to something," as though he knows for sure.

I ignore him and focus on the road ahead. The streetlights have come on and some fog rolls in off the water, so I am very cautious. I don't want Mr. Mendez to know I'm following him, even though I can't even see the taillights of his car anymore. Certain he's heading for school, I turn left onto First Street and head toward La Costa High. Man, is that place scary at night! Seriously, my mom isn't into making horror movies, but if she ever decides to, Costa High would be the perfect location. Hell, it's creepy enough during the day.

The back gate into the rear staff parking lot is chained and padlocked at night. I know because some of us kids, including me and J.C., have climbed the chain-link fence on occasion and wandered around the school just to scare ourselves. What can I say? There's not much to do in this town on weekends. All the action is in Manhattan or Redondo.

The gates are closed as I pull up and all is quiet. I cruise past the driveway and park on the street, killing the engine. There is a long moment of silence as our eyes adjust to the dark. We stare out the windshield at the parking lot, at least as much of it as we can see. The dim emergency lights provide some illumination, but there's no sign of Mendez's car.

"He must've gone somewhere else," J.C. whispers, even though we're in the car and no one else can hear us.

"Maybe." But I don't think so. "Let's check."

I pop open my door and the others do the same. As though we all have the same thought, we close our doors quietly, cutting off the interior light. The fog dims the streetlights to almost nothing. It swirls around my head and obscures my vision. Where did so much fog come from so fast?

I glance at J.C. and Laura beside me and then slip out my phone. Keeping close to the exterior fence, which is a good eight feet high, I scurry along to the gates, the others right behind me. J.C. is almost inside my shirt he's so close and I know he's spooked. Hell, so am I, especially with everything that's been going on.

I stop at the gate and engage the flashlight app on my phone. I shine the beam on the padlock. The shaft is firmly in place. I grip it and tug, but it's locked tight.

"That's it, then," J.C. whispers, sounding relieved. "He went someplace else."

I raise my phone and shine the beam into the vacant parking lot. Fog swirls through the light, splitting off like a prism in all directions. I see the white lines and concrete bumpers, but no cars.

"C'mon, Leo, let's jam," J.C. whispers with urgency. "I hate this place even more at night."

I sweep my beam around the visible part of the lot one more time. The ocean sounds in the distance are lulling, but no cars cruise past. Sunday nights in Costa are deader than dead. Something black catches my eye. I'd have missed it if not for the dirty white of the fog. I sweep my beam back. Bingo. The rear fender of a black car juts out from around the other side of the building.

"He's here," Laura says casually, stating the obvious.

I lower my light and turn to them. J.C. has a distressed look on his face, but Laura displays her usual calm demeanor.

"I say we climb over and see what he's up to," I whisper, not really sure why. A gut feeling, maybe?

"I'm down." That's Laura, sounding all badass and ready for business.

J.C. squirms and fidgets. First of all, I know he's worried about messing up his clothes. Second, he's not athletic and hates climbing this fence (the last time we'd done it we were freshmen and he wore old clothes—which for J.C. meant one month old.)

"What's this have to do with my situation?"

My gut tells me this is related. "I don't know. But I've got a feeling."

He gazes at me through the fog, but fortunately I can't focus on his eyes for too long because dense white mist keeps drifting past them. "For real?"

I nod.

"Okay." But he doesn't sound convinced.

I reach out and place a hand on his shoulder to let him know I'm here for him. He offers a tight little smile in return. I glance at Laura. "You're okay to climb this?"

"I was the pitcher on my softball team back home. Strong arms." She raises both arms and flexes like guys always do.

I turn to the gate, slip my fingers through the chain links and clamber up with ease. Thanks to gymnastics, anything that involves lifting my own bodyweight is a breeze. I'm up and over before Laura even grabs on. She's halfway to the top as I drop lightly to the pavement of the parking lot. I look through the links at J.C. He looks back, as though considering waiting at the car. Then, with an audible sigh, he grabs the links and starts to climb.

If I was a jerkwad like Chet Hamilton, I'd be hooting and laughing at the awkward and clumsy way J.C. climbs that fence. I'd call him unflattering names and say he climbs like a girl. Except Laura climbs better than most guys, so that idiotic insult wouldn't fly, as though it ever has. No, I whisper words of encouragement as his shoes press against the gate to help his arms with the ascent. The gate is solid chain link, so it doesn't bend inward, which helps him climb. J.C. is kind of weak for a sixteen-year-old guy, I guess, even though he's taller than me, but fortunately he's thin as a rail, so there's not a lot of weight to pull. Lean as I am, I still weigh twenty pounds more than J.C.'s one-thirty-five because I have more muscle.

Huffing and puffing, J.C. finally reaches the top and attempts to throw one leg up and over. He misses the first attempt and both feet lose their traction against the gate. He dangles a moment, cursing under his breath.

"Relax, J.C.," I whisper up to him as loudly as I dare. "Pull up as you throw your leg over."

He already knows this from other fences we've climbed over the years, but when people panic they forget the most basic stuff.

He follows my instructions and straddles the fence a moment while catching his breath. He looks down at us through the fog. I can just make out his face and it looks taut with fear.

"You're almost there," Laura whispers beside me, and that seems to spur him on. I guess having a girl best him is too much for J.C.'s pride. He swings over and plants his feet against the chain links and slowly scrambles down. Honestly, he looks about as graceful as a turtle, but I would never tell him that.

When he gets close enough, Laura and me reach up to grab his legs. He inches down another foot and then lets go. We step back as he lands on his feet and stumbles. I jump forward to block his fall and he ends up in my arms. He gives me a long look, which I can't meet for obvious reasons, but doesn't push himself away. Stabilizing him, I release my hold and step back.

Without another word, I turn and head toward Mr. Mendez's car. I already know where he's gone—the school boiler room, which doubles as the maintenance office. I've heard that the boilers have been renovated and upgraded over the years, but are still pretty old. With all the money in this town, La Costa High is still, in many ways, a throwback to, like, pre-World War II. So far as I know, the old heating and plumbing system is still in place with only minor upgrades.

This parking lot feels creepier than usual because of the fog and the mysterious nature of Mr. Mendez's behavior. Maybe I've been wrong in thinking he's a nice old man?

I hear the others behind me, but my gaze remains fixed ahead as I scan the area. Spotting the black fender looming out of the fog like a breaching orca, I dart closer. Of course, the car is empty. I move past it to the boiler room door. This is one of the older buildings, but the forest-green paint is new and the door is made of shiny metal. A lone, sickly looking bulb burns above it, likely a security light that probably stays on all night. The door is closed. I reach out and grip the knob. It turns easily.

Laura leans in, but J.C. hangs back.

"What is this place?" she asks in a low, nearly silent whisper.

"Boiler room," I mouth back in a whisper that matches hers.

She nods.

J.C. gazes at me with obvious trepidation.

"You don't have to go inside," I whisper. "You can stand guard out here."

He shakes his head. "I go where you go."

Oddly, that small declaration gives me a fleeting moment of warmth. I face the shiny metal, my hand still on the knob, twist slightly, and pull open the door with care. I don't want it to screech and alert Mr. Mendez.

I've never been in here before and I'm surprised to see that the boilers are down one level, accessed by a metal catwalk and stairs. The boilers do look incredibly old, but seem clean, at least. The walls of this basement are made of brick and pipes extend out from the large boiler tanks in all directions like a metallic spider web. The two largest tanks look to be over ten feet high, but it's hard to tell looking down at them from above. The body of each is vertically rectangular with a round "face" at the top. That's the only way to describe it. There's writing along the top part of the "face" that almost looks like bangs of hair in the dim glow from the overhead fluorescents. Then there's a line straight down the middle from the "hair" that sure looks like a nose and the two egg-shaped stamps on either side look like eyes. Seriously, these boilers are twisted versions of Thomas the Tank Engine's face.

I glance behind me at Laura and J.C. They wait for me to make a move. I guess that means I'm the point man. I nod for them to follow and creep along the catwalk where it turns past the boilers. So far, there's no sign of Mr. Mendez and, other than the slight rumbling sounds from the boilers them-selves, this place is crazy quiet, sending my nerves into high alert mode.

The metal catwalk creaks a bit, but I hope the rumble from the boilers is enough to drown it out. We inch our way far enough along so that the door we entered is now hidden behind the massive tanks and I look down onto an open area. There's a kind of office with a desk and lots of tool racks attached to the walls around it. Mr. Mendez sits at the desk unlocking a drawer. I pull back and bump into J.C. I guess he's nervous because I hear a slight grunt and then it's cut off quickly. I turn to find Laura with her hand across J.C.'s mouth. I point behind me and down.

"Mendez," I mouth.

Laura nods and releases J.C. He looks at me with wide eyes, and I whisper, "Let me do the watching."

They step back into the shadows cast by the boilers so I can creep forward unimpeded. I inch my way to where the tool area is revealed and crouch low, my hands gripping the catwalk railing. It's icy cold to the touch, but keeps me more stable as I hunker down.

Mr. Mendez slides open the drawer and pulls out a plastic bag of something I don't recognize. Pills, maybe? Then he reaches back into the drawer and slips out an object I can't quite see. As I watch, he presses his thumb against it and there's a *snap* sound. I force myself not to cry out in shock. It's a knife! The now-extended blade has to be at least six inches. And, while there's no way to be sure from this distance, that blade looks disturbingly like the one in my vision.

I hear the door to the parking lot open with a creak and spin around in fear. J.C. and Laura do the same. We listen. The door closes quietly. Muffled footsteps approach along the catwalk.

Crap, we're trapped!

I ignore the other two and take in my surroundings. There's a door behind us. With no time to even wonder where it leads, I scuttle over as the footsteps grow louder. In seconds, the newcomer will round the colossal boilers and see us. I grab the door handle and pull. It's not locked. I ease it open and find a large storage room with boxes and plastic jugs lined up on shelves and odd pieces of equipment in corners on the floor. Laura darts inside without hesitation, but J.C. looks at me uncertainly. I shove him harder than I intend and squeeze in right behind him. The footsteps clanking along the catwalk are almost around the corner when I ease the door closed and hold the inside handle tightly to keep it from rattling. I feel J.C.'s raspy breath on my neck and his body pressed in tightly against mine as I place one ear up against the cold metal door and listen.

The footfalls saunter on past as though the person doesn't have a care in the world and isn't worried about being detected. I hear a muffled greeting in Spanish, but it's not Mendez. My breath freezes as I recognize that voice: Chet Hamilton! How the hell does he know Spanish? He's in French class. And why is Mr. Mendez sounding like they're best buds when Chet treats him like dog crap?

I crack the door open a bit and peek out. Down below the catwalk, I see Chet standing next to Mendez's desk. The older man remains seated. The objects I'd seen him pull from the drawer are in Chet's hands. He turns over the bag. I hear the plastic crinkling as he examines the contents with casual disinterest, as though this is a routine activity for him. I can see the contents more clearly now and they *are* pills. I'm about to step aside for J.C. so he can listen in on the Spanish when Chet speaks English.

"Thanks. Mr. M. You outdid yourself this time."

Mendez cracks a lopsided smile. "For the money you pay me, Mr. Hamilton, I aim to please."

Chet chuckles.

J.C. pushes his head beside mine so our cheeks touch. I focus on the scene below.

Chet picks up the knife and folds the blade back into place. Then he presses that button on the hilt and the blade pops back out. Now it looks like ten inches beneath the fluorescent lighting, but I know that's just my imagination.

"Has a good weight to it."

Mendez grunts. "It'll gut a man, if that's what you want."

Chet laughs. "That's not for you to know."

I feel J.C. shudder.

"I understand," Mendez replies.

Mendez acts like he and Chet are friends. And Mendez's English sounds much better than when he talks to me. What the hell is going on here?

J.C. pushes closer to the two-inch opening between the door and the jam. His face pushes mine forward and I bump my head on the edge of the door. A *thunk* sound echoes around us and pain shoots into my temple. J.C. jerks back, mortified. Before either of us can react, I hear, "What was that?"

Chet heard the *thunk*.

I peer past J.C. through the crack and spot Chet looking around the boiler room with obvious anxiety.

Mendez chuckles. "Relax, señor. Just a rat or a pipe. I hear stuff all the time."

Chet relaxes. "This place gives me the creeps. Too much like...."

Mendez waits, but Chet falls silent.

"Like what?"

Chet shakes his head, like he got beaned and his brain's been scrambled for a few seconds. "Nothing. Childhood memory. Here's your money."

He fishes in the front pocket of his jeans and pulls out a wad of bills. I can't see how much, but trust me, it's a fat wad. Mendez takes the money and slips it into the pocket of his work pants without a word. I'm pretty sure this isn't the first exchange of cash between them.

"Let's blow this place." Chet glances around into the shadows beyond the boilers and looks almost afraid.

His nervousness intrigues me, but I can't think about it now because Mendez locks the drawer of his desk and stands. As they both turn toward the steps up to the catwalk, I yank my head back in and bump J.C., who stifles a small gasp. I ease the door shut again and hold the handle. Two sets of footsteps can be heard echoing outside and then striding past on the catwalk. The sounds recede and I hear nothing more.

We wait for at least a minute before I turn the knob and ease the door outward. The lights down by the desk area are off and the dark boiler room suddenly reminds me of a Stephen King book I read once called *The Shining*, the one about the old hotel with the haunted boiler room and tons of nasty ghosts. And the boy with supernatural powers. Kind of like me.

Slowly, I push open the door far enough for J.C. to stumble out. He's pressed so close to me that once there's an open space he pops out like a champagne cork. I stumble onto the catwalk and Laura spills out right behind me. Before any of us can move, I hear a sound that shoots dread straight into my heart—a key turning in a door lock.

"Oh, crap!" I hiss and scurry along the metal catwalk. My footfalls are muted because I know how to be light on my feet, but as I near the corner I guess J.C. and Laura must've figured out that sound, too, because they hurry after, not even trying to be quiet. I dart around the boilers and rush to the door leading outside. I grasp the knob, even though I already know what I'll find. I twist, but the knob doesn't move.

We're locked in.

I hear a car pulling away outside and then nothing more. I do something almost unheard of—I curse. J.C. is so startled he huffs loudly and Laura gives us a funny look. I'm weird by teen standards in many ways and one of those is my thinking that cuss words sound stupid, so I seldom use them.

"I'm sorry, you guys," I say, barely controlling my anger. "We're trapped and it's my fault!"

"How do you figure that?" Laura asks.

I glimpse the whites of her eyes, but little else in the pitch-blackness. "Because it was my idea to follow Mendez inside."

"You didn't exactly force us to come, you know," she replies while I fumble my phone from my pants pocket and engage the flashlight app.

I grunt in response to her comment. She's right, but I still feel responsible as I shine the cone of light on the doorknob. No keyhole on this side.

"Too bad," Laura says, sounding much calmer than I feel. "If there was a keyhole I could pick the lock."

"Yeah?" That's J.C. In the darkness with my phone light bouncing shadows off the side of his face, his disheveled black hair and hellishly long eyelashes make him look pretty damned scary.

I shift the light to Laura, who shrugs. "My dad used to lock me in my room a lot, so I taught myself how to pick locks with a paper clip."

Maybe it's the "lock me in my room" part, but her words shut me down and diffuse my anger at myself. At least my mother never did that!

J.C. glances at me, and even with the shadows dancing across his face I see his mouth open in shock. I look around and spot pipes twisting and rising high above us. I follow them with my eyes and note how close they are to a small window that looks maybe eight feet up. I can climb the pipes easily. That's gymnastics 101. But opening the window and dropping down to the parking lot outside, that would be a problem. Then there's the other issue about how I'd get the door unlocked. I guess Laura could, from what she says, but she'd have to climb up and drop down with me.

I step toward the array of pipes, figuring I'll climb on up and check out how the window is locked. J.C. puts a hand on my arm and opens his mouth to say something when I hear a key in the door lock behind me. I spin around and shine my light on the knob. It turns slightly. I freeze, and J.C. stiffens beside me. I switch off the light. None of us make a sound. We wait for the door to open.

Sweat dribbles from my underarms down the inside of my shirt as I glance at J.C. He's pressed up against me so close I feel his heart pounding in his chest.

But nothing happens.

The door doesn't open.

We wait for what feels like hours. A hand snakes around my back and taps my shoulder. I turn to find Laura's pale face floating in the darkness. She whispers, "I think I heard someone walking away."

I nod. I think I heard the same thing. Right after the knob rattled. I know what she wants me to do, so I reach out for the knob and grasp it. J.C. slaps a hand down on mine and I know what he's thinking. It could be a trap—if I open the door, Mendez will attack. Maybe I'm overconfident in my Aikido abilities, but I honestly think I can fend off an old man. I turn the knob and ease the door outward.

The same lone pool of light illuminates the asphalt outside, but I see no feet in that light. I decide to go for it and shove the door open. At the same time, I leap forward into a defensive stance, my hands raised to grab anyone who might try to attack. The door slams back against the side of the building as the whole of the parking lot comes into view.

It's empty.

I realize I'm holding my breath and release it as J.C. and Laura flank me. By now, my shirt is pretty damp with sweat and I'm more than ready to go home and hide in my room for the rest of the night.

J.C. blurts out, "What the hell just happened?" His shirt clings to his torso with wetness and I see he's even more shaken than me.

"Let's get out of here."

That's Laura, and I don't need to be told twice. I spin around to close the door and then sprint toward the gate. The black sedan is gone and the gate's still locked. I pause at the base of the fence for the others. J.C. starts to say something as he lopes up, but I shake my head and stoop down, cupping my hands together. He gets the message and grabs hold of the chain-link fence. Once he places his right foot into my cupped hands, I boost him up as far as I can. He claws his way up the fence as Laura leaps forward and joins him. Once I see they are both over, I grab hold and practically fly up and over to join them on the sidewalk outside.

Panting and slightly shaking from fear, I glance around the dimly lit street, but see no cars and no people. Together, we dash to my Prius and practically jump in. I gun the engine, and we're gone in seconds, leaving Costa High behind us in the darkness.

Laura asks the question we're all thinking: "Why would Mendez let us out if he knew we were spying on him?"

"How could he know we were there?" J.C. stares at me in the flickering illumination from passing street lights.

I don't know why they think I have all the answers. "He might be hoping we won't tell Harris what we saw."

"His ass would be arrested for sure," J.C. says, his voice returning to its normal tone. "And Hamilton buying drugs. We can use that against him."

"No."

I glance over as I roll to a stop for a red light and see J.C.'s mouth open wide in shocked surprise.

"Why not?"

I consider my answer. "First of all, we don't know what he bought. Then there's the fact that he's pretty chummy with Mendez in private, but talks mess in public."

"Yeah, that's weird," J.C. admits grudgingly. "It's like he was putting on a show the other day when he kicked the old guy's bucket over."

As I pull away from the light, there isn't much traffic so my mind has plenty of room to think about things other than driving. I bite my lower lip as I consider everything I've seen and heard tonight. Sure, most people, especially teens, put on "shows" for other people, posturing and pretending and hiding their true selves for fear of being rejected. Chet being chummy with Mendez in private and rude in public makes sense if the old man is supplying him with drugs. But what about how Chet reacted when he heard us make a noise? The expression on his face looked anything but haughty. It looked terrified.

We discuss what we'd seen until I drop Laura off at home, but reach no conclusions. We can't even decide what kind of drugs Chet bought. They were pills, but what kind?

J.C. is too rattled to sleep at his house, so he sends a text to his mom that he's staying with me and I'll drive him to school the next day. She sends a text back:

'Don't get each other pregnant. JK, sweetheart. Be good.'

J.C. burns with anger as he reads this aloud to me, and I'm even more speechless than usual. Why do adults think humiliating kids is funny?

"Ignore her, like always." I try to keep my anger in check, but he obviously hears it because he offers a tight smile.

"Thanks for being my friend, Leo."

"Back at you."

We drive the rest of the way in silence.

Since he's over at my house so often anyway, he keeps extra clothes and hygiene items in the spare room. Before he heads off to bed, he says, "We're never gonna find out who owns that jacket, are we?"

"Doesn't look like it."

We're both wrong.

CHAPTER NINE

YOU BETTER NOT TELL ANYONE WHAT YOU SAW

Mom's gone when J.C. and me get breakfast the next morning. That deal went through, so she's deep into pre-production on her latest hoped-for blockbuster and is barely home these days. As a child, I used to love going to the studio and hanging around the set while movies were being shot. But it was mostly because I wanted to be near my mom, not because watching movies being made is exciting. It's pretty tedious, actually. They shoot the same scene over and over again on sets that look fake in real life, even though they end up looking awesome onscreen.

Estella would bring me to the set, where we'd sit off to the side and she'd stay with me every minute. She wasn't comfortable with children being around "Hollywood types," as she called actors and directors, because they set bad examples for kids. At least, that's what she always told me. I just wanted to see my mom. After a while, I'd get bored and ask Estella to take me to the park to play, which she was more than happy to do. When I finally realized those movie sets were more important to my mom than I was, I hated them and haven't been back since I was eight.

I know J.C. is stressing before he utters the only words he says while we get ready for school: "Only five days left." He wears mismatched clothes for the second or third time since I've known him. His hair is usually so moussed up it won't move even in a gale. But today, it droops, still wet from the shower.

He doesn't even use the blow-dryer, so it straddles his eyebrows like dangling black thread.

The weather is cool today—the heat wave finally broke over the weekend—so J.C. wears a fancy jacket, while I throw on a black hoodie over my usual loose-fitting shirt and pants. As a finishing touch, I give my bushy hair a quick run-through with the brush. When that's done, I look up to find J.C. standing in the doorway to my bathroom staring at me as though not really looking. And that's when he says those four words: "Only five days left."

I feel his distress and want to say the right thing to comfort him, but nothing comes. We head out to my car in a silence that feels a lot thicker than usual.

We walk from the parking lot through the covered breezeway that leads to the quad and head for our usual spot to meet up with Laura. Normally, J.C. talks up a storm and I just nod occasionally. But today he seems too afraid to speak, like somehow talking will hasten his fast-approaching date with death. I think I understand how he's feeling and I really want to help him somehow, but I don't find anything useful to say and just trudge along feeling like the loser I've always been.

Laura sits at our outside table sipping an orange juice from the cafeteria. As we slide in beside her, she pushes two plastic bottles our way.

"Bought you some juice. Guys never eat healthy." She offers a smile meant to make us feel good, but it doesn't affect J.C. in the slightest, so I don't smile, either.

J.C. looks around at the milling students and the antique buildings with wide, lost eyes, as though knowing this week might be his last opportunity to see everything he's never paid attention to. Laura obviously senses the problem because she says, "We still have five days to figure this out, J.C."

He nods, but remains focused on the upper windows of the main building, as though hoping he'll find his answer in the sun's reflection. I twist the cap off my juice and take a swig, thinking Laura is kind of right—I probably wouldn't eat very well if not for Sylvia's cooking.

Before we can talk about the previous night, a large crowd of boisterous kids enters from the parking lot and starts across the quad in our direction. I see Chet Hamilton's head in the center because he's one of the tallest guys at Costa High, and it seems the other kids are surrounding him for some reason. I can't tell why everyone's so excited unless he's walking onto campus with no shirt on again so he can show off his buffness. Wouldn't be the first time Harris had to tell him to wear a shirt at all times while on school grounds, even if he's leaving for a surf competition.

I glance at Laura and she tosses off a casual shrug. I turn back to the group of chattering students and note that they have all stopped and Chet has his back turned. A bad feeling comes over me. I stand to get a better look, the juice still in my hand.

"What's up?"

That's Laura, but I don't respond. I don't know if J.C. is watching or not, but the crowd parts slightly and I get a quick glimpse of Chet's back. I drop my juice onto the table. It strikes the metal with a *clunk* and orange juice splashes out to drip through the corrugated holes of the table top.

J.C. mutters, "The hell, Leo!"

But my gaze remains riveted to Chet Hamilton's back. He's not shirtless, as I'd first suspected. He's wearing a jacket. A black leather jacket. The crowd closes around him before I can make out the design on that jacket, but the sick feeling in the pit of my stomach tells me I already know what it is. I step away from the table and walk slowly toward the moving swarm of kids. I hear, "Leo, what's wrong?" from J.C. behind me, but my gaze remains fixed on Chet Hamilton. I wait for an opening so I can glimpse the back of his jacket.

I sense J.C. and Laura rising to follow me, but I don't turn to look. I feel like I'm in a dream, walking in slow motion toward a fate I can't escape no matter what I do. Kids are prattling on about "cool threads" and "badass jacket" and "rad design" and offer other gushing compliments. I can't tell if they're just kissing up to Chet or if they really dig his jacket and I don't care either way. I just need to confirm for myself what I already know.

I push my way past several girls and catch their dirty looks from the corner of my eye. Chet's back is still facing me, but Wilson and Grady block my view. They're so close to Chet they might as well be glued. A girl up ahead shouts at them, "Move so we can see."

Wilson glances back and leers at the pretty blonde before stepping to one side and shoving Grady to the other. The crowd is still moving and I pace them. As Wilson and Grady step aside, Chet's jacket comes fully into view.

Despite knowing what I'll see, I groan loudly enough to be heard by kids on either side of me. The snake looks exactly like the one in my vision, the one drawn so expertly by Laura. I'm stunned. J.C. was right—it *is* Chet Hamilton who plans to kill him!

J.C. is suddenly at my side, his fists balled up in fury. "I told you, Leo!"

I sense Laura to my left, but Chet must've heard J.C. because he turns and those piercing blue eyes focus on us. He stops and the wave of students ebbs to a halt. The body of the snake twists around the front of the jacket in several coils before looping back to the rear. Chet grins in his usual haughty manner.

"Well, if it isn't Ninja Turtle and his Mexican boyfriend," he sneers. Then he glances at Laura beside me. "Laura the Lesbo, too." He chuckles. "Admiring my jacket, are you?" He tosses a thumb back over his shoulder at the cobra design. "Cool design, huh? One of a kind. Custom made. Bet Mexican boyfriend wishes he had one."

J.C. starts forward. "I knew it was you!"

I grab his arm and hold him back. "J.C.!"

Chet loses the grin for a moment. "Me?" Then it returns. "Oh, you mean I was the one who would always dress better than you? Course, I am."

Wilson and Grady laugh and a chuckle of amusement wafts through the crowd.

"Where'd you get the design?" That's Laura, thankfully distracting J.C. with her question.

Chet eyes her like he might a bug. "Had a friend draw it for me."

Laura stiffens with rage. "That's not—"

I elbow her harder than I intend, but she gets the point and doesn't finish her sentence.

Chet stares at us with a peculiar look on his face. I can't quite describe it. He looks like he wants to speak, but isn't quite sure what to say, which isn't like Chet Hamilton at all.

"I'm gonna stop you!" J.C. takes another angry step forward.

I don't want to fight Chet here in front of everyone, but I know I'll have to if J.C. keeps running his mouth. I squeeze his arm hard and he winces. Turning to me in anger, he snaps, "That hurt, Leo!"

"Leave it alone for now."

"But he—"

"I said leave it!" My voice comes out like the crack of a bullet and even I'm surprised at how forceful it sounds.

Wilson laughs. "Whoa, Chet, looks like we know who's the husband." He laughs and Grady reaches out to high five him.

J.C.'s face turns even stormier and I step in front of him. "Let's go. Now!"

Laura steps closer. "He's right, J.C."

J.C. looks over my shoulder at Chet and glowers. I push gently and he takes a step back. With a heavy exhalation of breath, he turns and stalks off past our table and out toward the football field. Amidst sniggers and nasty comments, Laura hurries after him. I turn one last time to eye Chet Hamilton. He looks stunned. That's the only way I can describe his expression. Even when Wilson says, "Losers" and generates a huge laugh from the gathered kids, Chet's expression doesn't change.

I turn and sprint after J.C. and Laura, catching up to them at the bleachers flanking the field. J.C. paces back and forth like a frustrated tiger and Laura is saying, "—still not sure because he lied about where he got the design."

"I told Leo it was him!" J.C. spits as I jog over. He stops pacing to glare at me. "You were wrong."

I feel choked up and muddled, like I let him down somehow. "Yeah. But at least we know now."

He struts up to me so fast I freeze into a defensive stance, like I would against an opponent who plans to strike me. He notes my posture and stops up short, looking abashed. "I would never hit you."

"You'd get your ass kicked if you did." I offer a tiny smile to assure him I wouldn't do that. At least, I hope I'd never have to.

His eyes widen, and then his angry look melts into his own tiny smile. "That's for sure."

"I won't let him hurt you, J.C.," I say, my voice sounding breathy, rather than strong like I want. I wish I could make eye contact, but I can't.

He squints with uncertainty. "You can't know that for sure."

"Yes, I can." This time my voice is steady.

"What if he brings Wilson and Grady and they triple team you?"

I hesitate only a moment, biting my lip. "I can take them, too." I'm not one hundred percent sure about that, depending on if they can get the drop on me somehow, but I don't admit this.

"I'll be there," Laura says with conviction. "It'll be three against three."

"Can you fight?" J.C. asks dolefully. "Because I sure as hell can't."

She offers a tight smile and waves her right arm in the air. "I got a helluva throwing arm. Perfect aim."

J.C. eyes me like I'm the leader of this group.

Me, a leader? I'd laugh if I weren't so stressed. "Sounds like a plan."

"We need to follow him tonight," J.C. says quietly. "And every night. See what he's up to." He looks at me with his mouth set in a straight, determined line.

I look away, but give a slight nod.

"That's a great idea," Laura says as she takes one of J.C.'s hands and one of mine. "Now let's get to class before Harris comes looking."

The three of us walk back toward the main building.

My second surprise of the day is inside my locker.

The lockers at Costa High are old school with tiny slats built into them, like breathing holes in animal travel boxes. I guess they're there for us losers who get sealed inside of lockers by bullies or upperclassmen. That way we don't suffocate before someone decides to show mercy and let us out.

Anyway, I spin my combo into the lock and pop open the door. A folded piece of paper tumbles out. J.C. has his locker open a few down from mine and he's holding a sheet of paper in his hands. He looks as pale as the paper. I unfold mine and my breath freezes. Typed onto the page is one sentence:

'You better not tell anyone what you saw in that boiler room.'

I glance at J.C. and his wide, fearful eyes tell me his note says the same thing. Laura pushes her way through the bustling crowd as the first period bell rips through the chatter of muted conversations. She holds a paper in her hands and has her mouth open to speak, but stops when she sees us clutching our own sheets of paper. Like magnets, the three of us drift together and scan each other's note. They're identical.

We don't speak. There's no need. We all know it has to be Chet or Mr. Mendez. They're the only two who we saw last night. My money is on Chet, but the bigger question swirling around in my head is, how did he see us? We kept well-hidden and neither of them even looked in our direction. Then I realize—Mendez let us out and later told Chet we were there!

I feel eyes on me and whip my head around. The hallway is clearing as kids push their way into open classrooms. My heart pounds and I nudge J.C. He and Laura follow my gaze and I hear a slight intake of breath from J.C.

Down the hall where the corridor branches off, Mr. Mendez swishes his mop around on the floor where I see some colored liquid, no doubt juice spilled by some kid. But the older man isn't looking at the spill he's mopping. His gaze is fixed on us, squarely, without a doubt. I stiffen. J.C. leans in to me and I feel the tremble in his arm. I glance at Laura, but she's good at hiding her emotions, so I can't tell if she's scared or not.

She turns to us. "Come on, let's get to class."

I shove the note into my pocket and grab my books while J.C. reluctantly does the same. He turns to me.

"Leo."

"I'll protect you. I promise," I say, but I'm not sure exactly how I'll do that since what we're up against seems to keep getting bigger by the day.

He nods, but his face remains twisted with fear.

"I'll see you guys later," Laura says and moves off down the hall.

Affecting an inner strength I don't feel, I start toward our first period classroom, J.C. trailing me like a puppy. I flash back to when I used to trail him like a puppy because he was filled with swagger and snark and his protective bubble made me feel lucky to have him. Now our roles have reversed and he's counting on me to save him. But can I?

J.C. and I have to sit through two classes with Chet insufferably showing off his new threads and bragging about how the jacket is one of a kind. We sit as far away from him and his homies as we can, but he still tosses a few smirks in our direction throughout the morning.

During lunch, we meet up with Laura at our table in the quad and plan our strategy. J.C. worries that Chet will have others with him on Friday and he wants us to be prepared. Given my experience with Chet backing down in the second grade, I agree with him, but confess I'm still surprised by this new turn of events. Chet Hamilton never seemed like the type to commit murder, if there is such a type. J.C. thinks murder is just the next step for a bully like Chet, but I'm not so sure. I recall those times I saw Chet's big brother chewing him out for looking weak in public. In truth, his brother made me happy to be an only child.

I suggest that maybe the older brother might have brainwashed Chet, but

J.C. will have none of it. "He's his own jerkwad!" he snaps, sneering. "Doesn't need his psycho brother to call the shots. 'Sides, Bob's in prison."

Chet's brother stabbed some guy in a bar fight a couple of years back and got twenty-five to life for second degree murder. His mom didn't even try to defend him, from what I remember. It was a pretty big scandal, as you can imagine, but I didn't pay too much attention.

"It was just a thought," I say and fall silent.

Laura shakes her head in dismay. "Some family. And mom's a cop, too."

Thankfully, we don't see the Chet Pack at all during lunch and don't have them in our afternoon classes, either. When the final bell rings, I hurry to my car to await J.C. and Laura, as we'd agreed. Students pour out into a parking lot that looks like a luxury car showroom and, as usual, they ignore me and my cheap-ass Prius. I keep my eyes open for J.C. and Laura—they have the last class of the day together—but really I watch for Chet to strut out to his loaded, spanking new BMW Z4. Pitch black, it reflects the sun like a mirror. Parked several rows away from mine, the two-door convertible awaits its haughty owner while several kids pause to admire its sleek curves on their way out the front gate.

J.C. and Laura arrive before Chet, breathless and panting slightly. We jump into my car and I join the queue to exit onto First Street. My hope is to wait down the street for Chet to cruise past and then follow him. Sure, my mom has produced tons of films and TV shows where people tail each other in their cars, but I've never tried it in real life and my palms sweat with nervous anticipation. What will I do if Chet notices? My car does pretty much stand out in this town.

Oh, well, I'll cross that bridge if I have to.

I park a block from school, letting my car idle in front of the CVS parking lot. It's just after three and the lot is busy, but traffic on First Street is light. In back, Laura has her head turned and stares out the back window. J.C. and I have our eyes glued on the rearview mirror. It doesn't take long before Chet's Z4 races up First Street from the direction of school. Normally, Wilson and Grady's equally fancy cars would be in pursuit or they'd be racing each other, but today it's only Chet. He whizzes past in a streak of black and I shift into gear to follow.

Fortunately, he's stopped by a light at the next block. There are several cars between his and mine and I intend to keep it that way. The light turns green and with a blast of an obviously cranked muffler, Chet peels out and hangs a quick turn onto Stafford Street. I pursue.

"Looks like he's headed for home," J.C. says in a quiet voice.

I nod, but focus on the driving.

J.C. turns out to be right. After several more quick turns amidst a screeching of his thick tires, Chet pulls up to his luxurious two-story home and zips into the driveway. The car lurches to a stop and I hear the gears grinding. I almost feel sorry for his transmission. I stop several houses back and roll to the curb in front of Mandy Michelson's home. She's a senior at Costa High who used to mock me almost daily in eighth-grade for being so shy. Mostly, I think she was mad because I didn't follow her around with my tongue hanging out like so many of the other boys did.

Chet exits his car and glances both ways up the street. I freeze, sure he knows he's been followed and will recognize my car. But it's only a glance he tosses in our direction before he struts to the front door and uses a key to let himself in. The door closes and I turn to J.C.

"Maybe he's just gonna stay home."

He grunts. "Maybe."

"If he's gonna do anything sketchy," Laura offers from the back seat, "it'll probably be at night." She leans in between the two front seats and awaits a response.

I glance at J.C. "I agree."

His eyes remain riveted to Chet's house, like somehow he'll have answers to all his questions just by staring. Slowly, like he's fighting against someone trying to twist his head around, J.C. looks over at me. "Yeah."

"So we head on back after dinner," Laura says. Her matter-of-fact tone calms my pounding heart. She's cool and collected and that's how we all need to be right now.

"Sounds like a plan," I say, waiting for J.C. to agree. He nods, but continues staring with squinting eyes at the two-story home with the Spanish-style terracotta roof tiles.

I shift into drive and make a U-turn. I have sense enough to not drive past Chet's house in case he might be looking out a window. I make a left at the corner and head home.

Laura texts her parents that she's 'hanging out with those same boys' and will be home after dinner. Her dad's reply causes her to burst into laughter and me to turn red when she reads it aloud: "Tell those boys to keep their hands off my daughter."

J.C. just grunts, but I feel humiliated.

We knock out our homework, though J.C. keeps checking his Facebook for any more threatening messages and never quite completes his essay. Sylvia had prepared tamales and salad, so we eat while we work. But my stomach roils with nervousness because I obsess over everything that can go wrong tonight as we tail Chet to who knows where. Part of me hopes he stays home, but the other part wants to know why he'd risk prison just to get back at J.C. for dissing him. It still makes no sense to me and I wonder if I misread my vision somehow.

As dusk approaches, we pack up our school stuff and shove it all into our backpacks. We don't even talk as we descend the stairs and head out the front door. My car is the only one in the driveway, which means Mom is still on set. We pile in and I drive down the darkening street in the direction of Chet Hamilton's house. None of us have any idea what we'll learn, if anything, which is why we don't talk, I guess. J.C. bites his fingernails, something he hasn't done since the second grade.

As before, we park down the street from Chet's house, this time in a darkened area between street lights so he can't spot my car. We don't have long to wait before he exits his front door and sprints to the Z4 still parked in his driveway. I only get a glimpse beneath the front house lights, but Chet looks like he's wearing a button down short sleeve shirt and really tight pants, maybe leather. It's tough to tell for sure and he's into his car too fast anyway. J.C. tosses me a raised eyebrow and I shrug. We'll know what he's up to soon enough. If I don't lose him, that is.

I focus on driving. The other two sit sin silence and don't distract me. I almost lose Chet on the freeway as he zips in and out of traffic, but manage to keep him in my line of sight. He takes the 405 to the 10 and heads toward L.A. My curiosity meter jumps even higher when he exits at La Cienega Boulevard and heads north. The surface streets, as always, are narrow and busy and I almost lose him three more times before he turns onto Santa Monica Boulevard in West Hollywood. This is a super busy street with tons of clubs and restaurants and places to shop or socialize.

Chet whips left onto a smaller street and swings around behind some kind of club. My window is down and I hear music blasting from the open front door as I pass. The name above the door is "Teen Rage" and beneath that "The Best Under 18 Club in L.A." I recall what Chet said about J.C. going to clubs down here in WeHo and that's when J.C. groans like he just got a serious stomach cramp.

I glance over. He's slumped down in his seat and looks like he might throw up. I want to ask what's wrong, but I need to keep an eye on Chet's car. There is a valet parking lot that looks like it serves several of the clubs in the area, but Chet passes it and slips down a side street to an open parking space very close to the rear of Teen Rage. I slow to a crawl, careful that no drivers are behind me who might honk and attract Chet's attention. He leaps from his car. Now I see his shirt is unbuttoned halfway down so even beneath the streetlights his muscular chest is evident. He struts up the side street and around toward the entrance to Teen Rage.

I confess I'm disappointed as I drive past Chet's car and find another space on the street to pull into. Chet's just clubbing. Nothing sinister about that. All the Costa kids are partiers, I think, except the three of us in this car. I park, kill the engine, and turn to J.C. He seriously looks sick to his stomach.

"'Sup, man? You okay?"

He nods, but says nothing. Two young guys walk along the sidewalk in the direction of the club. They look our age. J.C. slumps down farther in his seat as they pass by his window and I'm more bewildered. I twist around to Laura in back. From the look on her face, she's also mystified by his behavior.

"Looks like he's just clubbing," I say to her because I want to hear a human voice. J.C. is weirding me out right now.

"But why all the way out here?"

"Maybe there aren't many under eighteen clubs around," I suggest.

"I think we should go inside and scope the place out," she suggests. "See what he's up to. Just in case."

I hesitate. Crowds. Loud music. Noise. People bumping into me. Everything I hate is inside that building. My heart starts pounding. I dread going in. But then I see J.C.'s bloody corpse in my mind's eye and fight back my revulsion. "Okay."

I turn and grab my door handle when I feel J.C.'s hand on my other arm. I look at him in the darkened interior, but he refuses to even glance at me.

Still hunkered down, his gaze remains riveted up at the windshield. "I can't go in there."

His voice is so low I almost don't hear it. "Huh?"

"I can't go in with you guys," he whispers, his voice breathy and anxious.

"Why not?" And then I know. J.C. doesn't answer. He knows I figured it out. "How long you been coming to this club?"

"Three months."

I'm so stunned I think I stop breathing for a moment. Three months? How did I not know?

J.C. finally turns to me, but his eyes are in shadow, so I can only see the lower half of his face. "I'm sorry, Leo. I should've told you."

I say nothing. I don't know what to say or even if I'm supposed to respond. He knows me well enough to know I won't accuse him of ditching me or sneaking around behind my back. He also knows I wouldn't have come with him, but I guess being his friend I still think he should have told me. How hard would that have been? Maybe this is the beginning of the end of our friendship?

He must be reading my mind because he says, "I wasn't ditching you, Leo, honest. I just… I hate those kids in Costa, you know that. And I love to dance and you don't like dancing and crowds and… I just wanted to meet some other kids and have fun."

He stops talking, and even though I avoid looking into his eyes, I take stock of his expression because it seems confused. His averted eyes look fearful, but there's something like anger—or maybe it's a challenge—in the hard set of his mouth. I guess he's waiting for me to say something or get mad or whatever, but why would I? Everything he said is true. That's why no one but him ever hangs out with me. I'm the opposite of fun.

"I'm sorry, Leo," he whispers, lowering his gaze to the handbrake beside me. "I can't go in there. People know me."

My heartrate accelerates even more. He's as outgoing as they come. With me he can't be himself because I'm a deadbeat. I feel like someone punched me in the gut and actually knocked the wind out of me. That hasn't happened since I was very young and just learning Aikido, but I remember the humiliation I felt back then, and I feel the same way now.

"Laura and me'll go in." I don't wait for his answer. I grab the door handle and yank it up hard, flinging open the door.

"Leo!"

I don't turn back. I step out onto the pavement as Laura exits the back seat and looks at me with sympathy. I don't want her sympathy. I turn back to J.C. I don't even lean down to see his face. "If Chet heads to his car, text me."

I slam the door and start down the side street along the backside of the club. The music is louder now as Laura sprints up beside me and keeps pace.

"He didn't mean to hurt you."

My heart wobbles with uneasy fear. "I'm not hurt. I knew he'd ditch me some day."

"Did you hear his voice, Leo? If words could be tears, his would've been."

We pass behind various business establishments, each with a dumpster against the wall, and it seems ridiculous that I'm starting to sweat with anxiety in such a boring, ordinary place. I stop at the corner. The club entrance is just ahead and there's a small group of teens milling around, more than I'd have thought for a Monday night. I stare at them for a moment, picturing J.C. in the middle of that group, the center of attention and happy.

I don't plan to speak my thoughts, but I do. "I hold him back, Laura, don't you see? He's snarky as hell because he has to be. At Costa, everyone makes fun of him 'cause he's with me. That's why he didn't tell me. He was afraid I might've tagged along."

In the moody streetlight, her round face looks soft and gentle, but I avoid her eyes. Her blonde hair wafts in the cool breeze and her mouth curves into a frown. "I don't believe that, Leo. I only just got to know you guys, but he's your friend for real. And he's snarky because he wants to be. My girlfriend is the same. Defense mechanism, I always tell her."

I consider her words. Yeah, J.C. gets pretty damned sensitive about lots of things and he's been snarky since the second grade, so maybe it's not all about me after all.

"Thanks," I tell her, feeling a little better.

But then I turn and look back at the teens milling in front of the club and picture myself walking through them to get inside. I'm anxious all over again. I breathe deep.

"Now let's find Chet without being seen." I'll deal with the J.C. stuff after I save his life. He may have kept secrets, but he's still my best friend.

A mountainous bald guy who looks like the typical goon bodyguard right out of my mom's central casting office takes our ten-dollar cover charge and ushers us through the door. If I thought it was loud outside the club, inside is deafening. It's not the loudness that gets to me, it's the way I feel the music crowding into my brain and suffocating me. It's just like people swarming into my space. My heartrate speeds up the moment I step into that pounding techno beat among those dancing, bouncing bodies spinning past and brushing up against me. I break out in a cold sweat.

Laura takes my hand and leans in to my ear. "You okay?"

I nod, but I'm really not. I want out, and I want out now! The club has a colorful dancefloor—red and lit from below so it casts all the teen dancers into weird shadowy figures that look ghastly. There's a refreshment area on the other side, lit in garish neon colors where teens mill around eating and drinking and laughing. The club isn't so dark that we can't see faces on the dance floor and I spot Chet pretty fast. His height and broad shoulders make him stand out. I point and Laura looks into the crowd.

Chet seems popular. He dances through the writhing mass of bodies as though working the room. Several girls pull him into passionate kisses, rubbing their hands along his chest as they do. I squirm even more, wondering how I would feel if girls wanted to do that with me. Of course, they don't, but I often wonder what it would feel like to be popular and not, you know, a loser. I'm not sure I could handle it.

I'm surprised to see some of the boys grab Chet and dance with him as he mingles. And Chet doesn't object. Several of these boys rub his chest just like the girls did and Chet laughs and seems to like it. I look again at the dancers and finally understand that it's kind of a free-for-all. Boys dance with girls, girls with girls, boys with boys. I've never been anywhere like this before.

Laura leans in and says, "I've been to clubs like this in San Diego. No one cares who you're into."

That's obvious, but what shocks me is that Chet Hamilton doesn't care, given all the crap he gives me and J.C. and other kids at school. But here he's allowing boys to feel him up and he likes it! This whole thing gets crazier by the second. As Chet veers in our direction, I pull Laura back into a dark area off the dance floor where our faces won't be visible. I can't go any farther into the club, anyway. My social anxiety is in hyperdrive and I'll freak big time if I have to fight my way through this crowd.

Chet accepts a few more kisses from girls and gropes from boys as he turns toward the refreshment area and strikes up a conversation with a gorgeous brunette wearing a tight halter top and shorts that, even beneath the mood lighting, leave nothing to the imagination.

Laura lets go of my hand and pats me gently on the arm. "You stay here. I'll move closer and watch him."

I'm grateful for the shadows to hide my stressed-out expression. "Thanks."

She moves off along the fringe of the crowd and I glance at some of the other kids. They look around my age or a little older and they're all having fun. Why am I always the one who can't fit in? That's why J.C. comes to places like this, because he can hang out with fun kids instead of weirdoes like me.

I lose track of time and can't even see Laura anymore. The lighting shifts periodically in a swirling morass of color. Chet leaves the brunette after a while and mingles with other kids loitering in the refreshment area. He seems well liked by everyone, which also surprises me. I get a few texts from J.C., but I just send back the same terse reply:

'nothings happening stand by'

I guess I'm still mad about him hiding this place from me.

I'm so focused on Chet's totally different demeanor and his flirtatious behaviors with girls and boys that I don't even notice another kid suddenly beside me staring into the shadows at my face.

"Leo?"

I turn sharply and flinch away. I don't recognize this kid. He's Latino with dark hair, about my height, but dressed all preppy-like in a polo and what looks like designer pants. His clothes remind me of J.C. and he's gazing at me with squinted eyes.

"You are Leo, right?"

My inner alarm bells go off. "I don't know you."

"Name's Roberto," the kid says with a grin. "Friend of J.C."

J.C.? How many friends does J.C. have that I don't know about? "How do you know me?"

Roberto shifts a bit. He looks excited, like he's meeting a celebrity or something. "J.C. showed me pix of you. Including some from the beach. Man, you're hot." I guess I look surprised or maybe angry because his face shifts quickly. "I mean, you're, like, really buff and your face is…" He fumbles again and looks shyly at me. "When I saw you in this corner, I knew it was you."

My mind is reeling. I knew J.C. had pictures of me on his phone, but why is he showing this kid and why is the kid so nervous meeting me? No one gets nervous meeting me. I wish I could look into his eyes because I'd know a lot more, but I don't dare.

Roberto prattles on, "J.C. always said you hated places like this and here you are." He frowns. "He's not here, is he? J.C. always texts me when he's coming. He's my favorite dance partner."

I raise my eyebrows in surprise. "J.C. dances with you?"

Roberto laughs and I like the genuineness of that laugh. "When I can get him. Everybody here loves to dance with J.C. He's hella good. Especially hip hop. You seen him dance before?"

I nod. Roberto has this look on his face that prompts my next question, even though I'm not sure I want to know the answer. "Are you and J.C., uh, like… together or anything?"

He laughs again, but this time it's tinged with regret. "You'd know, right? I mean, you're all he talks about."

"I am?" My heart starts hammering again.

"Hell, yeah. Nonstop, man. He wishes he could be here with you, which, you know, doesn't make me feel so great, but he knows you hate places like this, so I guess I'm kind of a pretend Leo when he's here."

I'm so floored a slight breeze could knock me over. J.C. talks about me and wishes I was here? I see in my mind's eye me slamming the car door and ignoring his apologies and feel like gum on the bottom of somebody's shoe.

As though finally realizing, Roberto says, "But you're here. J.C. always said—"

Just then Laura is at my side grabbing my arm. "He's on the move."

Startled, I turn to her.

"Who's this?" She eyes Roberto suspiciously.

"Uh, Roberto, J.C.'s friend."

Roberto observes the two of us and looks disappointed. "Oh, you're with your girlfriend. J.C. didn't tell me about that."

Flummoxed, I stammer, "Uh, she's—"

Laura sticks out a hand. "I'm Laura."

Roberto shakes it and she pulls hers back. "We gotta go, Leo."

I want to explain to Roberto, but I don't know what to say. He looks confused and deflated, not excited like he was when he first approached me. I don't know what I did to upset him and I don't know how to fix it. "Uh, good meeting you, Roberto."

He nods. "Tell J.C. what's up for me."

"I will."

"Bye, Roberto." Laura grabs my arm and drags me back through the crowd toward the front entrance.

I know Chet is our target, but my mind can't get around how I need to make things right with J.C. We plow past the mountain man at the door and step into the coolness of the night air. Laura doesn't hesitate. She pulls me toward the corner.

"He went out the back."

I nod and pick up my pace. She lets go of my arm and we sprint down the sidewalk to the small street where the rear entrance is located. Rounding that corner, we slow because we don't want to call attention to ourselves. I see my car way up the street near the far corner and Chet's Z4 right behind the club. I turn to Laura, but movement catches my eye and I spot Chet emerging from the back door. He's the only one using that exit, which makes me think he snuck out against club rules. Why would he do that?

Then I notice someone step out of the shadows where the club building adjoins the one next to it. There's no one else on this street at the moment. The phone in my pocket vibrates and I know it's J.C., but I can't pull it out just now. Laura scoots onto the club property and presses up against the building. I copy her movements, wondering if she's ever tailed someone before.

We're about fifteen feet away from the other guy as Chet approaches him. Chet's back is to us, which is good. The shadows should keep us hidden from both of them as long as we don't move.

The other guy is Latino. I can tell by his face and hair beneath the street lights. He looks older than me, maybe early twenties, but it's hard to tell from this distance. He breaks into a big grin as Chet closes the gap and they embrace for a quick second. I guess I shouldn't be surprised after what I saw inside, but this feels different. For one thing, the guy is dressed in sloppy clothes, like he just got off work as a janitor or something.

Chet says, "Let's go." They walk to Chet's car and the older guy slips into the passenger seat as though he's done it a hundred times. Chet moves to the driver's side and glances around, like he suspects someone is watching. I press even closer to the building and feel Laura doing the same. Then Chet jumps into his car and revs the engine. In seconds, he's gone with a loud roar.

I'm about to step away from the building and ask Laura what she thinks when she shoves me back and points. I freeze and follow the direction of her finger. Two figures emerge from the shadows of the adjoining building, watching Chet's car pull away. I can't make out their faces until they turn to each other. It's Wilson and Grady! And Wilson holds up a phone, still aiming it at the retreating car. I hear them titter like little boys.

I stay pressed against the building while they sprint across the street to another parked car I recognize: Wilson's Mercedes. Had it been there when we arrived? I can't say for sure. But it's obvious they haven't seen my Prius parked up the street because they roar off in the same direction as Chet.

I glance at Laura. She looks as bewildered as I feel. The phone vibrating in my pocket startles me and I fumble to retrieve it. I slide open the message from J.C. 'Where are you he got away and you won't believe who followed him.'

I nod to Laura and we sprint to the sidewalk and hurry up the street to my car. I yank open the driver's door while Laura piles into the backseat.

"We saw everything," I tell J.C. as I catch my breath.

J.C. stares at me with expectation. "What the hell was that all about? And what happened inside?"

Laura does most of the talking, of course, describing Chet's totally un-Chet-like behavior in the club. She must sense that I don't want to talk about Roberto—she's right—and doesn't even mention him. I don't either. I'm not sure why, but I have a feeling J.C. might not like what Roberto told me, like he'd think of it as snitching or something, especially talking about me all the time and showing those pictures on his phone. I'm not sure how I feel about it, either, so I shove that issue aside to focus on the problem at hand.

Laura asks J.C. if he's ever seen Chet at this club before and he says, "No, but I haven't been here in a while. There's a couple of other dance clubs I like, too."

My stomach tightens and J.C. hangs his head, peering at me sideways in the gloom, looking guilty. Keeping the focus on Chet, we discuss who he might have driven off with and J.C. suspects the guy is a boyfriend. "You said Hamilton danced with boys and let them touch him."

"But he danced with more girls than boys," Laura said from in back. "And talked to more girls, too."

I want to remind J.C. that he dances with Roberto, so Chet dancing with guys doesn't mean he has a boyfriend, but I don't go there. "The bigger question is why were his homies following and filming him?" I say to redirect the conversation.

It works.

"Yeah," J.C. agrees. "That's crazy weird." He pauses. Then his face takes on a fearful look. "Think they're all in on the plan to kill me?"

"It's possible," I confess.

"I say we tail Chet again tomorrow if he comes here," Laura suggests as she leans in between the two seats so she can address both of us. "But this time we wait outside till he leaves and if he meets that guy again, we follow."

I nod. Sounds like a good plan to me.

J.C. agrees and falls silent. He gazes at me through the shadows and I already know what he's going to say. "Leo, I wasn't ditching you when I came here."

"I know. It's cool."

Maybe I don't sound convincing because he goes on, "I mean, it's just that I, well, you and me are kind of different and…" He trails off, like what he's trying to say is too hard.

"It's really okay, J.C.," I insist, hoping I sound sincere. "I shouldn't have gotten mad."

This time he nods and falls silent.

I glance back at Laura and the way she tilts her head looks like she's trying to ask me something silently. I decide she's wondering why I don't mention Roberto, but I say nothing more and start the car. The drive home is made in complete silence, with only road noise and honking horns interrupting my thoughts.

CHAPTER TEN

ARE YOU CRAZY?

J.C. PICKS ME UP THE NEXT morning for school, but seems quieter than ever and I feel like there's a wall between us now. I know it's because of the club and his friends there and his secret life apart from me. But I'm scared to talk about it, even in my own lame way. Ever since second grade, my biggest fear has been losing J.C.'s friendship. Now it might be coming true and I can't face it. I guess I would still have Laura, but there's something about your first friend that you've known almost your whole life that makes the relationship special. Besides, I *need* J.C. Without him, I'm *less* than nobody, so I ignore the subject entirely and we talk about homework as he swings by Laura's house.

She's waiting outside and hops into the back seat. Unlike us, she's full of energy. "We need to find out where Hamilton goes with that guy."

I grunt and J.C. says, "Yeah." We don't look at each other, another bad sign.

"And what are Wilson and Grady up to?" Laura goes on, leaning forward. "I thought they were all best buds."

I grunt again.

J.C. says, "Beats me."

There is an awkward moment of silence as Laura nods silently, sucking her bottom lip. She obviously senses the tension between Leo and me.

"Look guys, we have three days left. This isn't the time to go all drama about a dance club. Leo, J.C. likes to dance and you don't. Get over it. And J.C., you should've told him you wanted to go to clubs, but you didn't and now it's out in the open, so let's move on. Unless you don't care anymore about Friday?"

Her words sting. I notice J.C. flinch and glance over at him. His hands grip the steering wheel so hard as he turns onto Main Street that his knuckles look white.

"Uh, she-she's right, J.C."

He tosses me a look, eyebrows raised.

"Like I said last night," I go on, choosing my words with care. "It's cool, you going to the club. I'm not mad."

"Really?"

"Really."

He looks slightly relieved, but his shoulders look stiff and he's frowning slightly, so I think there's more about all this he wants to say, but can't. I think of what Roberto told me, but keep my mouth shut.

"That's better," Laura says, her tone laced with smugness.

As we pull into the student parking lot, we all agree to surreptitiously watch Chet, Wilson, and Grady as best we can throughout the day, and then after dinner we'll check out Chet's house to see if his car is gone. If so, it's back to the club for us.

We manage to avoid catching the attention of Chet or his homies throughout the morning. As far as I can see, they act like nothing is different. Chet wears dark sunglasses today, which he often does, but if he has any idea Wilson and Grady were following him last night, he doesn't show it. I wish I had some idea what was going on. Friday looms ever closer and, other than hiding in the haunted house, I don't have a real plan to save my best friend's life.

Laura, me, and J.C. are kicking it at our usual outside lunch spot when a shadow falls across the food in my lap and I look up at the silhouetted figure of Principal Harris.

Oh, crap, what'd I do now?

Harris wears his usual dark suit, this time with a pink tie. Seriously, it's, like, fluorescent pink. He grins like we're the best thing he's seen all day. "If it isn't my favorite group of nonconformists. How's your day so far."

Of course, I say nothing, but J.C. mumbles, "Peachy. Thanks for asking, Mr. Harris."

Laura tosses him a stern look, but J.C. knows how to play the game with Harris.

The principal's grin grows broader. "Excellent news. I want to thank you boys for not stirring up more trouble with Chet and his friends these past few days."

J.C. starts to say something and I kick him in the ankle. He closes his mouth and offers his most obsequious smile. "Well, just trying to keep the peace. Like you always say, a peaceful campus is a happy campus."

Harris reaches out and claps J.C. on the shoulder so hard I hear it loud and clear. "Exactly." He turns the grin on Laura. "These boys taking care of you, Laura?"

Sipping her juice, she nods, but says nothing.

"Splendid." Harris now focuses on me. "Anything you'd like to add, Shy Boy?"

"No, sir," I mutter, but don't look up.

"You really need to work on eye contact, Leo," Harris recommends in his smooth, *I'm your best bud giving you needed advice* tone. "It's a necessary trait for a man."

I glance up, but don't meet his eyes.

He grins again. "There, that wasn't so hard." Someone calls his name from across the quad and Harris raises a hand to let whoever it is know that he heard. "Well, I have to run. A principal's job is never done." He throws a thumbs up and saunters through the milling students toward the cafeteria building.

Laura snorts with derision. "He's a bigger doofus than my last principal."

I nod.

"Harris doesn't care what's going on under the water," J.C. puts in as he takes a bite from his quesadilla. "Kids could be kicking the crap out of each other, but as long as the surface looks calm, he's happy." He shakes his head in disgust.

We've been waiting only about thirty minutes before something happens. Chet's car is parked near where it was last night and J.C.'s is at the end of the block, at the opposite corner from the club. It's after ten o'clock when I spot someone exiting the building next to the club and locking the glass door. It's the same guy from last night, the one Chet went off with. Like before, he's dressed in grungy work clothes. I study the building more closely. It's two stories and looks like small offices. Maybe this guy is the after-hours janitor?

"Hamilton has good taste in boyfriends," Laura says from in back. "That guy's hot."

I turn back with a confused look on my face.

"Hot for a guy, anyway," Laura adds with a shrug.

"There's Hamilton," J.C. says and I whip my head around as he starts the engine.

As before, Chet greets janitor guy with a brief hug and a friendly smile. They slip into Chet's car and drive off. This time Wilson and Grady aren't hiding nearby. At least, I don't think so, but J.C. peels out so fast in pursuit of Chet that I might have missed them.

"No way I'm gonna lose him," J.C. whispers as he turns a quick right onto Santa Monica Boulevard. Chet's Z4 zips in and around a car up ahead, but J.C. keeps his eyes on the prize. I don't think I've ever seen him this focused except when he's dancing. He didn't even offer to let me drive tonight. I guess he knows my driving style fits my lame personality and I'd likely let Chet get away before exceeding the speed limit.

Chet swoops around a pickup truck and turns into a small parking lot, slipping into a space right beside a corner mart with LIQUOR lit up in red above the door. J.C. stops across the street and we watch. Traffic whizzes past on the boulevard, but I clearly see Chet's friend exit the car and enter the liquor store. I can make out two neon signs in the window, one that says "OPEN" and the other "ATM."

Silence fills J.C.'s car as we wait for the guy to exit. After only a few minutes, he emerges with a large grocery bag and lugs it to the car. The trunk pops open as he approaches and he slides the bag inside. Before the trunk lid eases itself closed, he reaches in and pulls out a bottle of something I can't make out. Then he raps on the driver's side window. The door pops open and Chet leaps out. He grabs the bottle and scoots around the hood to slide into the passenger seat, while janitor guy takes over the driving duties. Confused, I watch as the car pulls out of its space and back into traffic.

We follow them to the 10 freeway, where they head east. Traffic is always heavy on the 10, but J.C. manages to stay within three or four car lengths of the Z4. We pass downtown L.A. and my usual exit to Skid Row. Once again, I feel guilty for not being there.

We skirt downtown and enter Boyle Heights. This area I only know by reputation as being rife with poverty and violence, but J.C. drives the streets as though he's been here before. That piques my curiosity big time, but now isn't the moment to ask. Chet swings his car around a corner and pulls up to a dilapidated housing project called The Gardens. I know this because there's a big sign proclaiming the news, except what's behind the sign isn't much to proclaim. Run-down, two story buildings extend back from the sign in a kind of flat U shape. Every window that's visible has security bars on them. The doors, too.

J.C. eases to a stop down the street from where Chet parks. I watch the driver's side door of the Z4 pop open, and janitor guy steps out. Some kids playing football in the street scurry over and high-five him. But they barely notice the car, which tells me they've seen it before and it's nothing new. Janitor moves around to the passenger side and opens the door. He reaches in and pulls Chet out. Chet holds the large bottle in one hand and staggers slightly as janitor guy supports him. We can't hear what they say, but I hear Chet laughing as janitor guy locks the car with a *beep* and leads Chet onto the grounds of the housing project. Chet takes long swigs from the bottle, stumbling slightly so that janitor guy has to support him. He laughs and tosses the bottle into a small dumpster set into a recessed alcove. I'm stunned! Chet drank that whole bottle between the liquor store and here?

I can't see which apartment they go into and don't want us to drive closer because of those kids. They'll remember a fancy, unfamiliar car like J.C.'s and might tell janitor guy.

"Hamilton must be a pretty heavy drinker," Laura says, breaking the silence and echoing my thoughts exactly.

"Yeah." I eye J.C., but his gaze is fixed on those kids laughing and playing football.

"I have people in this part of town," J.C. says, his voice solemn and robotic. "My mother was born in the projects."

I'm stunned, and can't speak for a long moment. I gaze out the windshield at the squalor and poverty, the dirty street and tagged up houses. An awkward moment of silence passes, punctuated by cries from the kids of "touchdown" and more laughter. I find my voice. "You never told me that."

"Too embarrassed." J.C. turns to me. "Those kids are dirt poor. But look at 'em. They're enjoying life, even though they have nothing, and I'm not and I have everything. Crazy, messed up world we got, huh?"

There's another long silence because I don't know what to say.

"Why do you think Chet's here?" Laura asks from in back, I guess to redirect the conversation.

It works because J.C.'s face hardens. "I think he hired that guy to kill me."

"You don't know that," Laura insists quietly. "He could be just a boyfriend, like we said back at the club."

I consider J.C.'s words. In my vision, the guy wearing the jacket has the knife, but like we said about Wilson and Grady, that doesn't mean there aren't others present.

I turn back to face Laura. "He might be right. I still don't think Chet has the nerve to commit murder."

"If you say so." She doesn't look convinced.

"I'm gonna contact my people," J.C. whispers in a tone that scares me. "They'll get me a gun and I'm gonna kill Chet Hamilton."

I think I make a gagging sound, but I'm so floored I'm not sure I'm even breathing.

"What?" Laura leans in even more.

J.C. turns his head and his eyes look like they belong to Freddy Krueger. I've never seen such hate on his face before. "You heard me."

I finally find my voice. "Are you crazy?"

"No. Just tired of being kicked around by that bastard," he hisses, sounding like a real cobra. "He comes after me on Friday, I'm gonna shoot him like a dog."

My chest is tight and I feel almost weightless as I look at him in the shadowy gloom. "I can't let you do that."

J.C.'s face sort of collapses and then reassembles itself like a computer-generated image, and his eyes narrow even more. "Why are you always defending him?"

"I'm not defending him," I whisper because my voice is still shaky. "I'm protecting you."

"By letting him kill me?" The snark in his voice rips through me like a hunting knife.

"By keeping you out of prison. That what you want, to sit in prison with Chet's brother? 'Cause that's what'll happen if you shoot him like a dog."

"He's less than a dog and it would be self-defense."

"Would it?" I stare at his shadowed eyes because there's not enough light for me to see them fully.

He says nothing.

"Leo's right," Laura says, breaking the heavy silence. Her voice sounds a lot calmer than I feel.

J.C. turns to face forward. "We're going home." He starts the car and pulls away from the curb.

I glance at Laura, my heart pounding with wild unease. She looks concerned, but she doesn't know J.C. like I do. When he sulks, that's when he plans to do exactly what he wants.

I settle into my seat and stare out the window as J.C. navigates surface streets back toward the freeway. I see other run-down tenements and housing projects drift past my window, and more kids running or biking nearby, and I realize that J.C.'s never told me anything about his family's roots before tonight. I get that he's embarrassed to be anything other than the mayor's son and filthy rich, but I'd like to think he and I have a different relationship than he has with the rest of the world. I thought we were the kind of friends who tell each other everything. Does that mean he and I aren't best friends? This entire episode, ever since I saw his impending death, has fractured our friendship in significant ways. It's become like a cracked phone screen—the phone still works, but not everything is visible anymore. Will I end up saving his life and then lose him anyway? That question weighs on my mind for the rest of the drive.

I sleep poorly that night because of what happened and because J.C. doesn't even say good night when he drops me off. Him shutting me out hurts more than anything else that's happened lately and I slog upstairs to collapse onto my bed. I don't even take off my clothes.

For the first time in forever, I drive to school without J.C. I text him early the next morning to see if he wants a ride, but get no response. Laura returns my text and I swing by to pick her up. She says J.C. hasn't responded to her, either. I feel like my whole life is slipping away and I have no control over anything anymore. One of the great benefits of both gymnastics and Aikido is the necessity of learning self-control and I have tons of it by now. But I can't control anyone else, and I think I've just figured that out.

J.C.'s car isn't in the student parking lot and he doesn't show up for first period. I spot Chet eyeing J.C.'s empty seat for a split second before he resumes preening for the girls. I notice he's wearing the shades again, but can't get my mind off J.C. Where could he be? Is he so mad at me that he took the day off? Knowing that Harris will notify his mom has never been a deterrent to J.C. skipping school. He's just never done it before. Because I never have, I suddenly realize. He and I have had each other's back since the first day of freshman year. Except today. Because he's mad at me. Just because I don't want him to throw his life away? It's all too crazy for words and I struggle to concentrate on what my teacher is saying.

Second period rolls around and there's J.C. in his usual seat when I enter the room. I stop a moment and stare in surprise. He glances over and gives me the chin raise. Then he grabs his backpack to pull out a pen and his history book.

I navigate my way between desks and chattering kids and slide into my usual seat behind him. "You okay?"

He glances back. "Never better." He doesn't smile, but doesn't look mad anymore, either.

Mr. Morton steps into the room and J.C. turns to face forward. I fish through my own pack for supplies, wondering if his standoffish attitude is because he's still mad or because he knows I was right and doesn't want to admit it. Mr. Morton begins to speak and I do my best to listen.

It's strange to be near J.C. and not have him talking, but he says nothing as we toss books into our lockers just before lunch. We place our orders at the outside kiosk in silence and then enter the cafeteria where I spot Chet and his posse chatting up some hot girls. They don't look in our direction, but I notice J.C. mad dogging Chet something fierce as we stand in line to pick up our food.

I grab my bag and wait for J.C. to pick up his. He steps to my side, still not speaking, which is really creeping me out, and we head outside to meet up with Laura at our table. She's already there because her fourth period teacher lets them out a few minutes before the bell so they can get to the cafeteria ahead of the herd.

She tosses me a look that says, "How's J.C.?" I shrug and take my seat beside her. J.C. sits on her other side, rather than next to me like usual, and I feel that punch to the gut sensation again.

Laura swigs from her apple juice and eyes J.C., who makes a big production out of unwrapping his burrito. "You okay?"

"Never better," he says, echoing his words to me in second period, and then bites into the burrito. Hot sauce and cheese squeeze out and dribble down his chin. I wait for him to grab a napkin and swipe it away before anyone can notice, but he doesn't. His eyes look distant and his gaze unfocused. The sauce trails its way down to drop onto the ground beside his high-end Vans.

I decide now is the time to mention the plan I've come up with. "Um, I have an idea for Friday."

That catches J.C.'s attention and he whips his head around, mouth open in surprise. More sauce starts its way down his chin, but this time he snatches up a napkin and swishes it across to remove the offending condiment.

"What are you talking about?" His tone is almost accusatory.

Laura gives him the evil eye. "J.C., cut the attitude. Whatever he's thinking about is for you, so shut up and listen."

J.C.'s eyes bug out and I think mine do, too. I know my mouth drops open in surprise because I have to force myself to close it.

Laura doesn't back down. She squints at me. "All this drama queen stuff has to stop with you two so we can save this fool's life." She tosses a thumb in J.C.'s direction.

I drop my gaze and she turns to J.C. He obviously knows not to argue because he nods.

"Um, okay," I stammer, collecting my thoughts. "I've been, you know, thinking about this… power, I guess you'd call it… that I have and, well, I'm thinking that maybe if we change something in what I saw, it might change everything, like rebooting a computer."

I think I sound mixed up and uncertain, even though I've given this a lot of thought. J.C. stares at me in puzzlement, but Laura's eyes widen with understanding.

"I get it. We don't have to stop Hamilton at the moment he's going after J.C.," she says, putting my thoughts into better clarity than I did. "We just have to change something ahead of time so he doesn't get the chance."

I nod and J.C.'s face registers his comprehension, but he remains silent.

"So what's your plan?" Laura continues, setting her food down and leaning in so close to my face that other kids probably think we're kissing.

Normally, when someone invades my space that closely—other than J.C.—I break into cold sweats and back away. I guess I've gotten comfortable enough with Laura that nothing of the sort happens.

"I think we can lure Chet into a trap on Friday before he ever gets a chance to come after J.C. and then we hold him all night until morning. Since I saw J.C. killed that night, by morning the … uh, the timeline, I guess, should've changed."

"How will you know?"

"Guess I look into his eyes again." I glance at J.C. He looks like one of those poker-playing dudes on ESPN. Normally, I can read his face like a book, but somehow he's learned how to close it to me. I wait.

Finally, after several tense moments, he nods. "Worth a shot."

Laura looks relieved and pulls back slightly, but keeps her lips very close to my cheek, I guess so no one can overhear us. She repeats her earlier question. "So what's your plan?"

"We need to head to Redondo after school," I reply cryptically.

"What for?" J.C.'s eyes narrow with suspicion, and that hurts, too. It's like he doesn't trust me anymore.

"We need a fishing supply place."

Laura's eyebrows shoot up in surprise and J.C. starts to open his mouth, but Mr. Mendez is heading in our direction, multiple keys jangling from a ring on his belt. "I'll tell you on the way."

They both get the message and we set to our food. Mendez strides on past without so much as a glance and heads in the direction of the maintenance office. I glance up from my sandwich just as he prepares to round the corner. He pauses for a split second and flicks a look back over his shoulder. I'm sure it's in our direction, but then he's gone.

I feel J.C.'s eyes on me as I take a swig from my water bottle. I don't look up again and the other two eat their food in silence.

We meet up at my house and decide to Google fishing supply places in the vicinity. To my surprise and instant trepidation, there aren't any, not even as far away as Long Beach. I guess commercial fishing isn't as big a thing off the California coast as I thought.

"Now what?" J.C. asks, his tone derisive.

I come up empty, but thankfully Laura is thinking. "Online? I have Prime."

I glance at J.C. We both have Prime accounts, too.

"Worth a shot," I say as I call up the home page and type in 'commercial fishing nets.' A page appears that's filled with hits. The others lean in while I scroll down, checking out the size and strength of each. We finally agree on one that's twenty by twenty-five feet with one-inch holes. It looks tough enough for the job, but doesn't come with Prime shipping. It costs a ton to expedite the transport, but the net *will* arrive on Friday afternoon, guaranteed, and it's not like the three of us don't have money to burn.

We sit around refining my plan and agreeing on who will do what. Both Laura and I insist that J.C. remain in hiding at the haunted house—as previously sketched out—just in case the plan goes awry and Chet slips through our hands. J.C. doesn't like that part and protests vociferously. "There's no way Laura can handle that net alone."

"Let's scout out the location tomorrow after school and make sure," Laura tells me.

I nod. J.C. is right—the net might be tricky—but it's too dangerous for him to be present if we fail. He could be right and Chet will have others with him. It's too risky to have J.C. anywhere near the park when our trap is sprung.

I feel more alone than ever when J.C. decides to leave when Laura does. I'm still not sure what I did wrong, but my best friend suddenly isn't interested in hanging around me anymore. Alone in the big house, I launch into a fierce routine on the rings in my workout room and then spar with the dummies. I'm tired and dripping with sweat by the time I trudge into the kitchen to see what my dinner is for the night. Veggie enchiladas with salad and potatoes are all wrapped up neatly with saran wrap and a little note from Sylvia that reads: "Enjoy, Leo. See you tomorrow, honey."

She's called me "honey" since she started working here when I was eleven, and I confess it still makes me feel good. I've secretly hoped my mom would use that endearing term someday, but I know that's wishful thinking. I don't have much appetite, but eat because I'll need all my strength come Friday.

The next day at school, J.C. is cordial, but not chatty, and I almost feel like he doesn't want me around. But, as agreed, we pile into his car after school and cruise to nearby Shelby Park to scope out the place I've selected for our trap. It's close enough to our homes to make it easily accessible if running is required, and it's usually empty on Friday nights. There are no jungle gyms or kiddie attractions, so it's mostly old folks who go there to chill on the benches, and it's a tiny park, anyway. But it does have an enormous Moreton Bay Fig tree that was planted when the town began and its trunk is now at least thirty feet in circumference. Thick, leafy branches reach up and out to shade nearly the entire park. This tree is one of La Costa's most famous landmarks, and its mass and foliage make it the perfect location to carry out my plan.

I stroll around the colossal trunk to the spot I've already chosen in my mind. I know it's perfect because back when I was in first grade, some kids hid up in the tree and poured milk all over me as I played on the grass beneath. I cried all the way home, but never forgot the experience, or those wide branches, which have only gotten wider over the years.

I point and Laura looks up. She nods. "It's perfect."

J.C. squints up at the thick, twisting branches and large green leaves offering ample cover. "I still think I should be here to help her."

Laura and I look at him with fierce determination. "You need to stay hidden," she intones quietly. An old couple sits on one of the benches on the other side of the trunk. "Something could go wrong."

J.C. leans in. "That's why I need to be here."

"No," I say.

J.C. turns to me. My voice must've sounded intense because he doesn't speak.

"We don't know what he's planning," I continue, "or who he might have with him. You said it yourself—he could've hired that guy from the projects. If we blow this, at least you're safe. And that's the whole point, right?"

He doesn't look convinced, but backs down. "I guess."

I'm feeling anxious, maybe because we're only a day away from my vision coming true, but I feel open and exposed out here in broad daylight and have a strong sensation of being watched. I glance around, but don't see anyone entering the park or even strolling past.

"Let's head home and go over all the details."

"Okay." Laura starts back toward the car.

J.C. doesn't move. He's staring up into that tree as though looking for God within its branches.

I place an awkward hand on his shoulder. "He won't get you."

He turns toward me and I expect him to nod or say thanks or something, but his face hardens into a look of malice. "No, he won't." Then he turns away and follows Laura.

Contemplating his ominous words, I trot along after them.

We work out the kinks in my plan and Laura assures me she can handle the net on her own, rejecting J.C.'s continuing insistence that he should be there to help. I hope his reason is because he feels guilty that we'll be doing all the dirty work, but something in his face tightens my gut with disquiet and I wonder if he doesn't have some other motive in mind.

With all the details finally worked out, Laura and J.C. leave for home. Laura gives me a hug, which feels nice, I have to admit. But J.C. refuses to even look at me as he steps out the front door and strides down the walkway without looking back.

"He's stressed out about all this," she says, her hand lightly squeezing my upper arm in a comforting gesture. "He'll be back to normal after it's over."

I nod, but butterflies in my stomach make me think that nothing will ever be back to normal again.

CHAPTER ELEVEN

LEO, WHAT'S WRONG?

Friday is somber. That's the best word I can use to describe it. Knowing what might happen tonight has my body coiled into knots from the moment I wake up. Even a hard workout on the rings and parallel bars before my morning shower doesn't help.

Adding to my despair is the absence of J.C. on my way to school. I text him to ask if I can give him a ride, but he sends back two words:

'No, thanks.'

I can't describe the hurt I feel at him pushing me away like he has, especially since I have no idea what I did wrong. I wrack my brain on the way to school—so much so that I almost rear-end a VW because I didn't notice the light change—but I can't think of anything. I wonder if maybe Roberto told him we met at the club, but what could I have said about J.C. that would have made him mad? I barely said a word at that club.

Whatever the reason, J.C. hardly speaks to me the entire day. He's wearing a T-shirt and worn jeans, he's barely touched a comb to his hair, and he wanders around in a daze like a zombie on that TV show my mother loves. I know he's afraid. I get that. I am, too. But I can't help feeling rejected after all we've been through over the years. At lunch, some red sauce spills from my burrito, looking way too much like blood, and suddenly I have no appetite.

In class, the whiteboards might as well be blank and the teachers speaking ancient Greek for all the information I tune into.

Laura hangs with me as much as she can, but we don't talk either. What's left to say? Tonight is the night that will decide everything. The three of us sit together at lunch, like the friends we used to be, but don't speak. We nibble our food and search randomly on our phones for something to fill the void. It's like we're three statues in some bizarre modern art sculpture depicting 21st Century kids who don't know how to talk with each other in person anymore.

Oddly, Chet steers clear of us and I think he's doing it on purpose. While we're pretending to be modern art in the quad, he and his pack exit the cafeteria and head in our direction, Wilson leading the way. I glance up and my throat constricts with dread, expecting another confrontation. But Chet looks over at that moment and stares right at me. I freeze, unable to pull my gaze from that picture-perfect face. Thankfully, he's too far away to see into his eyes.

Then he does something odd. He grabs Wilson by the shoulder and points across the quad to where I can't see because of trees blocking my view. Wilson seems surprised, as though they'd already decided to go somewhere else. But he shrugs and follows Chet in the new direction. I wonder what that was all about, but come up empty.

It's now almost eight and darkness has fallen, leaving pools of soft light spilling onto the pavement from the overhead street lamps. The net arrived this afternoon, and Laura has taken up her position with the net in place across the tangle of branches in the Moreton Bay tree. The rest is up to me. It's a chilly evening, so I've got on sweats and a hoodie over a tank top—everything fits loose because I want to have freedom of movement if fighting is involved. I've got running shoes on too. Never hurts to be prepared.

As planned, I act like I'm out for a walk around the neighborhood, just in case Chet might be watching my place. Holding my phone in my right hand, I stroll past brightly lit homes in the direction of J.C.'s house. Never before has my street looked so much like the one in Haddonfield where Michael Myers killed all those people in *Halloween*. Every shadow seems to reach for me and I approach each hedge or tree with wary caution.

It's irrational, I know, since J.C. is the target, not me. But I can't help my roiling nerves and taut muscles as I round the corner onto J.C.'s street. I grip my phone with clenched fingers, and my sneakers against the sidewalk make squishy sounds, like they're filled with water. It's so quiet for a Friday night. Usually, there are parties in some of these houses, but not tonight.

My gaze flicks from one side of the street to the other. The homes are mostly old-school Victorian style, like mine, but many aren't mansions. Back in the day when the town was built, the residents didn't all have tons of money like they do now.

J.C.'s two story home comes into view just ahead on the opposite side of the street. I stop and crouch down, pretending to tie an errant shoelace. In reality, I'm scoping out the area around his house. A few lights burn in both downstairs and upstairs windows, but I know the house is empty because J.C.'s mom went to some fancy fundraising dinner. I guess she's looking to move on to the state level when her term as mayor is over. J.C. has always said he would never move if she did because he wouldn't leave me behind. Now, with all that's happened the past two weeks, those words don't seem so set in stone as they were when he said them.

I see no movement of any kind, and the night is so quiet I can hear the tide washing in and out, even though the beach is blocks from here. I stand up and continue on my way toward the Raley's house. It's just across from J.C.'s. They're an old, childless couple who always complain when kids in the area make too much noise. I've been at J.C.'s place a bunch of times when old Mrs. Raley called J.C.'s mom to complain about a party three houses away— like the mayor is responsible for that?

What makes their front yard the perfect place to hide is a six-foot high hedge that could easily obscure Michael Myers himself if he chose to scout this street for victims. The hedge wraps around their house and has a gate that opens onto a walkway leading to the front door. The gate is always locked and can only be opened from inside by some sort of remote system. Despite their desire to keep us kids out, there's a gap at the corner because there are two separate hedges trying to butt up against each other and not quite making it. Kids have dared each other for as long as I can remember to sneak in and ring the doorbell before busting a nut to get out before Mr. or Mrs. Raley attacked the yard with blindingly bright flood lights.

I'm still slim enough to squeeze between the hedges and from there I'll have a clear view of J.C.'s house. I pause again right in front of the Raley's place and glance around in all directions. I even check out every un-curtained window I see just to make sure no one is spying on me. Seeing nothing, I dart like a road runner to the small opening where the perfectly trimmed hedges just miss coming together, and slip in between them. My breathing is a bit ragged, but not from exertion, only nerves. I crouch down so as not to trip any motion sensor lights the Raley's might have installed to scare off intruders, and then press my face between the hedges, careful to watch for sharp extrusions that might cut me. J.C.'s house sits calm and peaceful across the street. Now all I have to do is wait.

J.C., Laura, and me already have a group text set up and, careful to shield the phone light with my body, I type:

'in place be ready'

Laura's blue box and her tiny photo appear:

'k'

But I get nothing from J.C. He should be safely tucked away in the haunted house by now, but I wish he'd send me a message so I don't worry.

I clutch my phone in my right hand and watch the street. No movement. This is the tricky part of our plan and where it can all go wrong. If Chet plans to get J.C. sometime tonight, he needs to know where to find him. In our brainstorming sessions, Laura and I felt certain that at some point, Chet would show up at J.C.'s house hoping to follow him. If that failed, he'd likely go to my house because he'd figure J.C. would be there. My job is to tail him and find out if he's meeting anyone else. If he's alone, then I have to lure him into the park. Like I say, this is the shaky part of the whole deal. So many things can go wrong. That's why I made sure J.C. is nowhere near me or the park.

I shift my position a few times over the next hour to keep my legs from cramping. Laura texts me two more times to ask for updates, but I tell her nothing's happening. I begin to think we need a new plan when I catch movement from the corner of my eye and spot a shadowy figure, dressed in black, from what I can tell by the streetlights, heading down the sidewalk. I hold my breath. The figure looks tall as it passes the hedge separating J.C.'s house from his neighbor's, but a hood shields the face so I can't make out any distinguishing features. Then I recognize the strut.

It's Chet!

He stops and surveys the house for a long, silent minute, at least. The porch lights burn with an inviting intensity, but Chet doesn't move. What's he doing? Just going to stand around until J.C. comes out and then stab him right there in the street?

Chet surprises me when he dashes up the walkway to the front door faster than I'd have thought for a guy with so much muscle packed onto a large frame. He depresses the doorbell and then darts across the front lawn like a gazelle to duck down behind tall bushes that will shield him from view of anyone opening the door. He waits and so do I. My only question is, what will he do when he realizes no one is home?

Chet waits another minute or so and when nothing happens, he rises to his full height and I spot his face beneath the hood. It's only a glimpse and he looks angry or worried, but I can't make out enough details from this distance. I stand on cramped legs and prepare to follow him in the direction of my house. But then he does something that surprises me. He returns to the sidewalk and starts off in the opposite direction. What the hell?

I freeze and my heart slams into my throat. He's headed in the direction of the haunted house! Coincidence? I don't see how it could be and I also don't have a clue how he could've guessed our hiding place. I speed text this message:

> 'Chets heading toward hh JC lay low Laura get ready Ill lure him to park'

I don't even await their responses. I feel the phone vibrate in my hand as I squeeze between the hedges and onto the shadowy sidewalk. I'd been so sure Chet would head to my house after finding out J.C. wasn't home that I didn't come up with a Plan B. My mind does somersaults of confusion. What can I...? And then it hits me. The plan is still the same. I just need to come at it from a different direction.

Chet is nearing the corner. I need to act fast so I sprint across the street to J.C.'s front lawn and stage a dramatic fall by "tripping" over a sprinkler head and sprawling into a tuck and roll onto the grass. I let out a loud, "Oh, crap!" as I tumble, knowing Chet can hear me. I land my roll perfectly—my years of Aikido see to that—but I clutch my ankle like I'm hurt. I wait. From the corner of my eye, I see Chet sprinting in my direction and I tense up. He's athletic and strong, but I've never really seen him full out run, so I'm like a cat ready to bolt as soon as I think he might chase me.

The hooded figure takes long strides and I look right at him so he knows who it is. My face is away from the porch lights, but there's enough illumination for him to recognize me.

"Leo?"

He stops and stares, and I freeze with indecision. He's never called me by my real name. Not ever. But's it's definitely his voice behind that billowing, shadowy hood. He starts forward. "I was—"

I don't wait for him to get within grabbing range. I spring to my feet and take off in the direction of my house like a cheetah chasing its next meal.

"Don't run from me!" I hear as I plow onward, phone clutched tightly in one hand, pacing my wind so it will last until I reach the park. I hear footsteps thudding against the pavement in pursuit and I focus on putting some distance between us.

I hear him panting as I leave the neighborhood behind and pelt up Second Street in the direction of Shelby Park. Panting is good, but the thudding steps are closer now. He's going full out and gaining ground. I have a sharp stich in my side, but I pour on the steam and widen the gap. I can't be too close once we pass under the tree or we'll both be caught in the net.

I dart across Second Street right in front of a sports car with music blaring. The brakes shriek and the horn pounds in my ears as I clear the car and enter the park. I hear profanity flung my way and then the engine revving. I don't look back to see where Chet is, but I hear the car roar off down the street.

The park has small lights along the pathways that provide enough illumination to see by, but not enough to fully reveal the Moreton Bay tree up ahead, which is another reason I chose it. With the car gone, I hear Chet's pounding feet still in pursuit. That's good. The tree looms closer. His footsteps grow stronger. I guess those long legs come in handy for running.

I inhale deeply and swing my arms side to side like an Olympic sprinter, the phone gripped so tightly I think it might actually break. I reach the outer perimeter of the shading branches of the tree and plow forward toward the trunk. Reaching it, I duck around the vast thickness and press my sweating back up against the rough bark. My breaths are hitching and I clamp a hand over my mouth. The running footsteps behind me cease.

I hear raspy breathing, so at least I gave him a run for his money.

"I… know," he gasps, "you're… there."

My heart pounds wildly like a snare drum.

I know you know. Come get me.

But I hear nothing more. What the hell? Laura should've done her thing by now. I lower the hand covering my mouth and listen.

"Come out, Leo."

My first name again! The hell is going on?

I know I can take him one-on-one, even if he has a knife. But what if he has some other weapon? Or he messaged his homies on the run over here? Knowing I have little choice, I ease myself away from the rough bark of the trunk and take the three steps needed to expose myself to whoever is on the other side. It's Chet and he's alone. He's still panting and clutching his side, but I see no evidence of the switchblade I saw him buy from Mr. Mendez and he makes no threatening moves. He's also just out of range of Laura and the net. Could he suspect? He's not looking up or around for anyone or anything, and that part's good. But I need to lure him closer.

I stare long and hard at him, but I don't move.

He stares right back. "Come here, Leo."

That haughty, commanding tone. A spoiled rich boy used to getting what he wants. I bristle, but don't budge. I finally find my voice. "You want me, come get me."

I take a couple of steps back and tighten my stance. If he gets past Laura, I'll be ready for him.

"Damn it, Leo!" He starts forward.

I stand my ground to lure him closer. A breeze ruffles the leaves above my head and I think it's Laura releasing the net. But nothing happens. Chet strides forward unimpeded. Something's gone wrong. I don't dare look up because I have to focus on Chet. He's close enough for me to kick when I hear pelting feet to my left and then, "Get away from him!"

Chet lurches to a startled stop at the same moment I whirl to the sound of that voice I know above all others.

"J.C.!" I blurt out, stunned by his presence, but forced into silence by the sight of the gun in his outstretched hand.

Chet makes some kind of profane exclamation and I hear Laura drop from the tree with a "J.C.!" but my eyes remain fixed on the best friend I've grown up with, the boy I thought I knew better than anyone in the world.

His face is twisted into an animal snarl of rage and his stride is filled with power and conviction, as though the gun has given him strength he never had before. He's wearing a sleeveless hoodie over a tee shirt and even in the dim lighting I see the cords in his forearm tight with tension. My eyes take in the taut finger wrapped around the trigger of what looks like a small pistol. I've never held a real gun, but sometimes on the sets of my mom's movies, the prop guys let me play with fake ones. Those *looked* real, but this one *is* real.

From the corner of my eye I see Chet freeze in place, with Laura paused just behind him.

"You've punked him for the last time, Hamilton!" J.C.'s raspy voice doesn't sound at all like him. It barely sounds human. He raises the gun higher and aims at Chet's head. His arm quivers with rage. His entire body trembles.

"J.C., no!" That's Laura's voice, but I don't look over at her. I focus on my friend's face and those wild, dangerously squinting eyes, and do the only thing I can think of—I leap forward and plant myself between Chet Hamilton and the gun that's about to end his life.

I hear Laura gasp and Chet issues a grunting noise of surprise from behind me. But I fix my gaze on J.C. and fight to keep from fainting. The muzzle of the gun is no more than a two feet from my face and the dark emptiness of that small barrel signifies my death if J.C. loses control of his finger. My legs almost buckle, but I force myself to remain standing.

J.C.'s twisted face mutates into one of stunned surprise, but he doesn't lower the gun. My mouth goes bone dry. I feel like I haven't had water in years. But I stand my ground. We all remain frozen, like some macabre exhibit at the Hollywood Wax Museum, waiting for death to show its ugly face.

"Leo!" Feral anger burns from J.C.'s eyes. "Get out of my way!"

My voice fails me. Of course, it does. It always does when I need it most. All I can do is shake my head.

The hand with the gun trembles even more. My gaze should be on the trigger finger, but I force myself to confront J.C.'s animalistic fury

"Leo!" The rasp is pure rage in vocal form.

I shake my head again. Damn my inhibition! If ever I needed to speak and say the right words, it's now.

"How can you protect him?" Spittle sprays from J.C.'s mouth. "After everything he's done?"

The gun arm shakes even more and I know he'll lose control any second. He's never been good at controlling his anger, but in the past I've always been able to help him defuse it. My tongue finally unsticks from the roof of my mouth and my voice comes out stronger than I'd have thought. "I can't let you kill him."

"Even though he's gonna kill me?" The gun shakes even more. I see my life down that narrow metal tube and think, *death might not be so bad.*

"I told you I wouldn't let him kill you and I keep my promises." My voice sounds steady, but my legs wobble.

"Leo!" He's pleading now. I hear it, despite the clenching of his teeth. "I don't wanna hurt you. Get out of my way! I have to finish this."

My hands remain at my sides and I make no sudden movements. The others are frozen behind me like marble statues. I can feel their fear without even turning. I force calm into my voice. "You'll have to kill me first."

J.C.'s mouth drops open in stunned exasperation. "What?"

I keep going while I still have the courage. "My life isn't worth much anyway. No one would even miss me." My mother's face flashes before my mind's eye, but I push it away. "If you kill him, you'll go to prison forever and I'd die from that, anyway."

J.C.'s rigid features crumble ever so slightly, like an old porcelain doll my mother had as a little girl. I dropped it when I was five and the face cracked and crumbled inward. That's what J.C.'s face reminds me of, but the gun remains aimed squarely at my forehead.

"Leo, *please*... you don't understand... I... I ... have... to..." He trails off, his voice wavering. His face, though. If I survive this moment, I'll never forget how it looks—piercing eyes filled with a tornado of hate and love and anguish and resolve and fear and uncertainty. His whole body shakes as if buffeted by this storm of emotions swirling around and around as he thrums with the intense need for one of them to triumph. He looks like he's going supernova.

I've never seen him like this before. I now understand why he's been avoiding me the past few days. He's been building up the rage to commit murder, and he knows I'm the only one who could defuse that rage.

I hope I still can.

He stares at me for another long, endless moment, then crumples and drops like a puppet with its strings cut, down onto his knees sobbing like a child whose beloved dog just died. Almost in slow motion, the loaded gun starts to slip from his suddenly slack grip, but Laura is there in a flash, catching it before it can hit the grass and go off.

From the corner of my eye I spot Chet coming around toward J.C., fists clenched. Lips drawn tight in an angry grimace, he growls, "You little—" but gets no further because I spin and hook one foot around his left ankle. I yank hard and he sprawls forward, arms outstretched to land in a clumsy heap on the grass between J.C. and me.

His face twists into a raging storm and he leaps to his feet, fists swinging on me. I sidestep with ease and slip into the moves I'd use against a close-quarters knife attack. My right hand grabs his right fist and twists it back. He yelps in agony. But I'm not done yet. He's still trying to rise so I swing my body around and pull his arm back while simultaneously jamming my left elbow into his right shoulder and bending him forward so he looks like he's gonna throw up. I apply pressure to both his wrist and the upper arm and press his head downward even more. He cries out several more times and then whimpers like an animal with its leg caught in a trap—equal parts fury, humiliation, and pain.

He tries to twist out of my hold and I clamp down harder. He bellows in agony. In the back of my mind I realize we're "causing a scene," as my mother would say, that could attract unwanted attention, like from the cops. But J.C. showing up with that gun has thrown everything into chaos.

"I will break your arm," I say quietly and without emotion. Chet stops struggling instantly, but my gaze remains fixed on the back of his head.

"You better let me go, you—"

I press harder, bending his wrist at a dangerous angle and yanking the arm against my side. "I *will* break your arm. Then I'll break your wrist. And then I'll dislocate your shoulder. If you make me."

Chet gags, like he can't believe this is happening. Or maybe he just can't believe I said so many words all at once. But I'm serious. I will hurt him if that's what it takes to stop him.

"Okay, okay," he mutters through gritted teeth. The words are steeped in pure misery. "I won't do anything. Just let me go, Leo."

My name again. It still unnerves me to hear it with his voice wrapped around it. "If I let go, you will stay down until I tell you to get up. Are we clear?"

I tremble with pent up fear, but my voice sounds steady. He nods, but that's not good enough for me.

"Look at me and tell me we're clear."

I'm not trying to be a hardass. I really need to see his face to know that he's telling the truth. I shift my body slightly to one side so he can twist his neck around and cast me a sideways look.

"We're clear," he grunts.

I press in a bit more for good measure, knowing that the next time I do so *will* break a bone. He winces and stares at me with wide, disbelieving eyes, as though he never imaged Chet Hamilton on his knees at the mercy of the town loser. I never imagined this moment either. Our eyes meet in that instant and I cry out in horror. Releasing Chet, I leap back. "No, oh, no!"

Laura is by my side. "Leo, what's wrong?"

"Oh, God no, oh, no, no, no!" I'm pacing back and forth, oblivious to everything around me except what I just saw in Chet Hamilton's eyes.

Then J.C. is before me, his cheeks stained with tears, his eyes wide with concern. He grabs my shoulders and forces me to stop. "Leo, what's wrong?"

"Dammit, J.C.," I snap, pushing his hands away. "Why didn't you stay hidden like I told you?"

J.C. flinches back and then Laura is by his side, her pretty face scrunched with worry. "Leo! Calm down and tell us."

My chest hitches with staccato breaths and I have to force air into my lungs. I look at both of them. "It isn't him!"

J.C.'s mouth drops open.

"What?" Laura looks aghast from me to Chet.

I glance over and see Chet still on his knees. He's rubbing his injured arm with his other hand and staring at us like we're escaped lunatics. That's when I see what I should've seen the moment I spotted him at J.C.'s house. I take two brisk steps forward and grab him by the collar of his hoodie, yanking him to his feet. He doesn't resist, which is good because I'm so keyed up I might seriously hurt him.

"Where's the jacket?"

He blinks in confusion. "Huh?"

I grip his collar more tightly and pull him down to my level so we could practically kiss. His eyes bulge with fear. "The one with the snake on it!"

Understanding, his eyes return to normal size. "Somebody stole it today outta my locker. When I get my hands on—"

I push him away, cutting off the rest of his threat, and turn to the others. J.C. stares at the hoodie Chet wears and I see he understands now. So does Laura.

"It's not him," I repeat, cursing this power I have and the limited information it provides. Here we are standing out in the open for anyone to see us. I spin around and take in the surrounding park and streets that flank it. A few cars drift past, but none stop and I don't see any pedestrians.

"Maybe he's got the jacket on under his hoodie," J.C. offers in a quiet, not-very-convincing voice.

Chet opens his mouth to speak, but I get there first. "It's not him, J.C."

"How do you know for sure?" J.C. still trembles from before, but the realization that we might have gotten everything wrong has clearly energized him.

I look from him to Laura's resolute face and back to him. "Because the same guy in that jacket is gonna kill him tonight, too."

"Oh, my God!" Laura still holds the gun in her right hand, but her left goes to her mouth in surprise. "And we're standing out here in the open."

She and I think alike. "Yeah. We need to hide. Now!" My voice comes out like a harsh bark, not at all like it usually sounds, but my body is tight with terror.

"What the hell are you idiots talking about?"

I turn to face Chet. He seems to be over his "cowering" mode and back to full-on "Chet" mode. His body is tensed to fight, his eyes narrow with wrath. He glares at J.C. so hard I think laser beams will shoot from his eyeballs. "You pulled a gun on me, you worthless little—"

I step toward him and he stops at once to back away. Any other time, seeing his fear of me would've felt good. Not now. "Back off, Chet. He thought you were gonna kill him."

"The hell?" Chet looks both shocked and confused.

I'm not sure what to say next and I can tell J.C. is still processing the reality that we pegged the wrong killer.

That's when Laura steps up and takes charge. I love how she can do that. "Leo can see when people will die just by looking into their eyes. He saw somebody wearing your jacket stabbing J.C., so we thought it was you. We were gonna snag you in a net, but it got stuck and… Anyway, we were wrong." She stares hard at him, her eyes narrowed and her expression grim, as though daring him to object.

He doesn't. He just looks at her with his eyebrows all scrunched like he's trying to figure out if she's nuts. Finally he shakes his head a little. "That's the stupidest—"

J.C. steps forward, his stance rigid and poised to fight. "Leo's not stupid!" He jabs an accusing finger at Chet. "You are. And you're gonna die tonight. Good! At least if they get me, they'll get your sorry ass, too!"

Despite being a full head taller than J.C., Chet takes a step back, his mouth open, his eyes wide with confused indecision.

"We don't have time for this," I hiss, my voice sounding as desperate as I feel. "We have to hide. Might already be too late." I scan the area again, but we still seem to be alone.

"Come on," Laura says, and starts walking in the direction of the haunted house. It's two blocks away and that's a lot of time in the open.

J.C. turns to follow after tossing Chet a final glower.

Chet turns to me. I can see on his face that he finally understands what's happening. "It's true, what they said?"

I nod. "We're going to hide. I hope if I can keep the killer away from J.C. all night, I'll change something, somehow, and he won't die."

Chet's eyes turn to saucers of fear. "What about me?"

"You can hide with us, if you want. The more, the better." I don't wait for an answer and hurry after the others. As I catch up to them, I hear footfalls on the grass behind me and then Chet is there, too.

J.C. whirls on me as soon as I'm close. "I don't want him here!" The narrow-eyed look of hatred doesn't look right on my best friend's face.

"It's not him, J.C. And he can help."

J.C. glowers at Chet before turning and striding toward the street. Laura glances at me before heading after him.

I turn to Chet, not really understanding why I'm helping him. "C'mon." I follow Laura and Chet follows me.

CHAPTER TWELVE

YOU'RE GOING UP TO THE THIRD FLOOR?

T HE HAUNTED HOUSE, WITH ITS blank windows and shadowed porch, looms dark and menacing as we sprint toward it. We'd broken into a run after leaving the park, but after only a block, J.C. was too winded to continue. The rest of us were doing fine. I expected to hear a nasty comment from Chet about J.C., but he's been uncharacteristically quiet. I guess the knowledge that someone wants to kill him is enough to shut up even Chet Hamilton.

I glance around anxiously as I near the house, just as I did on the run over here. Now that I know Chet isn't the killer, that means it could be anyone. Mr. Mendez, maybe? He easily could've stolen Chet's jacket. But why kill J.C.? Because he was rude to him? If that's the case, Mendez would want to kill every kid at Costa High. And why kill Chet? From what I saw the other night, they're pretty chummy. None of this makes any sense to me, but soon my attention is diverted as the creepy old house looms larger in my field of vision. Its glaring dormers and half-hidden doorways look more ominous now that I know the killer is still out here somewhere.

I notice a second-floor window is broken, most likely by kids throwing rocks at it. The two windows of the third-floor room look like dark eyes hiding something evil from the world. We had discussed laying low in that room so we could watch the street and would know if anyone was approaching, but we changed our minds. That was where the guy who murdered his family killed himself.

As we dart up the weed-strewn incline leading around to the backyard, I realize that I no longer hear Chet's footsteps behind me. I stop and turn. He stands on the sidewalk gazing up at the house with a look of sheer dread on his face. That's the only way I can describe it. Even in the poor light, I can see his usual tan has faded to a pale gray and he's raised his hand to cover his mouth as if he might vomit. It's like some internal terror—something more than the sight of a scary haunted house—is clawing at his soul.

"What's wrong?" My voice is barely a whisper, even though I don't see anyone around or looking out of neighboring windows.

Chet says nothing. Just stares at those dark rectangular 'eyes' on the third floor. His body is rigid and he looks like he'll bolt any second.

J.C. hurries to my side. "C'mon, Leo, we gotta hide!"

"There's something wrong with Chet."

J.C. snorts with disgust. "There's tons wrong with him. Let's go!"

I ignore him and study Chet's fight or flight posture. A memory surfaces from back in elementary school when we were all eight or nine. Kids whispered about how Chet's brother tied him to a chair in that third-floor room and left him there all night because Chet still slept with a night light at home.

"C'mon, Chet," I whisper. "That was a long time ago, what your brother did."

He yanks his gaze from the upper floor and fixes wide, accusing eyes on me. "How'd you know about that?"

I shrug, though it might be too dark for him to see. "When you're invisible like me, other kids say things around you that they wouldn't otherwise."

"I shut those kids up," Chet whispers, his breath coming in fits and starts. He really *is* terrified of going into this house.

I hear J.C. curse under his breath as I step closer to Chet. He flinches and steps back, like he's afraid I'll hurt him again. I hold up both hands in a nonthreatening gesture. "We're not going to the third floor," I assure him. "And we'll all be together this time."

He stares at me in utter amazement, like he can't believe any of this is happening. I can't believe it, either. He nods slightly and I turn back to J.C. "Let's get in there and seal the place up."

He tosses a stormy glare at Chet and then hurries to Laura. They continue along the sagging fence around to the back gate. Chet and I follow.

The ancient wooden gate is fastened securely with a rusted, but sturdy padlock, so that means we need to clamber up and over as quietly as possible. I don't want to embarrass J.C. so I quickly drop to a squat and cup my hands together for him to step into. He casts a quick look at Chet before stepping into my clasped hands with his right foot. The bottom is damp and bits of grass from the park smear my palms as I heft him up. He grabs hold of the six-foot-high gate and climbs up and over with more ease than I expected. I guess climbing the fence at school rejuvenated those long-forgotten muscles.

Laura leaps up after and pulls herself over with only a light *thud* sound as her sneakers strike the wood. I step back and motion Chet forward.

"Still don't trust me?" The voice wafts out from inside the shielding hood, which he replaced after the run.

"Just watching your back. They don't want *me* dead."

He flinches again, but his face beneath the hoodie remains shadowed and unreadable. Then he steps forward and easily scales the gate, up and over in seconds. I wipe my hands on my pants and follow.

The backyard is overgrown with weeds and strewn with broken bits of old paving stones. It doesn't appear that anyone has been here in forever, but it's really dark so we make our way slowly through the remnants of the garden and up onto the back porch. The wood beneath my feet creaks, sounding like gunshots in the utter silence.

Laura's in front, but she doesn't know the place like us locals do, so we switch places and she brings up the rear while I lead the way past the ancient, decaying rocker just outside the kitchen door. I already know we can't get in that way, so I turn right just past it. To my left are the rickety stairs leading up to one of the second-floor bedrooms. I wouldn't dare try them for fear they might collapse. The only point of entry—and the most unnerving—is the crawlspace.

Most of the town kids know about the crawlspace just under the stairs. One of my teachers in middle school said old houses often had them for workers or plumbers to get into hard-to-reach places. In this case, the crawlspace branches off in multiple directions once you enter it, and one of those offshoots goes into the basement through a small opening. It's not very large—literally a space to crawl through—but it will get us into the basement and into the house. I know because it's how J.C. and me got in that time we tried to stay the night.

Dirt and weeds have increased around the metal grate that covers the crawlspace and I squat down to pull the weeds back and dig away the hard-packed earth covering the lower lip of the grate. J.C. squats beside me and digs, too. I glance at him because this hard-packed earth means he never even tried to remove the grate earlier tonight. Which means he always planned on being at the park with the gun, and that realization scares me more than anything.

As though knowing what's in my mind, J.C. ignores me in favor of rapid thrusts and raking movements with his hands to pull dirt aside. I'm mildly surprised he's letting himself get dirty, but, of course, he's in fear of his life. At least when he thought it was Chet, everything sort of made sense. Now that the killer could be anyone, his world has turned upside down.

The entry cleared, I slip my long, slender fingers through the holes in the grate and tug backwards. It holds fast and I figure it's probably rusted and who knows what else. I glance at J.C. and he gets the message. I slip all of my fingers into one side of the grate while J.C. slides his into the opposite side. We tug hard and it pops out, knocking us onto our butts still clutching the now-dislodged grate between us. Ordinarily, we'd share a laugh over our klutziness and I half expect Chet, standing behind me, to toss out a snarky comment, but silence reigns and there's not so much as a giggle.

Nobody makes a move to enter, not even Laura.

"Okay, I'll go first," I offer as I right myself and eye the others, setting the rusty grate off to one side.

"I'll bring up the rear," Laura says, her tone all business.

Both J.C. and Chet stare at me, but pointedly ignore each other. I roll onto my knees and bend my head to peer into the crawlspace. Pitch darkness fills my field of vision. Of course it does. What was I expecting, lights to be on? I take my phone out of my pocket and engage the flashlight app. Using my hand, I shield my eyes from its brightness. With nothing more to be said, I lean in and begin to crawl. My head and shoulders are much bigger than when J.C. and me did this at age nine, but the space was made for grown men, so I don't feel like I'll get stuck. Once my body is halfway in, I turn my phone upward and shine the light ahead. The top and sides are made of rotting wood, but the ground is hard-packed earth. I wave the light around to make sure there are no nails or sharp rocks to cut open my hands or knees. Seeing none, I scurry forward cautiously, keeping a measured pace. I hear someone enter the tunnel behind me and figure its probably J.C., but there's no way to turn around and see.

About five feet ahead the tunnel branches off in a "T." From experience, I know the basement will be to my right. I've never explored what's to the left and don't plan to. I turn right and crawl onward. The removable panel into the basement is about six feet in front of me and I pick up the pace. I hear squeaking up ahead and the last thing I want is to be trapped in this tunnel with a bunch of rats.

There's lots more scrabbling and scuttling behind me, but the sounds are too big to be rats, so I figure J.C. and the others are close behind by the time I arrive at the wooden panel and shine my light through the slats into the basement. It looks pretty barren, just as it did when I was here before, only now it smells much worse, like maybe a skunk got in and died. A memory tickles the back of my mind, but I can't place it now and my stomach lurches from the odor trickling in through those slats, so I hold my breath and give the panel a gentle shove with my free hand. It pops out and clatters to the floor two feet below.

The foul stench is stronger as I clamber out of the tunnel and step onto the creaky wooden floor. I guess back in the day, concrete wasn't used for basement floors because this place is all rotting wood, slimy with mold and other things too disgusting to think about. As the others crawl out behind me, I move my light around the basement.

There's some junk scattered about, the same stuff I remember seeing when I was nine. Of course, at nine, the old tattered chairs and bureaus looked like monsters lurking in the shadows waiting to eat me alive. Now the old furniture just looks sad and forlorn and unwanted. I know that feeling. Leaning up against the stairs that lead into the house are rusty garden tools—a twisted rake, a sap-covered axe, a pickaxe, and a shovel. I shine my light on the shovel for a moment. Something seems off about it but—

"Leo!"

J.C.'s sharp whisper in my ear startles me and I whirl around with the light. He blinks furiously at the assault on his eyeballs and I quickly lower it. "Sorry. Just making sure the coast is clear down here."

He nods and I note Chet and Laura eyeing me in the pool of light from my phone. Once again, the invisible kid is the leader by default.

"C'mon." I hold out my light toward the stairs and we move in that direction.

"Smells like something died down here," Laura whispers.

"Probably just Hamilton," J.C. shoots back, pressing in closer to my back, for protection, I suppose.

I expect to hear a nasty comeback from Chet, but there's nothing. I aim the light up the battered old stairs toward a closed door. Shadows fill the edges of my vision and the silence is almost as heavy as the rancid smell. My body feels like a coiled spring and my heart pounds in my chest like it's trying to get out. I force myself to focus and start up the stairs leading to the kitchen

The wood groans in pain with every step I take and I hear creaks from the others behind me. I guess it's to be expected given the age of these stairs, but if there is someone in the house waiting to ambush us, they must know we're here by now.

I reach the top of the stairs and feel the others crowding in behind. The groaning stops with our movement and that creepy silence returns. The doorknob looks to be made of brass and it's tarnished beyond belief. I feel like my hand will be coated with grime as I grasp it, but the tarnish doesn't come off. I turn the knob and the door opens outward. So far, everything is just the same as the last time.

Why would it be any different, I ask myself as I push open the door and shine my light into the ancient kitchen. *It's not like anyone's lived here since then.*

I step onto the floor and shine my light around. The floor looks like real tile and it still seems pretty solid. I spot a few cracks beneath a heavy layer of dust, but that's all. I study the dust carefully. It doesn't cover the entire floor. Layers of it coat the area around the countertops and in front of green-painted cabinets. Dust also layers the floor around the old fridge, but the area around the sink looks clean. So does the floor leading into the hallway. And the area beneath my feet, right by the cellar door, is also pretty clean. My mind races with possibilities. Why would someone clean parts of the floor, but not all of it? I suppose no one has cooked here or used the fridge for years, but maybe some workmen needed the sink for something? But why near the cellar door? I saw nothing down there that looked like it hadn't been left ages ago.

I'm overthinking and I don't have time for that. We're hiding from a killer and our goal is to secure the house and hunker down for the night. I start across the floor toward the hallway entrance. I hear the others' footfalls against the tile, but don't bother looking back.

It's a short walk past several closed doors into a large entry hall with an ornately carved wooden ceiling, paneled walls, and a huge fireplace. I guess they did that back in the day. This place has fireplaces in almost every room, from what I can recall, so I guess that's how heating was done in 1918.

Near empty bookcases line several walls from floor to ceiling and a chandelier dangles just above the foot of the stairs. I'm sure it used to have real candles, but now it's one of those with fake electric candles jutting up from the ornate brass frame. The staircase leading to the upper floors is carpeted, I notice, with a faded design of flowers. My light falls on detailed carvings that cover the post and the bannister leading to the darkened second floor. I shine the light up at the landing, but don't see anything that catches my attention.

We have already agreed to stay in what I call the big living room, the one with the old piano and a fireplace big enough for Santa and all of his reindeer to fit through at the same time. So I lead the way past the stairs toward that room, which is just beyond the front door. I shine my light on the wood and beveled-glass door as I pass and make a mental note to check the lock after getting the others settled.

We enter the living room through wide double doors and I wonder, like I did before, why people would want doors for a living room. The stone fireplace is straight ahead. I shine my light along the columns flanking each side and at the pattern of small rocks embedded in the smooth stonework above it. There's no mantle, just that rock face and enormous opening fronted by a rusted metal grate. A few scattered, beat-up looking chairs rest in front of it as though awaiting cold bodies needing the heat of a fire to keep them warm. My light passes over the cobwebs stretching from chair to chair and I note that the large windows still have their heavy draperies intact, and closed. That's good. Less chance of this light being seen from the street. Still, I make sure not to aim it in that direction.

The old piano is layered with dust thicker than my phone and built-in floor-to-ceiling bookcases line almost every wall. I guess when no one bought the house after the murders, the owner let it deteriorate. That seems odd to me, given how close this place is to the beach, but I don't know anything about real estate.

I turn back to the others, keeping my light aimed at the floor. "I'm gonna check upstairs to make sure it's safe. You guys can hang down here."

"I'm coming, too," J.C. whispers sharply, like I'd somehow dissed him. "I'm not staying here with *him*." He nods toward Chet.

I glance at Chet, waiting for the sharp retort, but he's eyeing me with wide, uncertain eyes. "You're going up to the third floor?"

I nod.

He opens his mouth to say something and then thinks better of it. He bites his lip and turns away.

Laura looks resolute in the darkness. "I'll secure everything down here," she says with quiet assurance. "No one'll get in." She holds up J.C.'s gun in her right hand and I flinch back slightly. "Don't worry," she says with confidence. "My dad takes me to the shooting range all the time. He's what some people call a gun nut because he has a collection. I know how to use this."

I nod, a little amazed. Laura is full of surprises. I turn to J.C. "Ready?"

He nods this time, but says nothing. I head back into the hall, J.C. close beside me.

The old stairs creak with every step we take and I confess the sound is unnerving. I don't think anyone is in the house to hear us, except maybe the ghosts of J.C.'s imagination, but the dark and the creaking and the unsettling silence twist my heart into knots of dread.

The second floor has four bedrooms, two bathrooms, and a den—or maybe it's a library—for people to chill and read or talk. All the rooms are mostly devoid of furniture, but dust and decay are everywhere. Faded floral wallpaper peels off the bedroom walls in large strips and crazy-angled patches, like maybe the imaginary ghosts got tired of looking at the ugly patterns one night and just went wild.

J.C. and I don't talk as we creep through all the empty rooms. The windows in each are secure except for the one that has a jagged hole in it. I keep my light down because there are no drapes and this window faces out onto the street. Shards of glass and a rock the size of my fist lie on the floor beneath the sill. This is the broken one I noticed from the street. We close all the doors as we leave each room, so no trace of light from my phone can be seen.

We finally arrive at the final door on this floor—the one leading to the attic bedroom. I glance at J.C. and make out the anxiety on his face. We never went into this room before, but J.C. told everyone he did. Chet sneered when

J.C. described the room incorrectly and then bragged about how *he'd* spent the night there. Of course, he never admitted that the experience traumatized him.

I face the dark-paneled wood door and whisper, "I'll go first," reaching for the knob. J.C. doesn't argue. I grip the cold metal and twist, secretly hoping it will be locked. It isn't. The door lets out a sharp little scream as it opens and I almost jump out of my clothes.

"Everything okay up there?" Laura's voice sounds far away because she's trying not to be loud.

I step to the bannister and look down at the first floor. She stands in the shadows gazing up at me, Chet at her side.

"Yeah," I say as loudly as I dare. "Just a door squeaking. We'll be right down."

She nods and turns to head out of sight toward the living room. Chet stares up at me a moment longer and then hurries after her.

I head back to the open door, J.C. trailing close behind, and start up the narrow wooden stairs. I want to get this over with and go back down with the others. Like everything else in this old firetrap, these stairs creak and groan and the sounds are disquieting, but I plow on ahead and grab the tarnished brass knob to the narrow door at the top. Without so much as a glance back at J.C., who's nervous breath is warm against my neck, I turn the knob and push open the door.

Stepping into that attic sends a frigid chill throughout my body. Not because there are ghosts. No, it's because there's only one piece of furniture in the whole room—a single wooden straight-backed chair. And tossed haphazardly on the floor by its feet are long strands of rope.

J.C. stares at the rope and the chair with his mouth agape. "It's true? That story you heard back in third grade?" His voice is barely audible, like he can't bring himself to utter those words.

"Guess so," I mutter, as I try to imagine myself as a little boy tied to that chair in this dark, scary place all night long calling for help and having no one come. The two windows have heavy, tattered drapes over them, so only the tiniest slivers of light from the street lamps can sneak in. Chet would've been in near-total darkness, something that would've traumatized me for sure.

I'm so focused on the chair and the rope and my conflicted feelings about

Chet and his bullying behaviors over the years that I barely catch J.C.'s next statement. "I never would've shot you."

I glance over, startled, his words taking a few seconds to register. His eyes are wide, the whites almost glowing in the dark as if he's afraid of what I'll do, but in the pool of light from my phone I see the guilt on his face.

"I know."

"I could never hurt you, Leo." The voice sounds desperate, like I might not believe him.

"I know," I say again, louder this time. And I do know it. As scared as I'd been with the muzzle of that gun practically in my face, I never truly thought J.C. would pull the trigger—not on purpose. But he could have by accident and that recklessness still scares me. "I could never hurt you, either."

He looks abashed, even in the minimal light from my phone. "I'm *so* sorry about the gun. Just thinking about how I could have hurt you makes me wanna throw up."

He pauses, fighting to get his ragged breathing under control. He's actually trembling, but I don't think it's from the cold. I think his conscience is working overtime, and maybe that's a good thing.

"I got the gun from a relative in the projects," he goes on, his voice small and timid. "He promised it was untraceable."

My eyes widen in surprise and he stops again. I guess we're both thinking the same thing—this whole episode sounds like something from a TV show, only what happened at the park was all too real.

"That's why I couldn't talk to you the past couple of days. I knew you'd figure out about the gun if we spent too much time together."

He shakes his head a little as if in disbelief, and his lopsided grimace makes him look kind of shell-shocked. I get it, I think—he's seeing a part of himself he never suspected was there.

"I don't know what came over me except...." He pauses, peering at me through the gloom. "I was scared, okay? *Really* scared, and I wasn't sure you could protect me and...." He halts again and I do my thing—I wait. "When I saw him going after you at the park, I really snapped. All those times he mocked you and dissed you in front of everyone came flooding back and I lost it."

My mouth drops into an "O" of surprise. "You got that mad over me?"

He nods.

"Mad enough to shoot him?"

He nods again, looking embarrassed. "My temper just took over. I went crazy, Leo. And that scares the crap outta me." He pauses and looks down at the floor. "I almost…" He gulps, like he can't quite say the rest. Then it comes out in a hoarse whisper. "…murdered someone."

"But you didn't."

He looks up. "'Cause of you."

I try for a smile, but I'm so wound up with anxiety it probably looks like a frown. "What best friends are for, right?"

"So we're still best friends?" His voice sounds so wracked with need that I feel an urge to reach out and touch him. But I don't.

"For life." And I mean that, too.

He expels a breath of intense relief, like if I'd said "no" he might have jumped from this third-floor window.

"C'mon, J.C., let's go downstairs. This room gives me the creeps."

His eyes widen farther. "Only *this* room?"

I chuckle and that moment of camaraderie between us feels good, like old times. I lead him to the door and usher him through. I steal one final glance back at the chair, shuddering as I close the door.

CHAPTER THIRTEEN

SOMEONE TRACKED YOU

WHEN ME AND J.C. COME downstairs, Laura shows us some secret passages, wide enough to walk through, that she found behind two of the bookcases. Both passages start in the living room, but they go in different directions to exit outside the house. We make quick work of exploring them and find that the one near the double entry doors slinks around the side of the house where the kitchen is located. The other one, which starts next to the fireplace, connects to a study down the hall and then out to the back yard. We make sure both bookcase entryways are closed before we settle down to wait.

The living room is cold, maybe even colder than it is outside, and I shiver beneath my baggy hoodie. I stare into the empty fireplace wishing for logs and matches.

J.C. lounges in the chair right beside me while Chet sits about ten feet away staring at the closed drapes. Laura wanders the room with the gun, but mainly hangs by the windows, occasionally pulling back the drapes to examine the street outside. As she moves from window to window, she avoids an area of the floor just to the left of the fireplace.

"The wood's rotted there," she told us when we returned from upstairs. "Feels like the whole floor'll give way if we put too much weight on it."

We heed her warning and steer clear of that area.

As agreed beforehand, our phones are on mute with "Location Services" disengaged in case someone might try tracking J.C.'s phone, or mine. So we sit in gloom and heavy silence and wait for night to become day.

I'm eyeing Chet where he sits half-shadowed across the room when I hear J.C. say quietly, "I'm really sorry I went to those clubs without you, Leo."

I look over at him. My eyes have adjusted to the darkness and I can make out shame on his face. I guess this is his night for feeling guilty.

"I really wanted you with me, but I know how you hate places like that and…." He stops again and this time just stares at me. It's my turn, that look says.

"It's okay, like I said before," I reply, having given this a lot of thought since meeting Roberto. "I hold you back and that's not fair."

"Not true." But he doesn't continue, so I take his silence to mean he does think it's true.

"I talked to Roberto at the club." He frowns and ducks his head, as if he thinks I caught him doing something illicit, so I go on quickly. "Seems like a good guy. Really likes you." I pause to take in a deep breath and release it. "He said you talked about me."

"I'm sorry I showed him your pictures," J.C. says defensively. "We got to talking and I couldn't help bragging about you."

I stiffen with surprise. "I'm the town loser."

J.C.'s mouth drops open. "Oh, my God, Leo, you really don't get it, do you?"

I gaze back at him in silence, glad for the darkness obscuring his eyes. What's to get?

"I need you so much more than you'll *ever* need me," he says, his expression flat, as if his words are just an obvious everyday fact.

Now *my* mouth drops open. "But you have no other friends because of me, because I'm such a loser. You could be the most popular kid at school if it wasn't for me."

"Oh, man, Leo, for a guy who sees so much you really missed this one." He scoots his chair closer and leans in. "You're the most real kid in this stinking town. That's why no one relates to you. They're all about being fake and popular. And that's why I picked you for a friend, because I need to be more like *you*, not them."

I think a feather could push me over at that moment and I'm so beyond stunned I feel more tongue-tied than usual. I thought *I'd* picked *him* for a friend and always worried that he'd ditch me some day for more popular kids, like I thought he was doing at that club.

"I guess I gushed about you so much to Roberto that once he saw your picture he crushed on you big time."

My eyes grow even wider and I'm grateful the darkness hides the color rising to my cheeks. "He did?"

J.C. nods. "He was pretty bummed when he thought Laura was your girl-friend. He messaged me about it."

I glance over at Laura. She's standing by the largest drapery-covered window watching our conversation with interest. I notice Chet listening, too. I turn back to J.C. "That's crazy."

"Crazy that someone thinks you're awesome? No, it's not." He looks down in embarrassment and I suspect his own cheeks look flushed.

There is an awkward moment of heavy silence as I digest all this new and unbelievable information. "It's okay for best friends not to do everything to-gether, J.C."

"It is?"

I try for a little smile, even though he can't see it. "Hell, yeah. I could never get you into Aikido, remember?"

J.C. chuckles. "And I never got you into dancing."

We share a laugh.

"It's okay that you do things without me," I tell him. "Long as we're still friends."

"For life." He raises a fist and we bump.

Another long moment passes between us. Then I make out a sly grin on his face.

"Want me to tell Roberto you're available?"

I pull back in surprise and then offer my own grin. "Uh, no thanks."

We bump fists again.

J.C. looks over at Chet and his face turns stormy. "What'chu you lookin' at?"

I turn to find Chet staring at us without his usual coat of haughtiness. He just gazes at us as though he really wants to know something.

"Just wondering if you two are really…." He trails off, but I know what he means and so does J.C.

"What's the truth matter to you?" J.C.'s tone is filled with rising anger.

"You got the whole school believing it. Bet nobody knows about *your* boyfriend from the projects, do they? That he buys you booze and you get drunk before you even get to his place? Or how you let guys feel you up at the club. You're the biggest phony in a town of phonies!"

My hand on J.C.'s arm stops his tirade before it goes nuclear. I offer a gentle smile of reassurance and his face relaxes again. We both turn back to Chet and J.C. grins when he sees the look of horror on his enemy's face.

"You know about Pedro?" His voice comes out hoarse, like there's no timbre left in it.

"We followed you," Laura says, crossing the room and stand with us.

I feel certain Chet loses all the color in his face as his body sags like an old rag doll and his shoulders slump. He drops his arms to both knees and looks down at the floor. "It's not what you think."

"What's to think?" J.C. shoots back. "You call us gay and bully half the kids at Costa High and you're the one groping boys at the club and going home with some guy. That kinda says it all, Hamilton."

I squeeze J.C.'s arm gently and give him that calming look again. The tenseness in his body relaxes, and I look at the slumped and broken Chet. "We won't tell anyone."

"Only because Leo is a helluva lot nicer than me or you," J.C. grumbles. "If it was up to me, the whole town would know."

Chet looks up, wide-eyed and fearful. "No one can know. I can't be anything that looks weak. My brother'll kill me."

That comment catches me off-guard. "Uh, isn't Bob in prison?"

Chet looks down at the floor again. "He's got friends out here. Bad friends. If my mom tells him I'm anything less than top dog in town, I'll get beat up or—" He raises his head so fast I can almost hear his neck crack. "Oh, crap! That's why someone's after me! Damn, I should've thought of it before!"

"You're serious?" That comes from Laura, who looks stunned. "Your own brother would send someone to kill you?"

"He's psycho," Chet says, his breathing accelerating with rising fear. "That's no joke, either. He's been beating that macho crap thing into me all my life. He always said I better be the biggest, meanest, toughest kid in La Costa or else. I even copied stuff from high school bully movies so he'd get off my back. Mom let Bob 'work with me' because she thought I'd be a wimp otherwise. But she never knew how psycho he was until he killed that guy."

I remember my previous thought about Chet acting like every movie stereotype. Now I understand. I also recall those pills he bought from Mr. Mendez, and how lanky he was growing up—until high school when he buffed up pretty fast. "Is that why you buy steroids from Mendez?"

Chet looks startled, his wide eyes gleaming in the low light, and then nods. "I knew you were in the boiler room. I told Mendez the next day. But I didn't know how much you saw. I put those notes in your lockers 'cause I was panicked you'd tell Harris. That's why I went looking for you tonight, to talk. When you weren't home, I went to Rivera's house, figuring you'd be there."

I make another connection. "You're the one who let us out of the boiler room that night."

Chet nods again. "Saw your car parked on the street and went back. Mendez gave me an extra key when I first started buying from him."

"Where'd you really get that snake design?" Laura asks, her voice hard and accusing.

"Off the Internet," Chet answers quietly. "People were sharing it right and left and I thought it looked badass."

"Thanks. I drew it."

He looks startled, but doesn't respond.

"Who's Yury Muerte?" J.C. asks, watching Chet carefully.

Chet looks genuinely confused. "I don't know."

I believe him. J.C. and I exchange a look. That means the real killer is probably the secret messenger. I turn back to Chet. "So, who's Pedro? A guy you met at the club?"

Chet shakes his head. "He's twenty-one, too old for that place. He's the janitor at the building next door. I met him one night while he was getting off work and paid him money to buy me booze. My mom is a hawk on that stuff and practically measures every bottle in the house to make sure I'm not sneaking it anymore."

The big picture of Chet Hamilton that's made up of all the little ones I've observed over the years starts to take shape in my mind. I remember those episodes with his brother bullying him in the parking lot. I also recall in middle school how he looked red-eyed more than once when I happened to catch him with his shades off. And I think back on all the times he's worn sunglasses since high school began.

"How long you been drinking?"

Chet just stares at me and I confess it's kind of creepy. I almost prefer the badass jerk to this wreck of a kid. It's like watching Wolverine morph into the Cowardly Lion.

"Since I was twelve," he answers.

"Jeeze." That's from J.C. and he sounds genuinely shocked.

"Pedro buys me booze and lets me stay over," Chet goes on as though J.C. hadn't interrupted. "He's got three little brothers he takes care of and I buy them stuff they could never afford. Got more money than God, so why not, right?"

I confess I'm shocked. But on some level, maybe not. I always thought Chet didn't mess with me after first grade because he knew I wasn't afraid of him anymore. But maybe it was more than that. Maybe he sensed we're more alike than different.

Given our current situation, I ask the most logical question I can think of. "Do you think your mom found out about Pedro and told your brother?"

Chet considers a moment. "Maybe."

"Why would your brother want J.C. dead?"

"Yeah?" J.C. pipes up. "What did I ever do to him?"

Chet shrugs.

I think I understand.

"Maybe it's 'cause J.C. is the only one who can talk crap to you and get away with it?"

Chet sits up straighter. "Yeah. I'm sure my mom told Bob about that at some point."

"Great," J.C. says with derision. "Once again everything is your fault, Hamilton! Why didn't you just drink yourself to death when you were twelve?"

"J.C.!" I stare at him, aghast. I've always seen his mean streak, but that was low even for him. Now I understand his earlier words about needing me to make him better.

J.C. looks at me and must see the horror in my eyes because his face kind of collapses in disgrace. "Sorry."

Before I can respond, Chet whispers, "I tried hard, Rivera. But for some crazy reason, I'm still here."

J.C. looks startled and we both stare at him. This whole conversation makes me uncomfortable. Too much like my mom's favorite old movie, *The*

Breakfast Club. It's about a bunch of stereotypes who get detention together and find their "real" selves. I hated that film and here we are acting it out. I just want to focus on staying alive.

"Is your brother the reason you bought that knife from Mendez?"

Chet nods. "Protection. Especially with me going to the clubs and those projects all the time."

"Why is he even in prison?" That's Laura. "I thought rich people never went to prison 'cause they get the best lawyers."

"He killed the wrong guy in that bar fight," Chet answers solemnly. "Senator's son. Politics and wealth trump just plain wealth."

Laura nods and I see she understands. We're all rich, so we know how much rich people get away with in this country. But there's a line, even for us.

That's when I hear the sound of breaking glass from somewhere at the very back of the house. It's faint, but distinct.

J.C. jumps slightly and Laura lifts the gun toward the closed living room doors. My mind whirls. How could anyone have found us? Our phones are off. No one knew we were coming here. Chet stares at me with wide, terrified eyes. He's looking at me to protect him, even though Laura has the gun.

That's when I notice the phone clutched in Chet's right hand. I whisper, "You have your GPS on, don't you?"

Chet looks surprised. "Guess so," he whispers back.

I want to shout my anger to the ceiling, but keep it contained. "Someone tracked you."

Chet lifts the phone and makes to turn it off, but Laura hisses, "No!"

We all turn to her.

"I have an idea."

CHAPTER FOURTEEN

THERE'S SOMEONE UP THERE

I HAVE TO SAY LAURA IS crafty. J.C. and me huddle against one another in the secret passage next to the fireplace. Chet and Laura hide inside the one next to the double entry doors. The owners must've been really paranoid because some of the books are fake and peepholes allow us to see into the living room from the secret passage.

I stare through the peepholes at Chet's phone resting on the chair he'd been sitting on. Only now the chair is in a different spot. Now it sits on the rotted floorboards. It was Laura's idea to leave it there with the GPS still on so whoever is tracking Chet will find it. Then we'll know who our enemy is and hopefully trap him in the basement when the floor gives way. To mask the sound of the creaking wood, we covered that section with a faded oval rug that was in front of the fireplace. Like I said, Laura is crafty.

I hear footsteps approaching from the entry hall. Sounds like only one person. I glance toward J.C. and even in the pitch black of the secret passage, I know he's terrified. I feel him shivering as he presses firmly against my body. I peer again through the cleverly disguised peepholes into the room as the footfalls grow louder. Whoever it is walks normally, as though visiting an old friend instead of skulking around an empty, possibly haunted house. That casual walk strikes me as odd, but I have no time to contemplate it before the doors open inward and a figure enters the living room, looking around at the empty space. I feel J.C. flinch beside me.

It's Matt Wilson!

"Hey Chet, you in here?" Wilson looks around the room and then down at the phone in his hand. He steps farther into the room and spots the chair with Chet's phone resting on it. Slipping his phone back into his pocket, Wilson strides across the room to the chair and scoops up Chet's. "Chet? Where are you, man?"

My mind reels with questions. Wilson? Could he be the killer? That doesn't make sense. He's Chet's best friend. Then I study his clothes. He wears designer jeans and a fancy Abercrombie hoodie and high-end kicks, but not the snake jacket. What the hell is going on?

Before I can even react, the bookcase across the room pushes open and Chet steps out. Wilson whirls around in surprise and I'm silently screaming at Chet for revealing Laura when he quickly closes the bookcase before Wilson can see what's inside.

"What are you doing here, Matt?"

Wilson chuckles with relief. "Damn, fool, you scared me. Why are you hiding in there?"

Chet shrugs, but to his credit he doesn't approach close enough to stand beside his friend. He knows the floor is weak. But he doesn't warn Wilson either, which I find odd.

"I heard something break, so I hid in a secret room I found," Chet answers casually. "How'd you know I was here?"

Wilson flashes that charming smile the girls at Costa High swoon over and holds out Chet's phone. "Tracked your phone."

"Why?" Now Chet sounds suspicious and I don't blame him. I wonder if he suspects Wilson and Grady followed him to the club.

"Been worried about you, man," Wilson says in a voice that sounds sincere. "You been acting kinda weird lately."

Chet stiffens slightly, but his face displays the usual cocky sneer he wears every day at school. "I don't act weird, Wilson. You better watch your mouth."

I catch the bravado in his voice, but, maybe because of everything I heard from him tonight, I also detect a trace of fear.

I guess Wilson does, too, because he doesn't cower. He grins even more broadly. "Drop the act, Hamilton. It won't work."

Chet's face crumbles with shock, but before he can respond, Wilson calls, "Come on out, guys."

Before I know what's happening, I'm shoved hard from behind and feel J.C. lurching forward beside me. We strike the bookcase door and it swings open, sending both of us tumbling to the hardwood floor of the living room. I hear Laura's voice protesting and see her from the corner of my eye as I roll over. She's stumbling from her own hiding place, the gun no longer in her hand.

J.C. is sprawled beside me looking around, wide-eyed with fear. I lurch to my feet to get my bearings, but another shove from behind sends me back down to the floor.

"Stay on the floor, all of you," Wilson barks, his piercing gaze roaming the room.

Whoever shoved us must've turned on a lantern because a large glow emanates from behind me and casts the room in a cold, bluish light. I see Wilson holding a large gleaming knife. It looks like a kitchen knife.

Chet stares at the knife as though considering how to take it away from him, but stops when the voice behind Laura says, "Hey, Matt, looky what Laura gave us. A gun."

Wilson whistles with surprise. "Right on. Might come in handy with all these extra people." He chuckles at Chet. "So, what have you and the other queers been up to over here, eh, Chet? We didn't expect to find a party."

"The hell's going on, Matt?" Chet snaps, taking a step closer to Wilson, despite the extended knife.

"Don't try anything, Chet," says the voice behind Laura. Out of the darkness of the secret passage steps Randy Cranston, the fourth wheel of the Chet Pack. I thought he was Chet's friend. I thought they all were…

Chet turns and then freezes in surprise when he sees Cranston pointing the gun at him.

Cranston shoves down on Laura's shoulder. "On the floor."

She crumples, but retains her balance enough not to bang her knees. She breaks her fall with outstretched arms and ends up facing me. We exchange a quick look and what I read in her eyes is the same thing she must see in mine—uncertainty, worry, and fear. This situation is bigger than we ever imagined and I curse myself for not planning our defenses better.

Chet stares at the knife in Wilson's very steady hand and to his credit, the tightening of muscles under his eyes look more like anger than fright. "Why the hell would you wanna kill me? We're friends."

Wilson's face twists into disgust, mixed with fury. "We've never been friends!" His voice sounds like he's spitting. "And why would I go to prison for you?"

"But Leo said—"

"Chet!" My voice cracks like a whip and everyone looks at me.

Wilson sniggers with delight. "So, you and Ninja Turtle are on a first-name basis now, eh? This just gets better and better." He looks at whoever shoved me and J.C. "Looks like you won't be the only movie star tonight, Jonny."

I glance over my shoulder and have to keep myself from gasping. Grady stands behind me wearing a black wig and Chet's snake jacket. He holds a kitchen knife in one hand and a lantern sits on the floor near his feet. My confusion soars. What is going on here?

"What the hell is this about?" Chet takes an angry step forward, but Wilson raises the knife and points the tip of the blade at Chet's chest.

"I won't kill you, Hamilton," he snaps, his eyes narrowed, "but I *will* make you bleed."

Chet stops, fists clenched at his side. For all his swagger at school, it's obvious he has no clue what to do right now.

I also sense this whole scene is about Chet and not me or J.C. It's pretty clear Wilson didn't expect to find us here, so I look for any opening I might have to disarm Grady hovering behind me.

"Sit down, Chet!" Wilson snaps, waving the knife at the chair while slipping Chet's phone into the front pocket of his pants.

Chet glances over at me as he stiffly sits in the chair. I make no move, especially when I hear the floor beneath the chair groan.

Wilson slips off his backpack. "Keep him covered, Randy."

Cranston keeps glancing at Laura on her knees in front of him, but the gun remains fixed on Chet.

Wilson sets down the knife and unzips his pack. He extracts a long length of rope—the kind people use to tie stuff to the tops of cars. He moves behind Chet. "Hands behind the chair."

The way Chet complies, jerking his hands behind the chair and glaring, makes it clear he's furious. But he's clearly afraid too. Wilson squats down and ties the rope around his hands and then secures it to the wooden frame of the chair, so if Chet does try to stand he'll bring the chair with him.

Wilson retrieves the knife and moves back in front. "I've waited for this payback since the first time you did a swirly on me," he purrs, obviously enjoying the moment. "All of us have." He waves the blade of the knife around the room and I note the others nodding. "My father never let me hear the end of it when I caved in and joined you instead of beating your ass. Called me a coward and lots worse. I swore on his deathbed that I'd get even with you and now I am."

"We were friends after that," Chet says feebly, but I can see by the downward turn of his mouth that he's beginning to understand.

Each time Wilson moves, I wonder just how much longer the floor beneath him will hold out.

"We were never friends!" Wilson plants his face right in front of Chet's, sneering as though he's getting ready to spit on him. "You have no friends, Hamilton. You forced us to be your slaves. No one at Costa likes you. You made everyone scared of you, but that's 'cause they don't know you're a girly boy like these two." He points the knife at J.C. and me. I glance at J.C., but he's too frightened to be offended by the insult.

Wilson pulls back from Chet and reaches into another pocket. He slips out his cell phone and holds it up. "We've been following you a lot lately and boy do we have some great footage."

Chet's eyes bulge, but he says nothing.

Sniggering, Wilson taps his screen a few times. Loud techno music pours from the phone and Wilson quickly mutes it. He holds the phone out and Chet visibly deflates like a balloon losing air.

"You sure like having those guys feel you up, Hamilton," Wilson says, and I hear laughter from behind me. "Yeah, you danced with some chicks and made out with a few, but we'll edit that stuff out."

Chet groans then, but not from Wilson's words. Something he sees on the screen shocks him.

Wilson leans in and grins. "Oh, yeah, the Mexican boyfriend. We got tons of footage of you going home with him. The booze shots are good, too, you swigging from the bottles. I knew you drank, but not that much, and it's nothing compared to the boyfriend. See, we're gonna edit this footage together, but make it look loose and kinda raw so people won't think anyone messed with it. Once it's on the Net, especially after we add in tonight's fun and games, you're done for in this town. You'll have to move to San Francisco to feel at home."

Cranston laughs. "You always been trash, Hamilton," he says, "But I never figured you for a queer boy, too."

"You don't know anything." That's all Chet says, but he's looking straight at me when he says it.

"Don't matter what we know," Wilson says quietly. "Once it's on the Internet, it's true. 'Specially when there's video."

"What're you gonna do?" Chet stares up at Wilson, his features unsettled as if unsure what emotion to focus on, his body jerking slightly as he struggles to free his hands.

Wilson sniggers like a little boy about to pull the best prank ever. "Here's the plan. We gave Grady a wig that matches the hair color of your Mexican boyfriend and he's wearing your jacket."

Chet suddenly comes to the realization that Grady has his jacket and his face becomes stormy again. "You broke into my locker?"

Wilson laughs. "We thought the vid would be better with your boyfriend wearing that jacket. Since we couldn't be sure you'd have it on, we had to steal it."

"I reported it to Harris," Chet says, his cocky tone resurfacing. "Everyone will know it was stolen."

Wilson chuckles again. He's really enjoying himself and I consider for just a moment how much hate he must have kept inside to have waited this long for revenge.

"Of course, you'd lie and tell Harris it was stolen," Wilson goes on, smiling slightly, his voice purring like a new car engine. "You sure can't tell him you gave it to your boyfriend, right?"

Chet flinches and I recognize the truth of Wilson's words. Once these videos hit the Net, anything Chet says to try and explain them away will be seen as lies.

"What our film is missing is the money shot," Wilson goes on and eyes me. "Ninja Turtle knows what that means, don't you?"

I nod.

"What is that?" Chet asks, his voice cracking ever so slightly.

Wilson holds up his phone. "That's the big scene in a movie, the one the audience will always remember," he explains with glee. "For our movie, that means you and the boyfriend in a nice, romantic kiss. You know, the kind that'll make the girls go 'aaahh.'" He laughs at the horrified expression on Chet's face. "We kept hoping you'd kiss the real boyfriend, but you never did. In public, anyway."

"He's *not* my boyfriend," Chet asserts with anger. "Now let me go and I won't tell my mom about this."

Wilson smirks and I know that can't be good. "Oh, yeah, your mom. She's very worried about you. She asked us if we knew where you stayed when you weren't home all night."

Chet's eyes widen with surprise.

"Of course, we told her we didn't know, that you've been hiding stuff from us, too. We acted real concerned for our best friend and I think we deserve an Oscar for our acting." He turns to me. "What say, Ninja Turtle? Think your mom could get us nominated?" He laughs again and I start to realize something else. He's not just filled with hate. He's unhinged. His blind hate for Chet has pushed him over the edge.

"Uh, Matt?"

That's Grady behind me. I glance back. He looks almost sheepish, like he's afraid of how Wilson might react. Maybe he senses the unhinged part, too. "What're we gonna do about them?" He waves his knife around at J.C., me, and Laura. "They'll tell what we did."

My heart freezes in my chest. He's right! We're witnesses who weren't supposed to be here. Could Wilson be unhinged enough to kill us, despite saying he wasn't planning to kill anyone?

Wilson looks at Grady like he's an idiot. "They won't say anything anyone will believe 'cause they're gonna be in the film, too."

"The hell?" That's J.C. beside me.

I jerk my head around to face Wilson. "What're you talking about?" My voice sounds small and timid.

Wilson steps toward me. I hear a creak from the wood beneath the throw rug, but he seems oblivious to anything but his fun. He stops and stares down at J.C. and me like we're two bugs he'd gleefully crush underfoot. He casts an uncertain look at Laura before returning his piercing gaze to us.

"I got no idea why she's here, but Hamilton obviously brought you two for some action." He shakes his head in amusement. "Funny. I thought you guys were only into each other, but I guess a pretty boy like Hamilton is too much to resist."

"We are not—"

That's all J.C. gets out before Wilson kicks out with one sneakered foot and connects with his midsection. J.C. grunts as the air whooshes from his lungs and he doubles over. Fury washes over me and I start to rise. I feel a sharp poke in the back of my neck and a trickle of moisture that can only be blood dribbles down my upper back, soaking into my tank top.

"Don't try anything, Ninja Turtle," Wilson says derisively. "You don't have moves like the real Leonardo. Hate to see you get hurt."

I freeze, not because I fear Wilson. No, it's because he doesn't know what I really *can* do and I might be able to use his ignorance to my advantage. I catch Chet staring at me. He's clearly waiting for me to make a move.

Wilson looks over my head at Grady. "To answer your question, you're not the only one who's gonna kiss our enemy. So will they." He indicates J.C. and me.

Still doubled over from the kick, J.C. spits out, "Never," in a breathless voice.

My breathing halts for a moment at Wilson's words, but my mind continues to spin with ideas.

Wilson grins, revealing bright, perfect teeth in the lantern light. "You two are icing on the cake. Hamilton making out with every guy he finds. It'll be perfect once it's edited in with the stuff from the club. We kill three birds with one vid." He laughs and raises his free hand for a high five. I can't see Grady's face, but the slap he gives sounds like the crack of a whip.

My gaze sweeps the "set" without being obvious and I think back on the movies I watched being filmed as a kid. I recall the special effects guys proudly showing me their tricks of the trade, especially the "in-camera" tricks that are shot live, and the way they set up fight scenes. I focus a moment on the phone in Wilson's hand and then glance at Laura. She's watching me, not Wilson. She knows I have an idea. And I do. But then Wilson speaks and my idea is thrown into disarray.

"The Mexican queer goes first."

Back on his knees, J.C. looks at Wilson in defiance. "Never."

"But this has to be a dream come true, to kiss the guy who outed you?" Wilson laughs. "It's so TMZ."

J.C. glowers at Chet again. "I will never kiss that—" He freezes as Wilson signals to Grady and the point of the knife once more presses into my neck.

"Your lover boy will bleed if you refuse," Wilson says coldly. He fixes hard, emotionless eyes on J.C. "Well, Mexican? Your choice."

J.C. turns to me with wide, desperate eyes. I know he's going to say yes, to prove his words up on the third floor. He would never hurt me or let me *be* hurt.

Still focused on my best friend, I say with quiet forcefulness, "I'll do it."

Wilson sneers. "Course you will. After the Mexican."

I turn my head and sit up higher. Grady backs up a step and I feel the knife eased away from my neck. I know Grady won't kill me. He doesn't have it in him. "No. I'll give you a real make out session with Chet if you leave J.C. out of this."

"Leo!" J.C. stares at me aghast, his mouth hanging open.

Wilson steps closer. "He means that much to you?"

I remain silent, but the answer is written all over my face. Wilson actually looks impressed. He's obviously never had a real friend before.

"No, Leo," J.C. pleads. "I can't let you do this. You'll be the laughing stock of the town."

I turn to my friend and offer a sad smile. "I already am, J.C. I don't matter to anyone."

"You matter to me," J.C. whispers, lowering his gaze as his cheeks redden.

"I told you I'd protect you," I say quietly, hoping he'll look into my face again. He does. "Trust me. I got this."

His expression relaxes as understanding blooms on his face and he nods, then returns his gaze to the floor.

"Okay, Ninja Turtle," Wilson snorts. "Let's see what you got. Grady, give him the jacket."

I hear Grady rustling around behind me and then he's handing me the jacket faster than I would have thought possible. Maybe he's having second thoughts?

I stand, clutching the snake jacket in my right hand, and stare at Wilson.

"Take off the hoodie and put it on."

I shrug out of my hoodie, tossing it to the floor. I hear a slight intake of breath and look up to find Chet staring at me in amazement. So is Wilson. I realize that none of them have ever seen me in a tank top or at the beach and I guess they didn't expect a dweeb to be built.

Wilson whistles. "Ninja Turtle is pretty buff. Turns you on, doesn't it, Hamilton?"

I glance at Chet and he just stares at me as though Wilson doesn't exist. I can't quite read his expression, but disbelief comes close. First, I kick his butt in the park and now he sees I'm built without using steroids like him. And I don't go around bragging about my body. I think that's so foreign to him that he's beyond stunned.

"Well, buff boy," Wilson says, waving the knife toward Chet. "Put on the jacket and get to work. The camera awaits." He holds up his phone and wiggles it back and forth.

I notice that he's keeping his distance from me and that's not good. I need to lure him closer so I can make my move. I'm not so worried about Grady, but Cranston has the gun and that's the biggest threat. He stands behind Laura waving the weapon around like it's a toy. The idiot grin on his face tells me he's never held a real gun before and that can't be good for any of us.

I slip the jacket around my shoulders, but don't put it on. I need freedom of movement.

"I said put it on, Ninja Turtle!" barks Wilson, enjoying his dual roles as both director *and* dictator.

"Um," I begin, sounding as timid as possible, "I've seen lots of movies being made, you know, and I think it looks, well, you know, more romantic if the jacket's draped over my shoulders." I'm embarrassed even saying this and the blush in my cheeks is genuine. "Like he put it over me 'cause I'm cold or something."

I stop and wait. Wilson's glare turns into a broad grin. "I like that."

Inwardly, I release my breath. He bought it. Now for the rest.

Thankfully, Wilson helps. "Any other ideas, film boy?"

I guess it would kill him to use my real name. No matter.

"Uh, well, I was thinking if you, well, want Laura in the movie, right there is a good place to put her." I point to a spot just to the side of Chet's chair. Laura would be looking across Chet at Cranston and that's what I want.

Wilson's eyes narrow to slits. "Why there?"

I move slowly onto the throw rug, choosing my steps with care. Creaks and groans abound, but Wilson stares at me so intently he doesn't notice. I stop between Laura and Chet. "If you, uh, film from here you'll get a nice profile shot of me and Chet, with Laura looking on in the background just a phone's throw away."

Wilson pulls a confused face. "Don't you mean a stone's throw?"

"Oh, yeah. My bad." I glance down at Laura. I see in that instant she understands my plan.

Wilson eyes me a long moment. "I like it." He waves the knife at Laura. "You heard him. On the other side of the chair."

Laura scuttles around Chet to the opposite side of his chair. More creaks and groaning of wood accompany her movements. She turns and hunkers down on her knees, gazing at Wilson in fury. He smirks and turns to Cranston. I catch a slight movement as Laura's hand moves to her pants pocket.

"Keep 'em covered while I film, Randy."

"No sweat."

I glance back to see Cranston take a step closer. If that gun goes off, my head'll have a hole the size of a golf ball right through it. Forcing myself to remain calm, I step closer to Chet. The floor groans again. This wood is stronger than I thought. Chet looks up at me from the chair, the astonished look still on his face.

"You're really gonna do this?"

I nod.

His eyes widen, but I avoid them. I guess standing by your friends is also foreign to him.

I drop to a squat right in front of him and rest my hands on his knees. They're trembling. I glance sideways at Laura for a split second and note her right hand at her side, hidden from Wilson's view. Then I glance to my left to gauge how close Wilson is to me now. As I suspected, putting my hands on Chet's knees where they are clearly visible lowers Wilson's guard. Keeping the knife in his left hand, he holds out the phone and frames his shot, grinning the whole time.

"Okay, lover boy, let's see you put the moves on Hamilton."

I eye him a moment longer. He's not close enough. "You might want to start with a tight close-up of our lips together and then move back with the phone to reveal who's kissing. It's more dramatic that way."

Wilson eyes me with suspicion. "Man, you're getting into this, aren't you?"

I shrug. "If I'm gonna be humiliated on the Internet, might as well do it with style." That sounds like a dumb line from one of my mom's dumb movies, but it has the desired effect.

Wilson grins even more broadly. "Hell, yeah!"

He steps right up to us, eyeing my hands as he does. I keep them firmly clamped on to Chet's trembling knees. For whatever reason, I'm not scared. Not for me, anyway.

Satisfied I'm not going to make a grab for him, Wilson uses the thumb of his knife hand to tap the phone's screen and motions for me to begin. I lean in slowly toward Chet's face, focusing my eyes on his nose. He stares back, but I can't tell what he's feeling. He doesn't try to pull away. Maybe he's figured out I'm up to something.

My face is mere inches from his and I move my head closer, my lips puckered for a kiss. Since I've never kissed anyone before, I have no idea if I'm doing this right. Just going with what I've seen in the movies. I flick my eyes to the left and see Wilson right by my face with the phone and that's when I make my move.

Snaking out my left foot, I hook it around Wilson's ankle and kick backwards. At the same moment I see in my peripheral vision Laura rise like a phoenix, her right arm back and cocked. As Wilson makes a short, startled exclamation of surprise, Laura's arm swings over her head and a phone flies from her grasp at an astonishing speed. I duck and the phone whizzes over my head straight at Cranston.

I hear a loud grunt and Cranston's body crashes to the floor, but my attention is caught by the gun skittering along the throw rug. It lands by Wilson's feet as they fly out from under him and he sails backward. I rise as Wilson slams hard onto the rug. The *crack* sound is so loud I think it's the gun going off. But I feel the floor sinking beneath me and make a wild leap forward. I land in a roll, Chet's jacket sliding off my shoulders, and right myself in time to see the entire floor in front of the fireplace give way and drop out of sight like a massive sinkhole.

Chet cries out as his chair tilts sideways and vanishes along with Wilson's screaming form. Before I can even react, Grady has leapt backward and the floor beneath J.C. crumbles and collapses. With a loud cry of terror, my best friend vanishes through the hole along with Grady's lantern and I hear a series of muffled *thuds* from below as everything crashes hard onto the old wooden floor of the basement.

With a look of horror on his face, Grady turns and bolts from the living room. His footsteps vanish in the direction of the kitchen. I glance over at Cranston. He's rolling around by the living room doors clutching at his bleeding face. I crawl to the edge of the massive hole, Laura by my side. The basement floor is at least fifteen feet down. I whip out my phone and switch on the flashlight, shining the beam into the dark hole. Chet's chair has shattered from the impact, but his arms remain tied to the back and his left leg juts out at a crazy angle. He doesn't move. Wilson lies in a heap beside him and a couple of feet away I see J.C. unmoving and covered in dust and wood debris. I can't tell if he's dead or alive. That goes for all of them. The lantern must've broken on impact because my phone provides the only illumination. Grit and dust swirls through my beam of light as I shine it right onto J.C. Blood streaks the back of his head. I quickly move the light to the other two. No visible blood on Wilson, but Chet's leg is covered with something shiny.

I swing the light back to J.C. He's stirring. "J.C.!"

He opens his eyes and blinks against the light. "Leo?"

His voice sounds so far away and so weak. My heart lurches with fear. "Are you okay?"

J.C. sits up slowly, looking disoriented and confused. He sees blood on his shirt and reaches behind his head. He winces with pain and pulls back a bloody hand. "Oh, God, Leo, I'm hurt!"

I feel so helpless and have to fight the urge to jump down and help my friend. But I know I'll break an ankle, at least, and then I won't be able to help any of them. I make out the panic on J.C.'s face and need to redirect him. "You're okay, J.C. I can tell from here. Chet doesn't look so good. Check on him while I call 911."

He nods and begins a slow, deliberate crawl toward Chet's twisted body. "Ow!"

"What's wrong?" I aim the beam at him again.

He clutches his right ankle, his face twisted with pain. "My ankle. Think it's broken."

"Hang on," I call down. "Getting help now."

As I open the keypad on my phone, the jagged floorboards beneath my knees give way and I start to pitch forward. Hands grab me from behind and yank me back. The phone slips from my grasp and as I tumble backwards into Laura I see my phone drop out of sight into the hole. A moment later there's the sound of shattering glass.

"Crap!" I turn back to her terrified expression. "Thanks for grabbing me." My mind whirls. We need to get help. Now. "Your phone!"

Her eyes light up and she lets me go, rising to her feet. But then she stops, frozen in place like a museum exhibit. I twist around and follow her gaze toward the spot where Cranston had been knocked down. He's gone. And so is Laura's phone.

"Leo, what the hell's going on here?" Laura sounds scared to death.

I know the feeling because I have it, too. I'm trembling and force air into my lungs to calm myself. I stand and stare at the empty space where the semiconscious Cranston had been only minutes before.

"He must've taken off while we were looking down the hole," I say because I want to hear a calm voice at that moment.

"With my phone?"

I look at her in the darkness and I can see both fear and bewilderment on her face.

"We gotta get down to the basement. Let's go."

Laura follows as I sprint out of the living room and across the entry hall. I see no one and hear nothing, which is good, right? We're in the kitchen moments later standing in front of the door leading down to the basement. The very door we'd used to enter the house. Only now it's locked. With a padlock.

"What the hell?" whispers Laura, her fingers reaching out in the gloom to touch the shiny new lock. She and I look at each other and reach the same conclusion at the same time—we're *not* the only ones in this house.

"What do we do?"

I've never seen her so scared and I've never *felt* so scared, not even when I realized Mr. Franklin gave me the power over life and death. "We need to find another way down to the basement." Right now, helping J.C. is my first priority.

"We need to call the cops," she says breathlessly, her gaze flitting about in the darkness.

I know she's right, but I won't leave my friend. Then I think of Chet. He's not my friend, but he's badly hurt. We need help and we need it now.

Thoughts of Chet remind me of that upstairs room. The chair. And the rope! I grab Laura by the shoulders. "There's rope upstairs. You get out of this house and bring help. I'm gonna climb down that hole and help them till the paramedics arrive."

"What about…?" Her gaze flits to the padlock glinting in the moonlight streaming through the kitchen window.

"I can handle whoever it is." I say this, but I'm not convinced. The gun tumbled down into the basement and so did Chet's knife. Grady's gone, so he must've escaped and took his knife with him. "Don't worry about me. Just get help."

She runs toward the back door leading into the yard. I move with her to make sure she gets out, but when she grips the knob to turn, it's locked. Of course, it would be locked, I stupidly tell myself. This house is abandoned and the doors are probably secured from the outside by those real estate padlocks. She looks at me questioningly.

"Find a way out. Break a window if you have to. I'm going for that rope."

She nods and I sprint from the kitchen and back into the entry hall. Then I take the stairs two at a time. Whoever's in the house already knows we're here, so there's no point in being quiet. My eyes are well-adjusted to the dark by now and I keep them roving as I step out onto the second-floor landing and check out the doors. All closed. Everything looks just the way J.C. and me left it. I break into a run down the hall to the third-floor door and fling it open. I look up at pitch blackness. Someone could be there at the top, waiting to ambush me and I won't know till it happens. I see in my mind's eye J.C.'s bloody head and Chet's twisted form and know I that don't have a choice. I begin my ascent.

Creaks and groans accompany my every step, but I go slow just in case a trap has been laid. I won't be any use to J.C. if I get hurt. My heart thumps with anger and frustration. I promised him I'd keep him safe and now everything's gone to crap. He's hurt and trapped and the killer is somewhere in the house.

I reach the top without being attacked and fumble in the dark for the doorknob. Finding it, I grip and turn, half expecting it to be locked. It isn't. I swing the door inward, my body crouched into a fighting stance in case I need to leap at someone who's lurking within. Moonlight filters through those tiny tears in the drapes. The rope and chair are still there, but otherwise the room is empty. Releasing my breath, I dash inside and scoop up the long pieces of rope in my shaking hands. In seconds I'm back down the stairs and running along the second-floor landing.

There's no sign of Laura when I reach the entry hall, so I figure she found a way out and that means help will get here soon. Now I just need to get down into the basement to help J.C. and Chet. Wilson, too. He looked unconscious and that can't be good.

The hole looks even bigger than before as I gingerly cross the weakened floor and crouch low near the jagged lip. I don't have any light source, so gaping darkness is all I see. "J.C., you okay down there?"

"Yeah, Leo, but Hamilton's in bad shape," wafts up from below. "Wilson, too. It's too dark for me to see injuries because my phone got smashed to crap when I fell. But at least they're both breathing."

"I sent Laura for help," I call down. "And I got that rope from upstairs. I'm gonna tie it off and climb down to help you till the paramedics get here." I consider telling him about the locked basement door, but change my mind. With the door locked, I'm in more danger than him. I glance around to make sure no one is sneaking up or creeping out of the two secret passageways. I detect no movement in the darkness and set about tying the two pieces of rope together. I can't tell how long each piece is, but once I have them secured by a tight knot, I'm pretty sure it's long enough to get me down there. Now where to tie it off?

I scan the area. The fireplace is close, so I cautiously make my way around the edge of the hole and search for something that might hold my weight. The screen won't work, but it's held in place by two large, heavy-looking ornamental metal lion sculptures. I grab one to move it aside so I can take out the screen, but it won't budge. It's anchored to the marble hearth. My heart beats with excitement. I grab on with both hands and pull with all my strength. It doesn't move. Perfect!

Wrapping the rope around the lion, I tie it off and yank a few times to make sure it's secure. A sound somewhere in the house prompts me to whirl around, my breath on hold. I have no weapon—only the rope. I search the darkness of the entry hall as best I can from where I'm crouched, but detect no movement. On hands and knees, I scuttle to the edge of the hole.

"Rope coming down," I say, but not so loudly this time. With someone in the house, the safest place to be is the basement until the cops get here.

"I see it," J.C. calls up from below. "Hurry, Leo."

He sounds urgent and desperate and afraid, exactly how I feel right now as I squat down and take the rope in my hands. It's about three-quarters of an inch in diameter and provides a good grip. The edge of the hole groans as I turn toward the fireplace so I can lower my legs down into the darkness. As my knees leave the relative safety of the floor and my legs dangle, a loud crack erupts all around me as more boards give way. The wood pressing into my midsection crumbles and then I'm falling.

The rope yanks taut and my shoulders shriek with pain, like they're being pulled from the sockets.

"Leo!"

I dare not look down and couldn't see J.C. even if I tried. "I'm okay."

My heart threatens to erupt from my chest as I focus on steadying my swinging body so I can continue the descent. I'm only just over the edge, but with the hole now larger and closer to the hearth, I realize I have more rope to aid me. Hand under hand, I lower myself ever so carefully. Despite the ache in my shoulders, I still have enough arm strength to not use my legs and the going is faster without them. I think I'm about halfway down when I hear something.

Footsteps.

Right overhead.

I freeze as the footfalls move closer to the hole. Dust rains down on me from the deteriorating wood with each step on the floorboards above and I blink furiously to clear my vision. The movement ceases and all is silent once again. I look back up and expect to see a face leaning over the hole, but no one appears. I know enough to know it's not a cop or paramedic. They would have announced themselves.

This is the killer.

I resume my descent, hoping against hope that whoever it is isn't athletic enough to climb down a rope. I hear nothing from below, which means J.C. must've heard the footsteps, too, and isn't moving. I'm almost there—I think—when I hear a loud *thunk* hit the floor above, like an ax or machete striking the wood, and then I'm in free fall. Having my legs dangling freely probably prevented a broken leg. I strike the basement floor hard and immediately let go of the rope to dive into a roll. I land painfully on one shoulder.

Sharp stabs of fire shoot from my shoulder straight into my brain as I complete the awkward roll and slam into something soft.

Not something.

Someone.

"Leo!"

J.C.'s arms loop around me as I land on top of him and knock him backwards. We settle into a tangled heap of arms and legs, but he doesn't release me. He hugs me tight like he'll never let go. "Oh, God, Leo, I'm so scared. When you fell…."

"I'm okay," I grunt, the wind knocked out of me as I struggle to sit up. I feel J.C.'s arms leave my torso and almost wish he'd put them back. For a moment, I think this might all be a terrible nightmare and when I wake up J.C. and me will be sitting on the beach gazing out at the ocean like we used to.

But this is no dream.

I turn and reach out with my hands. They wrap around his face and my heart calms a bit. But then I slide them around to the back of his head and feel the blood. "Damn, you're bleeding like crazy."

"I'm okay," he says. "My ankle's worse, I think. The others are in bad shape."

"You first," I whisper as I strip off my tank top and wrap it around his head. He winces. "Sorry, but I have to stop the bleeding." I pull the shirt into a tight knot and he cries out with pain, but the fabric, now soaked with blood, feels tight enough to staunch the bleeding. Basic First Aid was required by my Aikido instructor. I thought it a waste of time then. Now I'm grateful. I feel J.C.'s cold hands on my naked torso and shiver.

"That was your only shirt," he says, stating the obvious. "You'll freeze down here."

It's cold, and that rancid smell permeates the air, but those are the least of our worries. I look up at the gaping hole, expecting to see whoever cut the rope. But there's no one visible and no more footsteps.

"Shssh." I point at the hole and it's like he suddenly remembers.

"Who's up there?"

My eyes are adjusting to the dark and I look directly at him. I don't need to speak because we know each other too well and he can see the answer written all over my face like a mural.

"Oh, no…"

"I *will* protect you," I whisper with a fierceness that surprises even me.

Chet moans in the darkness and I release J.C. to scramble forward over the broken pieces of chair. I squint in the dark and note that Chet is now untied. A few feet from him lies the unmoving form of Wilson.

J.C. drags himself to my side. "I untied him, but I think he's got a broken leg and arm," he whispers into my ear. "I felt around for blood. His leg's soaked in it."

I nod and lean in toward Chet's head. He's moaning louder now as he wakes up. "Quiet, Chet," I whisper. "There's someone up there."

His face feels coated with dirt as I clap a hand to his forehead. He's cold to the touch, but that could be the frigid air of this basement. Or he could be in shock from his injuries.

"Can you breathe all right?" I whisper.

His wide eyes focus on me as he comes around. "Leo?" He must realize that he's no longer tied to the chair because he asks, "Did you untie me?"

"J.C. did."

His eyes bulge as he takes in J.C. beside me. Then he tries to move and shrieks with pain. "I can't move! I think my arm's broke."

"Your leg, too," J.C. adds quietly. "Better stay put till help arrives."

I explain about Laura going for help. "But there's someone in the house."

"Who?" His voice is raspy and I can hear the intense pain he must be feeling.

"The guy who wants us dead," J.C. says softly, like he just realized that he and Chet finally have something in common.

"Can you get out through the crawlspace?" Chet croaks.

J.C. and me look at each other and then over at the wall, now hidden in darkness, where we came in through the grate.

"No way I can get you and Wilson through it," I whisper to Chet.

He gags and coughs. A dribble of blood exits his mouth and trickles down his chin. He must have internal injuries, too.

"Not for us." He flicks his eyes at J.C. "You should get away while you can. Both of you."

I look at J.C. He's staring at Chet, almost dumbfounded. "Even with your ankle, I bet you could crawl out, J.C.," I suggest hopefully. "I can stay until—"

"No!" J.C. barks sharply. "I'm not leaving you."

"But the killer doesn't—"

"No!"

Despite my fear, his words warm my heart.

I'm about to suggest we splint Chet's arm and leg when I hear rattling from above. No, not above. From the stairs, off in the dark on the other side of the basement. From the door that was locked. The rattling continues, like someone is up there fiddling with the padlock. My night vision is better now, but the stairs remain a vague shape.

"What do you think that is?" J.C. stammers.

I glance over and see that he already knows the answer.

It's the killer.

And he's coming down to finish the job.

CHAPTER FIFTEEN

WHY DO YOU WANT TO KILL ME?

T HE RATTLING STOPS AND THEN there's a *crack*, like the padlock was dropped onto the tile floor.

I turn to J.C. "Get behind me."

He shakes his head. "No. We face him together."

I study what I can of his face and in the hard set of his mouth I see something that's never been there before—resolve. I nod as the sound of a door creaking open fills the basement and then light spills down the stairs. The beam is large, too large for a phone light. It looks like a real industrial-size flashlight beam wobbling and jerking its way down the stairs.

"Mr. Hamilton, I can't let you report me for selling them drugs."

I whirl to face J.C.'s wide-eyed expression.

Mendez!

I look down at Chet and he looks stunned. He shakes his head, his meaning clear: don't answer.

It won't matter anyway because as soon as the old man steps onto the basement floor and waves the light around, he's got us.

I hear his measured footfalls on each creaky stair, but the darkness is too thick to make out anything but the light. Then he appears behind a giant glaring beam. From the quick glimpse I catch, it looks like he's carrying Chet's jacket over one arm. Maybe he plans to wear it when he kills us? I don't wait to find out. The beam turns and blinds me with its harsh invasion of white light. I lurch to my feet and barrel forward straight at it.

I hear "Leo!" from behind, but my focus is on that light. Mendez looks startled at seeing my forward momentum and tries to step back, but he's not fast enough. I plow into him like a football player, knocking the flashlight from his hands and shoving him backward. My foot catches on the flashlight and I stumble as Mendez slams hard into the stone wall and collapses to the dirty wooden floor. He moans and shifts slightly, but doesn't get up.

I stoop and snatch up the flashlight, swinging the beam over to illuminate his prone form. His head lolls slightly and then he stops moving, but I see his chest rising and falling, so I know he's not dead. I swing the light around. The snake jacket lies in a heap at the foot of the stairs to my right.

"Leo!" J.C. shouts from behind.

Panting with fear, I shine the beam in his direction, careful not to blind him. "I'm good. I think he's out."

J.C. exhales with relief.

The bright light makes everything so much clearer and I see just how badly hurt Chet really is. His left leg is twisted at an obscenely grotesque angle away from his body. A sharp extrusion of bone pokes through the skin of his thigh, looking red and jagged. Blood oozes out in a steady stream. The pain must be unbearable, especially when I see his left arm is broken at the elbow and twisted under him. He eyes me in the light and I see what could be taken for gratitude, but it's hard to say because he's grimacing so much from the pain.

I move the light toward Wilson and spot my discarded hoodie. It must've fallen through the floor. I see no sign of the gun, however. I hurry to the hoodie and scoop it into my hands, passing the flashlight to J.C. Then I bend down to Chet. "I'm gonna tie off your leg."

He nods weakly.

"It's gonna hurt."

"Like it doesn't already?" Same old Chet.

I press the main part of the hoodie over the wound that's oozing blood and then wrap the sleeves around his thigh. I twist the sleeves into a knot and pull tightly. He grunts and his leg spasms twice.

He offers me a tight smile, but then a voice from the top of the stairs makes me freeze.

"The police are on their way."

J.C. and I lock eyes. The voice sounds muffled, like the person is speaking into a cloth napkin, but it's definitely *not* Laura's voice. Warning bells chime in the back of my mind and I shake my head so J.C. doesn't call out.

He grips the heavy flashlight like a weapon as more footfalls descend the stairs. A large pool of light grows bigger and bigger until it reaches the ground floor. For a split second, J.C.'s flashlight beam does battle with the new light source and there's so much glare I can't see anything. I blink furiously at the sudden invasion until J.C. lowers his light, aiming it at a pair of legs wearing dark pants and dark shoes. My eyes adjust enough to see that the light source isn't a flashlight, but a camping lantern. It looks a lot like the one Grady had, but whoever holds this one remains obscured behind the bright glow.

"Leo?"

I gasp as the man lowers the lantern enough for me to see his face.

"Principal Harris!"

"My God, what happened to you boys?"

He moves the lantern moves around to take in the whole of the basement and I blink repeatedly, my eyes struggling to accept the added brightness. With the sudden illumination, I see Chet's twisted form more clearly and he looks pasty gray in the face. His blue eyes are fixed on Harris, but he says nothing. Wilson lies where he fell, but now I see the blood pooling around his head.

"Behind you," J.C. tells Harris, and the principal spins quickly, the light arcing around the room to settle on the unmoving form of Mr. Mendez. "He tried to kill us."

I watch Harris carefully. He bends to examine Mendez, the lantern light dipping and rising like Tinkerbell swooping around the room. Then Harris and the light rise and swing back around to us. He steps closer. "I followed him here. I've been suspicious of him for months."

"You have?" J.C. asks, his voice filled with shock.

Harris nods, but his gaze is on me. "You look unhurt, Leo."

"I didn't fall as far as them."

Harris eyes Chet and Wilson gravely. "You can help me with these two until the paramedics arrive. I see you know some basic first aid." He points to my shirt tied around J.C.'s head.

"Yes, sir."

Harris spots the rope on the floor near Chet and holds his light over it. "Use that rope to tie up Mendez," he orders in his principal voice that's accustomed to having his commands obeyed.

Something feels wrong, but I'm too frazzled to figure out what, so I grab the rope and hurry across the basement floor to where Mendez lies unconscious. The lantern light follows me and hovers like an umbrella while I truss the janitor's hands and feet with the two sections of rope.

I turn back to Harris and he looks like he's about to pat me on the head.

"Excellent, Leo. Now let's help Mr. Hamilton and Mr. Wilson with their injuries."

He sounds so calm, I'm thinking. That's what's off. *How can he be so calm stumbling onto something like this?* "Uh, how long ago did you call 911, sir?"

"When I found the bodies upstairs," he answers matter-of-factly.

I hear J.C. gasp loudly, but my throat goes so dry I can't speak for a moment. "Who…?"

Harris eyes me through the lantern light and acts like he's reciting a math problem. "Let's see. There was Mr. Cranston and Mr. Grady. Oh, and your friend Laura."

My heart soars into my throat. I slowly rise to my feet, but my legs feel wobbly. Laura? So she never got out? "Are they…?"

"Dead?" Harris says conversationally. "The boys, yes. The girl, no. She's merely unconscious."

I feel my lungs relax slightly, but my heart still races. Something is terribly wrong here. "Maybe I should go up and check on her."

I start to ease around him toward the stairs, but he casually sidesteps and blocks my path. "She's fine. Your friends down here are in much greater need of help." He extends his free hand toward J.C., who's staring at us open-mouthed. It's obvious he knows something's wrong, too. Harris has always been loopy, but this behavior is downright disturbing.

My legs feel like they weigh a hundred pounds each as I slog my way back toward J.C. I seriously consider spinning around and attacking my principal, even though I'd be expelled for sure, especially since he's just acting weird and not threatening us or anything. I decide to wait a bit longer, but my mind whispers troubling thoughts into my consciousness—thoughts like *no help is coming* and *you're on your own*.

I stop beside J.C. and, needing to say something, point to his swollen ankle. "He broke his ankle pretty bad, so he can't help much."

Harris smiles. In the lantern light, it somehow looks hellish and demonic. "No worries. We don't need him. You look more than fit enough to take care of the others, even without my help."

His comment makes me shiver and I feel very exposed in my shirtless state. It's almost as though he knows comments like that unnerve me because of my shyness and that's why he said it.

"You look stronger than I'd have guessed, Leo," Harris says in his smooth voice, that trace of a Midwest accent coming out more than usual.

I glance at J.C. He looks worried now, *very* worried.

"Combined with your Aikido abilities, that could prove problematic," Harris adds cryptically.

My mind is spinning. How does he know about me and Aikido? No one does at Costa High except J.C. and Laura and they wouldn't have told him. He must've checked me out. But why? I notice he keeps his distance, like he's afraid of me. And he should be. If I can get close enough, I might be able to overpower him, even though he's much bigger. But do I need to? He's acting bizarre, sure, but he's my principal and I've seen him almost every day for three years. He's never seemed *dangerous* before.

"It looks like Mr. Wilson might have a head wound," Harris says calmly, pointing at Wilson, but keeping his eyes on me. He shrugs off a plain jacket that looks like something he got from a thrift shop. Underneath it, he wears a black, long-sleeved shirt. "Use this to staunch the bleeding." He tosses the jacket to the floor by my feet and I pick it up.

Harris steps back slightly as I scoot around J.C. and Chet and squat down beside Wilson. His wound isn't bleeding as much as J.C.'s, but when I gently lift his head to wrap the ratty jacket around the back, I feel part of his skull kind of caved-in. I shudder as I tie the jacket off across his forehead with the sleeves.

I'm just starting to turn around when I hear J.C. yell, "Leo, look out!"

It's too late. I feel something press into my upper back accompanied by a jolt of pain and a sharp crackling sound. My back arches involuntarily and fire surges through my skin, torching my insides with burning agony. The crackling continues, like a circuit shorting out, and my nerves sing with pain. I feel the hair on my arms rising and grit my teeth to keep from biting my tongue.

After what feels like an eternity of torture, the object is removed and I collapse to the floor, flopping around like a fish out of water. My arms and legs twitch and vibrate, my vision wafts in and out of focus, and I fight to stay conscious.

"It's highly unlikely you could overpower me with those muscles of yours, Leo," I hear Harris say as though from a great distance. "I do outweigh you by a good fifty pounds, at least. Still, best not to take chances, don't you think? Anticipate the unexpected, like I've always taught you kids."

"Leo!" That's J.C.'s voice, but I can't speak. I roll over onto my back and struggle to focus on the man standing over me. He still holds the lantern in his left hand, but there's something in his right, now. At first, I think it's a gun and maybe he shot me in the back?

"Leo, are you all right?" It's J.C. again, but I still can't respond.

"He's fine," I hear Harris saying with a slight chuckle, like he finds himself very amusing. He holds up the object and I can make out that it's not a gun, but my vision still swims, so I can't discern details except that it's black and seems to fit into the palm of his hand. A phone? His head is angled toward J.C., but I'm still writhing with pain and can't even look in that direction.

"It's a cattle prod," Harris goes on like he's explaining a science lab we're supposed to do. "Souvenir of my days on the farm. Course, this is a smaller, handheld version I bought off the Internet, but it does the trick, wouldn't you say, Leo?" He looks down at me and grins. I can still barely move and my hands feel like they're encased in lead. My feet, too. Vaguely I wonder how many volts of electricity he shot into me. It feels like a million.

He moves out of my line of sight. I hear skittering, scraping movements and then, "I didn't give you permission to move, Mr. Rivera."

"I'm checking on my friend," J.C. shoots back, sounding more fearless than he ever did standing up to Chet. With Chet, he knew he had some level of protection. But not with Harris, and he clearly doesn't care.

I hear Harris chuckle again. "I guess the rumors about you two are true, after all."

J.C.'s face hovers above mine and he ignores the taunt. "Leo, say something. Please be all right!" He cups his hands on either side of my face.

"Hurts," I grunt with major difficulty. It's like my brain has a short circuit in it and nothing works the way it's supposed to.

J.C. scoots around and cradles my head in his lap. I feel his pants against the back of my head, but not fully. I guess nerves take time to come back after being shocked. But the new angle of my head allows me to see what Harris is doing. I want to groan, but I can't. J.C. makes a low rumbling sound of despair that comes from deep within his chest. I feel his erratic breathing and thumping heart.

What we see is Harris bending down and picking up Chet's jacket.

The snake jacket.

He stands and holds it out, admiring the artwork on the back. "Such a gorgeous jacket. I wish I could keep it. Would make a fine souvenir of my sojourn in this city. Alas, it must be left behind as evidence against our old friend, Mr. Mendez." He turns it around in his hand, holding up the lantern to admire it more fully. "Still, it wouldn't hurt for me to put it on while I take care of business. It'll look more realistic with blood on it."

J.C. makes a gagging sound from deep in his throat as Harris sets the lantern on the floor by his feet and in the pool of light we watch him slip on the jacket and turn toward us like he's a runway model. "How do I look?"

I inwardly groan as I replay the vision in my head, the one that started all of this. I focus not on the jacket this time, but on the pants just below it. Black pants. The black pants Mr. Harris is wearing. J.C. pulls me in closer for protection and I realize he'll fight for me no matter what happens to him. I wish I could thank him, but more importantly, I want to help. I feel stupid and useless as I watch Harris step closer to J.C. and me, leaving the lantern on the floor for illumination. His foot strikes something and he stops to look down. I follow his gaze and catch my breath in surprise—it's the gun!

"Now what have we here?" Harris asks in that maddeningly conversational tone as he bends to retrieve the gun. He examines it carefully, shaking his head in consternation, and I finally realize he's wearing gloves. "How many times have I told you kids that firearms are dangerous, especially with the safety off."

Still holding the cattle prod in his right hand, he uses that index finger to press something on the side of the gun near the trigger and then slips the weapon into the left pocket of the jacket. "I better hold on to this," he adds, smirking at J.C. and me. "Can't have it fall into the wrong hands and be used against me, now can I?" Then he snaps his fingers, as though the best idea in the world just came to him, though with the gloves on his fingers don't actually make a *snap* sound. "I know. It'll be the perfect instrument for the conscience-stricken Mr. Mendez to take his own life. I'd planned on him us-ing the knife, but a gun is so much more manly, isn't it boys?" He laughs and fixes that intense gaze on J.C. "Did you like the Facebook messages I sent, Rivera? I thought they were a nice touch. I knew you'd conclude they were from Hamilton. You did, didn't you?"

"Why?" J.C.'s voice quavers, but comes out stronger than I thought it would. "Why do you want to kill me? What have I ever done to you?"

Harris offers a sneering grimace of distaste. "You, Mister Rivera, are a parasite. So is Hamilton and the other parasites upstairs. My original plan had been to just kill you two, but since you offered me the opportunity to rid the world of a few others, I took advantage of it."

"How did you know we were here?"

J.C. is clearly stalling until I can recover and I want to hug him for being so clear-headed.

Harris slips his phone from his pants pocket. "An app, of course. It's designed for jealous people to track the movements of their significant other, but it works well with any phone GPS. You were clever enough to turn yours off, but Hamilton's signal originated from this location, so I tracked him. Finding you here was a pleasant surprise. Two birds with one stone. Mendez will be my cover, the drug-dealer turned murderer. I sent him a message he thought was from Hamilton threatening to turn him over to the police. The old man was stupid enough to believe it and came here to work out a deal. It's all so perfect." He slides the phone back into his pocket.

I'm beginning to recover and I want to defend J.C., but I also don't want Harris to know I'm getting my strength back. If I can catch him off-guard...

"I've made it my life's work to rid the world of selfish, entitled, narcissistic, leeches like you, *Mister* Rivera, and these others," Harris goes on calmly, in full teacher mode as he indicates Chet and Wilson. "Everywhere I've been principal I find trash like you—spoiled, self-absorbed punks who become spoiled, self-absorbed adults and suck resources away from decent people who need them. You don't deserve to exhale, let alone breathe in oxygen that others need for survival. With every one of you I've killed, I've made the world a better place."

J.C. glances at me in wide-eyed horror, but I pretend I can't respond. He looks back at Harris and I feel him shudder. "How many kids have you killed?"

"Sadly, only nineteen before tonight," Harris answers with a heavy sigh. "That number includes the three who went missing from other South Bay schools. They were gifts to my fellow principals and are buried underneath you, by the way. The smell's a bit strong, but no one ever comes to this house, so it was the perfect hiding place."

My mind races as I try to absorb all this information. Harris killed the kids who went missing and they're buried underneath me? The shovel! Now I know what was off about it. The shovel looked brand new while the other tools were old and rusted out. I also understand the smell now and remember where I experienced it before—in the vision of J.C. being killed. I actually *smelled* this place. I curse my stupidity for not putting the pieces together when I first entered the basement.

"As much as I love watching you leeches whimper and plead as I bleed you out," Harris adds in a gleeful tone that reminds me of The Joker in that *Dark Knight* movie, "I do feel a twinge of remorse for having to kill you, Leo."

My eyes bug out in surprise. "Why?" I croak, though my voice is now strong enough to actually talk.

"I love killing, don't get me wrong on that score," Harris goes on, looking positively excited at the prospect, like a teacher with a lesson plan he's gleeful about presenting to the class. "You kids think partying and drugs are the big high. Trust me, they can't hold a candle to murder. The thrill of watching someone's life drain out of them simply can't be equaled."

I stare at him with my mouth open. J.C. groans and trembles beneath me, but I pretend not to notice. The fact that I can feel his every shudder means my nerves are coming back.

"Sorry, I become giddy when a kill is close at hand," Harris says. Shadows distort his face into The Joker's smile and he giggles. No joke. He giggles, and I shiver. "You, Leo, are one of the good kids, the ones I'm trying to help by ridding the world of scum like Rivera and Hamilton. Their kind corrupt the good ones and turn them into self-aggrandizing vermin. You probably would have been a productive adult, Leo, once I severed the unhealthy relationship you have with *him*." He practically spits out the last word right at J.C. and I realize that my principal, the man who's told terrible jokes and talked about peace and brotherhood for the past three years is more insane than The Joker could ever be.

"You're crazy," J.C. says quietly.

Harris smiles. "That's what everyone says when I tell them I enjoy being a high school principal." He laughs with delight, but when we don't react he loses the smug expression. "My humor has always been wasted on you kids."

He pauses and puts his free hand to his mouth, as though deep in thought. I see he still holds the small shock tool he said was a cattle prod. Two metal prongs extend out from the front and I can confirm that they pack a serious punch. I feel a moment's sympathy for cows. Something to my right moves at the very corner of my vision. If I'd been fully recovered, I'd have swung my head over quickly and tipped off Harris. But my neck is so stiff I can barely shift my gaze in that direction. Bare feet are visible on the stairs. The rest of the person is still hidden behind the wall.

Harris studies Chet for a moment. I force myself not to look over, fearing Chet might already be dead. "Hamilton might die before I get to him, which will be a great pity. Wilson, too." He fixes his burning eyes on to J.C. and my heart begins hammering. "Let's start with you, Rivera. I'll finally silence that nasty mouth of yours."

He switches the cattle prod to his left hand. From the corner of my eye, I spot movement as Laura rushes forward swinging the pickaxe like it's a softball bat. The floor beneath her bare feet creaks at just the wrong moment. Harris simultaneously ducks and twists his body around. Laura's forward momentum sends her slamming into him. Flashes of light and a sound like a shorting electrical fuse fill the basement as Harris jams the cattle prod into her neck. Laura screams in pain before Harris kicks her feet out from under her and she goes down hard, the pickaxe spinning away to slam into the far wall, where it drops to the ground with a clatter. I hear Laura's head make a *crack* sound as it strikes the floor and she doesn't move after that.

I'm burning with frustration, but almost recovered enough to make my move. I'll have to be fast and he has to be really close because my muscles and joints are still too stiff for a protracted fight. If he zaps me again, I'm finished.

Panting slightly from his exertion, Harris stands to his full height and nudges Laura with the toe of his black shoe. She doesn't move. "This one is tough," he says, a touch of admiration in his voice. "I thought I'd knocked her out upstairs. I caught her from behind and she never saw me, so I planned on letting her live. Too late for that. I'll slit her throat later." He turns and eyes J.C. like someone staring at his favorite food. "But first, as my biggest thorn in the side, you will bleed out while I cut and slice and dice your pretty face to ribbons. And that's just for starters, boy."

He leans down so fast it stuns me. He grabs J.C. by his shirt collar, shoves me aside and yanks him to his feet. J.C. cries out in agony as his full weight lands on the broken ankle.

"Yes!" taunts Harris, his ecstatic grin making it clear he's savoring the moment. He kicks J.C. viciously, landing the blow right where the swelling in his ankle is the greatest. J.C. shrieks and crumples. Harris lets him drop into a whimpering heap onto the floor.

I'm on my back now and it's clear I can't wait any longer. I have to act or J.C. is dead. Summoning all my strength, I breathe in deeply and let it out as Harris bends down toward my best friend. He seems to have forgotten me in his zealous desire to murder J.C. and I know I won't get another chance.

I push upward, propelling myself right at Harris, reaching out to incapacitate the hand holding the cattle prod. But Harris whirls around and I realize he baited me. He must know how long it takes for the shock to wear off.

But I can't stop my forward momentum now, even if I wanted to. I reach for the prod. Something sharp and gleaming pops out of Harris right sleeve just as I grab his left wrist and start to bend. He grunts, but I gasp as a sharp pain in my stomach sucks the air from my lungs. I hear a ripping sound and feel liquid pouring into my sweatpants. My body goes numb with sudden shock and I release his wrist to stagger back.

"Leo!" J.C. screams in horror.

Harris laughs as he holds up the bloody knife blade that's attached to his wrist. It was obviously hidden beneath the sleeve of his shirt until he needed it. Pain assails my nervous system again, but this pain is sharp and stabbing and I instinctively press both hands against a jagged hole in my midsection. I look down and see blood forcing its way between my fingers and pooling onto the floor at my feet. My mouth hangs open and I feel tears of pain and helpless defeat leak out of my eyes. I look up and see J.C.'s horrified face from where he lies crumpled on the floor.

I failed you, my mind says, but I can't force the words out of my mouth. I can't let them be true. I turn and look at Harris, inching my way to the side so I'm between him and J.C. I'm losing blood fast and already feel light-headed. But my will is stronger than this wound.

"I won't let you kill him," I snarl, sounding to my own ears exactly like a rabid dog.

Harris chuckles. "You're in no position to stop me."

"Knife or no knife," I spit, droplets of blood striking the leather jacket. "I will break your neck if you try to hurt him."

Harris's eyes narrow and his cruel smile falters. I keep my fists clenched tight as I press against the wound in my abdomen, and the fire of rage I feel must show in my eyes because he hesitates.

"This piece of scum means that much to you?"

"He's the best friend I'll ever have."

I hear J.C. groan behind me, but my misty eyes remain fixed on Harris's shadowed face.

"Very well, then, Leo," Harris says with a heavy sigh, like he's about to excuse me from detention. "To spare you the pain of losing your best friend, I'll finish you off first."

Behind me, J.C. screams, "No!"

Harris takes a quick step forward. I reach for him as the knife plunges toward me and grab hold of his hand. My fingers almost slip off from all the blood, but I manage to bend his wrist back enough to cause a grimace of pain on his face. The sudden agony forces him to drop the cattle prod and with that free hand he grips my throat and squeezes. I'm weak and can't hold him off for long.

"J.C.," I croak, struggling to breathe.

I hear J.C. crawling along the floor by my feet and then Harris grunts in pain and releases my throat to kick out at J.C. I glance down and see my friend swinging at Harris's legs with a broken piece of the chair, hammering against the principal's left thigh and calf.

Harris grunts and kicks out again with his right foot, connecting with J.C.'s face and flinging him backwards onto Chet. Chet groans in pain, so I know he's alive, but J.C. looks momentarily stunned. I turn back to face Harris as he uses his free hand to pry my fingers off his wrist. We struggle a moment and I know I'm going to lose. The blood loss is having its way with me. My sweatpants are soaked and I feel weaker than I ever have before.

I lock eyes with Harris, and gasp.

Releasing his wrist, I lurch back.

Surprised, Harris gazes at me warily. "Finally giving up, Leo?"

"I… know…when…you're going… to die… Mr. Harris," I stammer, my voice wheezy.

Harris laughs and raises the knife. "Oh yeah? And when might that be?"

I drop like a sack of potatoes to the floor. I hear J.C. cry out a muffled, "Leo!" as I land in a heap at Harris's feet. He looks down just as a large two-by-four that once supported the ceiling above swings downward in a perfect arc right past where I'd been standing and slams into Harris's forehead with a loud *thunk*.

Still attached to the ceiling above, the board just misses Harris's nose. His eyes bug out with stunned surprise, but he doesn't drop to the floor. The board holds him in place like he's a model posing for a painting. Blood erupts from beneath the wood where it rests against his forehead. The wide, shocked eyes hold on me a moment longer before glazing over. Almost in slow motion, Harris tips backward and falls. A sucking, tearing sound fills the room when his forehead pulls free of the long rusty nail protruding from the two-by-four. As he collapses dead to the floor, I have a split second to notice the blood and brain matter coating the nail that saved J.C.'s life.

"Right now," I wheeze, answering Harris's question as the vision I'd seen in his eyes plays out exactly as I saw it.

I glance over at J.C. I don't have much time left. Like Harris said, I can feel my life force leaving my body with every drop of blood.

"Promised… to save you," I croak, offering the best smile I can muster. Blood dribbles from my mouth and my vision blurs.

"Leo!" J.C.'s scream of anguish pierces my brain and I'm vaguely aware that he's by my side, cradling my head again in his lap. "Hang on, Leo, please! I need you!"

He's crying, blubbering. I see tears rolling down his cheeks and hear the anguish in his voice.

"Best friends… for life," I whisper.

"I won't let you die! I won't!"

"It's… okay," I mutter as my vision blurs. "Kept… my…promise."

I think I feel him moving away from me, but I can't be sure because everything goes dim. My last thought is, *I wonder if Mom will miss me,* and then darkness takes me into its comforting arms.

CHAPTER SIXTEEN

IS HE OKAY?

I'M NOT SURE WHERE I am, but it's quiet and peaceful and there's no pain. I guess I'm dreaming, but I don't know for sure. All I know is that I feel safe. Everything's misty so I can't see clearly, but I think I'm at the beach. Yeah, I am. I hear the water lapping at the sand, and above me a wide sky glows reddish orange from the setting sun. I breathe in deeply. The salty air is clean and intoxicating. I glance to my right and now I see that my best friend in the world sits beside me. We wear board shorts and no shoes and I feel warm sand between my toes. This moment would be perfect except J.C. is crying, his head bent forward onto his knees.

Why are you crying?

That's what I want to ask him, but I can't speak. I can only sit and watch him sob. I want to comfort him, but I'm too lame with words even if I could speak. I want to put an arm around his shoulders, but I can't move my body either. How could such a peaceful moment be sad?

What could have happened?

The image breaks up into tiny droplets of sea spray, wafting away and fading into darkness.

And then there's nothing.

I open my eyes. There's light, but it's dim. I hear strange beeping and whooshing sounds and the muffled conversations of people somewhere not too far away. Where am I? I feel weak and can't even lift my head, but there's a pillow beneath it so I must be in bed. But not my bed. The ceiling above is stark white and unfamiliar.

I hear soft crying from off to my left. Turning my head takes major effort, but there's no pain. I feel sluggish and, well, drunk? At least, what drunk looks like on people I've seen at my mom's parties. I've never tried getting drunk 'cause it looks dumb, but I feel like I am now because I can't quite control my body.

The soft crying continues. It's a woman! Why would a woman be crying? I forcefully turn my head to the left. I feel like I'm a slo-mo special effect in some video game, but I gradually make out a woman seated in a chair. She's definitely crying. Her head is bent and her long auburn hair has spilled about her face, so I can't see it clearly, but I'd know that hair anywhere.

"Mom?" My voice comes out like a frog that's smoked too many cigarettes.

She jerks her head upward in stunned surprise. Then she leaps from the chair. "Leonardo!"

She practically screams my name and the sound pierces my fogged-up eardrums. The door flies open and some lady in white rushes into the room.

"He's awake!" Mom shouts, even though the lady—a nurse, I think—is only a few feet away.

The nurse bends down to me. She's pretty young for a nurse and offers me a very sweet smile. "Can you hear me, Leo?"

"Yes," I croak. "Water." Then I remember to add, "Please."

She lifts a pitcher from the table next to my bed and pours a small amount of water into a cup while Mom hovers anxiously by her side like a lioness guarding her cub. The nurse holds out the cup to me in very delicate-looking hands sporting turquoise nail polish. There's a straw. She bends the straw toward my parched lips and I wrap them around it, sucking greedily at the cool, soothing water. It feels so good going down my throat, but there's barely any there.

"I can't give you much," she says, offering that kind smile again. "Your insides were pretty badly damaged." I wonder if nurses have to go to smile school as part of their training so they learn how to make people feel good without words. She removes the straw.

"Thanks." My voice still sounds like it belongs to someone else.

The nurse sets the cup down onto the table and says to my mom, "I'll let the doctor know he's awake." She turns back to me again. "Are you in a lot of pain?"

My whole stomach area throbs and I nod.

"We'll get more pain meds going into your IV." She points to the tube running out of my right arm into a plastic bag hanging next to the bed. "The doctor needed to make sure you woke up before giving you too much." She flashes the perfect smile again "I'm happy to have you back with us, Leo. We were all pretty worried." She pats my arm and leaves the room.

I look at Mom, but she just stares at me, completely at a loss for words.

"What did she mean?" I say, my voice starting to sound less raspy. "About being worried?"

Mom sniffles and dabs at her eyes with some tissue. She doesn't have any makeup on, which is weird because she always wears makeup, and she's not even swagged out in her clothing, which is beyond weird.

"You were badly hurt, Leonardo. You lost a lot of blood. The doctors didn't think…." She trails off, but I see the rest on her worn features.

"Am I gonna be okay now?"

She nods as more tears force their way out. "They said if you woke up, that meant you were out of the woods."

I absorb this information and pause to reflect on what happened to me. Then it all floods back in—Harris, Mendez, Wilson, Chet, Laura, and—

"J.C.! Is he okay?" My heart pounds as I await her answer. I recall the dream of J.C. crying on the beach.

She nods again. "His ankle is broken and he needed stitches on his head, but he's alive. You saved his life."

"What about the others?"

"The girl, Laura, is okay," Mom says, looking more comfortable talking about something other than her own feelings. "Chet Hamilton was in bad shape, but he's going to make it. Matty Wilson is in a coma. They say he'll probably have permanent brain damage, if he wakes up at all. My God, Leonardo, Principal Harris… it's like a horror movie plot."

I don't say anything for a long moment as I digest this news. "How long have you been here?"

"Since last night when they brought you in," she answers with another swipe at her eyes. "You were in surgery for hours. I was so afraid…."

She stops again, once more unable to say what she really feels. No wonder I'm such an emotional vacuum with her as my role model. "It's okay, Mom. I'll be fine now. You can go back to work."

Her expression shifts to one of momentary shock, maybe even hurt. "I belong here with you."

I stare up at her, this woman I barely know, who I've tried to please my entire life. "But you don't even like me." I say it without thinking, but not in anger, just as a simple fact.

Her face crumples like a Halloween mask caving in on itself and more tears erupt from her eyes. "That's not true." She pauses, and I wait. This could be the longest conversation we've ever had and I almost had to die to earn it. She wrings her hands, crushing the tissue into a tiny ball as she struggles to think of what to say.

She clears her throat and when she speaks her voice comes out like it's being filtered through a voice changing machine. "You're almost a young man, Leonardo, and you need to understand something. Just like many men should never be fathers, some women aren't cut out to be mothers." She pauses and I wait to hear more. So far she hasn't told me anything I don't know. "I'm one of those women. It was a mistake to have you."

I feel like sinking through the bed and disappearing from the earth. "Thanks," I mutter, unable to disguise the sarcasm. So now I'm a mistake on top of everything else.

Her face shifts again into a look of embarrassment. "No, that's not what I meant. *I'm* the mistake in *your* life. You're everything a mother could want in a son, but I'm not a mother. I do love you, Leonardo, in my own way, and I think when you're grown up we might even be friends, sort of. But I don't know how to be a mother. I'm sorry."

I lie there stunned. This is the most she's ever said to me in my sixteen years.

"So you don't hate me?" It's stupid, sure, but it's all I can think of to say.

"Of course not," she insists and I hear the truth in her voice. Then she bows her head. "I don't even know you."

I feel choked up with so many emotions that I can't separate them out into the one I think I should be feeling. But I see an opening to establish some kind of relationship with her, so I say, "What would you like to know?"

She looks confused by the question. "I don't know… are you and J.C. …." She trails off, but I know the rest.

Just hearing his name brings a smile to my face. "He's my best friend, mom. My only friend. Don't you have someone like that? Someone you can tell anything to and know they won't ditch you?"

She gives me a blank look, like no one ever asked her this question. "No, I don't."

Hearing those three words, I understand my mother better than I ever have, and instead of resenting her standoffishness as a mom, I think I feel sorry for her more than anything else. Her work is her life, as superficial as the movie business is to the rest of us. To her, it's how she keeps herself at a distance and prevents closeness to anyone else.

"It's okay, Mom," I say, my voice soft and gentle. "You don't have to stay. I'll be all right. I'm sure you're needed at the studio."

She brightens and wipes away the last of her tears. "As a matter of fact, the studio is hoping I'll develop a project based on what happened to you and the others. They want to fast track it and have me produce it. I know you hate being in front of a camera, Leonardo, but they'd love it if you could play yourself. We could cast J.C. and Chet, too, and Laura and, well, it would be a great opportunity for you and me to spend some quality time together."

I want to laugh, but I don't have the energy. Mom is still Mom and I guess that won't ever change. "Sure, Mom, that sounds like a plan."

Her face explodes with delight. "Really?"

"Really."

"Oh, this will be so exciting, Leonardo," she gushes as she hurries to snatch her purse off the floor by the chair. "This has been a terrible tragedy for the town, but in the long run maybe this film can help with the healing process."

"Maybe," I mutter, already bored with this topic. "Where's J.C.?"

Her face freezes a moment at the change in topic. "Oh, he's been here all day, so I sent him to the cafeteria for food. He told his mother he wouldn't leave the hospital until he knew you were all right." She pauses a moment and eyes me with what I swear is envy. "I'm happy he's your friend." She waits by the door, as though debating whether or not to leave.

"It's okay, Mom. You can go. I'm tired, anyway."

And I hurt. Hope the nurse gets back with the pain meds soon.

She nods, looking more relieved than worried. "The nurses have my number if you need anything."

"Okay."

She grabs the large handle and pulls open the door.

"Mom?"

She turns back. "Yes, Leonardo?"

I choke up a moment. "I love you." I watch her face for any reaction.

She smiles. "I know you do." Then she's through the door and gone.

Inwardly, I sigh. That's probably the most real talk I'll ever have with her and I need to savor it. I lie in bed a few more minutes listening to the heart monitor go *beep, beep, beep,* and the other machines chirp out my vital signs. The door opens and a man wearing a white coat steps into the room, followed by the pretty young nurse.

"Hello, Leo, I'm Doctor Cavendish. I operated on you." He has short black hair with graying temples.

I offer the best smile I can muster. "Thanks for saving my life."

He chuckles. "A life worth saving," he says as he examines the machines and then hooks his stethoscope into his ears to listen to my heart. The metal feels cold against my skin. Draping the stethoscope around his neck again, he pulls down the covers and slides up the gown I'm wearing to examine my abdomen. I angle my eyes downward and see a large, blood-soaked bandage covering my stomach area.

Cavendish peeks underneath the bandage, easing it up carefully, and then turns to the nurse. "When he's more awake and has had some food, I'll need you to clean the wound and replace the bandage."

"Yes, doctor." She flashes the smile that makes me feel good.

He lowers the gown back over my stomach and then takes a syringe from the nurse. Pulling off the cap, he injects something into the IV tube attached to my arm. "Pain medication, to help you sleep."

I smile and already feel less throbbing in my abdominal area. Must be strong stuff.

Cavendish caps the empty syringe and hands it to the nurse, gazing down at me with admiration. "You're the local hero, Leo."

That shocks me. "I am? Why?"

"Your friends told everyone how you saved them and stopped Principal Harris from killing more kids. That makes you a big-time hero in my book. The media is outside and the police want to talk to you, but you need rest first. Other than family, no one else is allowed in until I say so."

"What about J.C.?"

The doctor eyes me a moment. "Oh, yes, the mayor's son. I couldn't keep him out if I tried." He grins. "I'll send him in."

He and the nurse leave the room and I'm alone for a few moments. Then the door opens again and J.C. hobbles in. He's on crutches and sports a boot the size of a small waste basket around his right foot. He's also got a thick white bandage wrapped around his head and a big bruise on his cheek, but my heart soars at the sight of his grinning face as he struggles into the room, bumping the door with his crutch when it swings shut.

"You scared the crap out of me, Leo," he announces in that *how dare you do that to me* tone he excels at.

I just grin and let him go on.

"I thought you were dead for sure, but there was no way I was gonna let you go without a fight, so I crawled over to Harris—he looked really nasty with that hole in his head and his brains leaking out, by the way—and got the phone from his pocket to call 911. Then I copied what you did with me and used my shirt to tie around you to stop the bleeding and—what?" He stares at my grinning face like I'm insulting him or something.

"I'm just happy to see you."

He pauses and catches his breath. Then he smiles. "I'm happy to see you, too."

"Pull up a chair and tell me what happened after I passed out." I'm starting to feel sleepy already and hope I can stay awake long enough to hear his story.

With great awkwardness, he slides the chair over, having to hold both crutches under one arm so he has a free hand. After a few difficult moments, he has the chair up near my head and plops into it like an old man.

"These things are a pain, let me tell you," he says as he rests the crutches up against the bedside table. And then he recounts his story.

"The paramedics got to the house pretty fast and stabilized you. I told 911 there were a few people injured so there was more than one ambulance. I made them wait to treat me until you were in one of them and on your way here."

My heart soars with gratitude and I try to thank him, but he just prattles on and I close my mouth.

"I made them take the others, too, since I just had the broken ankle and all. Well, the head wound, too, but whatever. Anyway, the cops swarmed all over the house, but I only told them a little before the paramedics said I had to get to the emergency room. Harris told the truth about Grady and Cranston. They were dead upstairs." He looks at me gravely. "He cut their throats, Leo."

I shiver. Our principal, a serial killer. I still can't believe it.

"Anyway," J.C. prattles on, "Laura needed stiches and has a concussion, but they released her already and she went home. Chet's in the next room over. He's in bad shape, but he'll pull through. Probably never surf again because of his leg, but at least he'll be alive."

I nod, noting in my mind that J.C. called him "Chet," rather than "Hamilton." I guess almost getting killed together has the effect of making even our worst enemies seem human after all.

"Did the police tell you anything?" I ask, stifling a yawn. I almost feel like I'm floating.

He shakes his head. "No, but my mom did after talking with them. They've been searching Harris's apartment all day. They found a key to the haunted house, but don't know where he got it. And they found some kind of journal. He wasn't joking when he said he's been killing kids all over the country. Mom said that he was a narcissist—isn't that what he called me?"

I nod.

"I didn't know what it meant, but Mom said it's someone who's totally in love with himself and everything he does. Anyway, he kept a record of the kids he killed and even where he buried them."

I shiver again. "Damn." I picture the families of those kids and wonder how they'll react when they hear the news. At least with their kids missing there was still hope they might be alive. Then something else occurs to me. "What about Mr. Mendez?"

"He was selling Chet the roids 'cause he needed the money, but Harris knew what he was doing and decided to frame him for the murders, like he told us. He planted stuff he'd taken from the murdered kids down in that boiler room for the cops to find."

"Damn," I mutter again. Harris really *was* crazier than The Joker. "Uh, what about the gun?"

He knows what I mean without my having to explain. "I guess Harris holding the gun with those gloves wiped off the other fingerprints 'cause the cops figure he brought it with him."

I nod, eyeing him, waiting for the rest.

"Never again will I touch one," he says quietly. "I've learned my lesson. And the guy who got it for me won't say anything." He pauses and considers a long moment. "I almost murdered someone, Leo." His voice is barely a whisper now.

I nod again, but my head feels like it's filled with cotton.

He lets out a big breath and stares at me with more gravity than ever before. "I can't ever get that mad again or I could turn into Harris. Do you think that's possible?"

"Never. But yeah, you can't lose control like that anymore."

He nods now, looking thoughtful and afraid.

Wanting to change the subject because that episode revealed a side of my friend I wish I'd never seen, I ask, "Is Mendez okay?"

Clearly relieved to move on to another subject, J.C. replies, "Yeah, he's gonna make it, but he's in big trouble for selling the roids." He pauses and scrunches up his face as though a revelation just hit him. "You know something?"

"What?"

"Today was the longest talk I ever had with my mom."

I smile. I know the feeling.

"I don't think she hates me after all, Leo," he adds, his voice going all soft and introspective. "She even said she was proud of me for keeping you alive."

A smile fills up my face. "So am I. Thanks."

He gives me that look he's perfected that says, *are you an idiot, or what?*

"Leo, you're the big hero. Without you I'd be dead and so would the others. That's what I told the news people, too."

"The news?"

"This is a huge story, man, national media stuff. They can't wait to interview you."

My throat feels very dry again. "Great. Me in front of a camera. My favorite."

He reaches out and takes my hand in his and clasps it like we've always done since we were little. "I'll be there with you. Best friends for life, right?"

I feel a lump in my throat. I might not have a real mom, but as long as I have a best friend, life is good. "You know it." Then I yawn. I almost feel euphoric and all the pain has vanished.

"You sleep," he says, letting go of my hand and leaning back in the chair. "I'll stand guard in case any of those doctors try anything."

He grins and I return it. My eyelids feel so heavy that I can't even keep them open. The last thing I see is J.C.'s grinning face and then I'm gone.

I spend ten days in the hospital and more people talk to me than ever in my life. Besides the police, I get a visit from two guys in gray suits. I know they're FBI before they even flip their badges open because they look just like the Feds in the movies. They're part of the investigation because Harris killed kids in other states. When I ask the agents about the families of those kids, they say the parents are grateful to me for stopping the man who murdered their children. That surprises me, but I don't say anything. I can't offer much, but I answer their questions as best I can.

The police investigation recovered Wilson's phone with all the stuff about Chet, but Chet's mom deemed the footage irrelevant to what Harris did and so the media doesn't know. She comes to see me the day after I woke up and says she's already talked with Laura and J.C. about what happened and now it's my turn.

She's always been mean and scary-looking, in my opinion, with her short hair and pinched face that looks like it doesn't remember how to smile anymore. The official uniform—with its dark blue pleats and angles and the badge gleaming beneath the fluorescent lights—makes her look especially intimidating. She pulls the chair over and sits, shifting her holster to one side, and stares at me with squinting, suspicious eyes. I note the gun and my mind flashes back to J.C. pointing his weapon at me. I shudder.

"I know he doesn't think so, but I love Chet and almost losing him reminded me of that fact," she says in a confessional tone, which surprises me.

"I allowed Bob to toughen him up because Chet was a weak little boy and I didn't want him to be stepped on his whole life. Thanks to us, Chet became a bold and confident child, even in grade school, and I thought he admired us for helping him become that way. Now I know it's all been a sham. If anything, Chet is more fragile than ever because I wanted him to be someone he isn't. And because I didn't see how deeply disturbed his brother really was. Not much of a cop, am I, missing the evidence right before my eyes?"

I lie there and listen because I sense that's all she wants. It's what I'm best at, anyway.

"He's going to stop the drinking asap. I'll see to that."

I suspect it will be a lot harder for Chet to stop than his mother thinks, but I don't say that.

She sighs and looks at me, but I sense she's not really seeing me, like most people don't see me. She's mostly talking to herself and just needs someone to be there. "I knew Chet stole alcohol from me, but I don't believe he's an alcoholic and I definitely didn't know about that club or, well, him and other boys."

She says this last part with a sharp note of distaste in her voice, as though it makes Chet worse than a serial killer. "Having everyone in La Costa find out about Chet's, how shall I put this, *activities*, will humiliate him. And me. I can't force you, Leo, but I'm asking you not to tell the media what was on Matty's phone."

It's funny that grownups still call us by our little kid names even when we're old enough to drive. "I won't."

She gives me a long, appraising look, like she's waiting for the "catch" in the deal. When I add nothing more, she says, "Thank you."

Another pause, another thoughtful look. I sense she's done more soul-searching today than maybe ever before. "I heard rumors over the years, but no one officially charged Chet with bullying, and he was such a great athlete I ignored those rumors. And I failed to notice the rapid changes in his physique. Even cops don't see what we choose not to see." She pauses a moment and then adds, "He's learned his lesson."

But have you learned yours, I wonder, as she goes silent again, apparently unsure how to continue. I wait.

"I never knew Chet until today when we really talked for the first time," she finally says, her eyes looking kind of distant and far away. "I should say I *listened* for the first time. Him helping that poor family shocked me, I confess. He said he got the idea from someone he really *does* admire." She looks embarrassed. "Unfortunately, that someone isn't me." Then she stands and leaves the room without another word.

I'm left in a state of confusion because she didn't ask me a single question, but I'm too tired and drugged up to think much about it. I drift off to sleep a few minutes later.

On the fourth day, when I can sit up in a wheelchair, Dr. Cavendish allows the media people with their cameras to interview me and J.C. in a kind of open-air atrium on the roof of the hospital. I let J.C. do most of the talking because I can barely look directly at the cameras and I'm embarrassed by all the hero talk they keep laying on me. I'm just a guy who stood up for his best friend. That's what I tell them. Needless to say, I don't tell them how I knew J.C. was in danger in the first place. So far, only J.C., Laura, Chet, and Mrs. Santini, the school librarian, know about my "power." I don't dare tell my mom or she'll want to work it into the movie script.

We stick to the version of the story as laid out by Chet's mother in her official capacity as police chief. It goes like this: Because of those Facebook messages to J.C., he and I and Laura decided to hide out in the haunted house because we thought the threats were from Chet and we'd spotted him loitering by J.C.'s house. We didn't know that Chet spotted us, too, and followed us, bringing Wilson and the others like he always did. The steroids aspect couldn't be hidden because of Mendez, so Chet's truthful explanation that he wanted to convince us not to say anything about them explained why he followed us to the haunted house. Harris tracked Chet's phone and that's how everything went down. It's kind of a lame story, but it fits the evidence and worked for the FBI, whose main focus is locating Harris's victims in other states.

I allow the media folks to snap what seems like a gazillion pictures of me and J.C. and then Dr. Cavendish finally tells them I need to rest. I seriously want to hug him for that.

Wilson is awake now, but the extent of his brain damage hasn't been fully assessed. He'll have a long road back, if he ever does get back to where he was. Oh, and the net Laura set up in the Moreton Bay Fig tree was discovered yesterday by an old couple sitting on one of the benches, but the police can't determine who put it there and we don't volunteer to tell them.

Mom drops by once in a while to bring me lunch and chatter on about all the big TV talk shows wanting to interview me and how the script for the movie is shaping up, but never about how I feel or what I think. Some people can't or won't change and I guess that's how it will always be.

I'm really happy when Mrs. Santini comes to visit. Her dress is all bright colors, and her reading glasses hanging on a beaded chain around her neck make her seem so casual. She brings bright flowers in a Superman vase and when she sees me sitting up, she stands at the end of my bed, grinning happily. Setting the vase onto my little table, she looks me up and down.

"You don't need to tell me, Leonardo, but I strongly suspect all of this has to do with the *gift* that old man gave you."

My eyebrows shoot up in surprise.

Her smile is warm and she chuckles. "Now do you understand my words to you that day in the library?"

I grin and nod, feeling too choked up to answer.

She pats me lightly on one arm and then slips a large purse off her shoulder and fishes around inside. In a moment, she pulls out a book and hands it to me.

I clutch it in both hands and read the title: *Young Heroes in World History,* by Robin K. Berson. I look at her quizzically.

"These are all courageous young people who made wise choices," she answers in that calm, quiet library voice. "Like you."

Embarrassed, I look down. I need to avoid her eyes, anyway, and she knows that, but the deep admiration I spotted on her smiling face fills me with warmth. "Thanks, Mrs. Santini. You're the best."

"No," she says, smiling over her shoulder before she heads out my door. "You are."

Her words make me feel special.

On the morning of the day before I'm supposed to go home, there's a knock at my door.

"Come in."

I'm in a regular room now with no monitoring machines, so the only sounds are people talking and moving around out in the corridor. The door opens and a middle-aged nurse pushes a wheelchair into my room. It's Chet. His head is so bandaged he looks like he's wearing a white beanie, while both his left arm and left leg sport massively thick casts of white plaster.

Chet turns to the nurse. "Can I call you when I need to go back to my room?"

"Of course. Have a nice visit." She offers her version of the smile-school look and leaves the room.

"How are you?" Chet asks, looking even more unsure of himself than he did back in the haunted house.

"They had to sew me up inside and I'll have a nasty scar across my abs, but I'll live. You?"

"No more sports for me, they say, but I'll live too. Thanks to you."

I look down at the white sheet pulled up to my waist. I'm sitting up in bed—I was reading the book Mrs. Santini brought me. I fiddle with the book, at a loss for words, like always.

"I'm glad you're alive," I say, because I mean it. Chet has spent his whole life trying to be someone his brother and mother invented. I hope now he'll have the courage to be himself, whoever that turns out to be.

There's an awkward moment of heavy silence. Then he says in a quiet voice, "I don't deserve what you did for me."

That catches me off guard. "Sure you do," I say, and I believe it. "Everybody can change and be better." Except my mom, but I don't say that. Recalling what Chet's mother said, I offer, "I think it's cool, you helping Pedro's family."

He looks surprised, but I detect the tiniest trace of a smile, like hearing that from me was something he really needed. There's a quiet moment between us and I wait to see if there's more.

"Nobody from school's come to see me," he finally says, his voice soft and full of resignation. "But some kids from the club came by to check on me, which is kind of cool, I guess." His face clouds over and he looks down at his cast. "They uploaded pix of me from the club, not to be mean or anything, but 'cause they were worried and wanted people to pray for me." He laughs, but it's hollow. "I'm sure everyone in town knows about me by now. Maybe it's better that way."

I don't know what to say to that, so I don't say anything.

"Anyway, I just wanted to say thanks."

I nod.

He looks at me with those helpless, lost blue eyes and says, "Uh, could you call the nurse? I can't wheel myself with only one arm."

I shove aside my book and the covers and slip my feet out from under and onto the floor. "I can walk now. I'll take you."

He gazes wide-eyed as I alight to the floor and stand without support. I could only do this as of yesterday and feel proud to succeed on my own without help.

Chet looks impressed. "You're a tough kid, Leo. Much stronger than me."

I know what he means and it's not physical strength he's talking about. "I guess being the town loser can make a guy tough like that. Plus, I really don't care what people think of me."

"Wish I could be like that."

My eyes go wide, but I don't respond.

"Can I see your scar?" He looks curious, like a real kid instead of someone trying to be all things to all people.

I grin and pull up the billowy gown. There's a bandage covering my stomach and lower abs, but there's no blood soaking through anymore.

"Damn." He cracks a shy smile. "Another cut for your six-pack."

I laugh as I drop the gown. Then I turn and rifle through the stuff on the table that Mom brought me, and snatch up a pen. Turning back to Chet, I hold it up. "Can I sign your cast?"

This time he laughs. "Sure."

I hobble over and scrawl my name on both casts and then, without another word, I wheel him outside and down the hall to his room. The middle-aged nurse spots us and runs over in a dither telling me I shouldn't be doing that, but she lets me finish the job of getting Chet back to his room before escorting me back to mine. As I leave, Chet gives me a hesitant smile and I see gratitude in his eyes, but I think it's about more than just saving his life. I think it's because he knows I understand him.

After lunch, J.C. sits by my bed and we play Uno on my tray table. That's when something hits me like a lightning bolt. "J.C., look at me."

He looks up from the cards spread out in his right hand, a questioning expression on his face. "What?"

I lean in close and stare into his eyes, deeply and with purpose. Then I grin.

"What?" he says again, and then realizes what I'm doing. "Oh, no. What did you see?"

My grin spreads across my face. "Nothing."

"Huh?"

"There's nothing, just like I hoped," I say, wanting to grab him and pull him into a hug, but my abs are too tender to make sudden moves.

"I don't get it."

I formulate my thoughts and try to explain the best way I can. "I've been thinking about this all week, this *power* I have inside me." I pause to think of the best way to express this.

"Yeah, so why didn't you see anything in my eyes?"

"Because we stopped what was supposed to happen."

He looks confused. "I still don't get it."

"I'm not sure I do either, but we stopped you from dying when you were supposed to and now I see nothing in your eyes at all. I guess that's how this power works. Maybe I can only see the original way someone's going to die, but nothing if I'm able to change it."

He looks more confused. "So I'm never gonna die? That's crazy."

"No, you'll die," I say quietly. "Everybody dies. But you won't know when or how and I can't help you find out."

He frowns. "That means it could be any time."

"It's better not to know, don't you see? You live your life like you'll hit a hundred and whatever happens, happens. As long as you don't do stupid stuff to put your life in danger, of course. I'll kick your butt if you do that."

He cracks a smile. "Don't worry. The past few weeks are enough excitement to last my whole life."

I chuckle and we fall silent a moment, the game forgotten. I hear cart wheels roll by my door as I formulate how to express this next part. "I also think I know why that man gave me this power."

J.C.'s eyes go wide and his eyebrows shoot up, but he waits for me to finish.

"Like Mrs. Santini says, he knew I'd only use it to help people, like I helped you. Looking into your eyes, well, it set everything in motion that brought down Harris. Chet would never even have had that jacket if I hadn't seen it and Laura hadn't drawn it. Don't you see, it's like some crazy loop that came full circle."

"So now you're gonna go around and look in everyone's eyes so you can stop serial killers?"

"Yeah, right. Shy Boy here." I laugh, but it's kind of a sad laugh because I do wish I wasn't Shy Boy. But I am who I am, just like my mom is who she is and Chet is who he is and so is J.C. "But in cases where I do happen to see, and there's something that can be done, I'll try to fix it, like I did for you."

He grins. "It really is kind of like a super power, you know, and your best friend will be at your side the whole time. Batman and Robin."

I laugh, for real this time. "You're crazy."

He laughs, too, and we return to our game, just two friends happy to be alive and in each other's company. And the best part? I can look into my best friend's eyes again, for as long as we both live. That makes me giddy with joy. Then I suddenly realize I can also look into Chet's and I shake my head at the ironic way everything turned out.

Laura drops by and joins in the game. She has a small bandage on the back of her head that she covers with a beanie. We three really haven't been together without other people present since everything went down, so we savor this time alone. Laura might not be girlfriend material, but she's awesome second-best friend material and, like with J.C., I believe she'll be my friend forever. We laugh and yuck it up as we play the game and just relish being together. I think the greatest gift life can give us is each other in the bonds of friendship, which makes me the luckiest kid on earth.

It's two more weeks before I'm allowed to return to school. J.C. and Laura have already been back and they've been bringing my assignments every day and filling me in on all the gossip. There's been a ton of nasty stuff about Chet all over the Internet, but I haven't paid attention. J.C. says the kids at school are happy Chet has been "brought down," and some even said he should have been killed instead of Cranston and Grady. I don't think any of them deserved to die.

Laura turns a friendly smirk on me and says, "All the girls suddenly think you're the hottest guy on campus."

I blush furiously at that. "You're joking, right?"

She shakes her head and the smirk turns to a smile.

J.C.'s grinning like he's in on the best joke ever. "She's telling it straight up, Leo The girls even talk to me. We're like, superstars or something." He chuckles. "Enjoy it while it lasts. You know those kids. Somebody else will be the big man on campus pretty soon."

I nod, because I know he's right. "Let's see how many of those chicks'll go to the homeless shelters with me."

J.C. laughs and we high five.

Sure enough, I'm swamped with attention the moment I set foot on campus. At first, everyone stops and stares at me, J.C.—using his crutches with ease now—and Laura as we enter the grounds from the student parking lot my first day back. My stitches are gone now and there's no more bandage. The scar is long and jagged since Harris twisted the knife inside of me, but who cares? I'm alive and have no intention of taking shirtless selfies, so it's all good. The other kids clamor to see my scar, but I refuse to pull up my shirt.

Girls and guys surround us and pepper me with questions from all directions as I try to enter the cafeteria for breakfast. They already got the eyewitness account from J.C. and Laura, but I'm the "hero boy," according to the media, so they're excited to hear my side.

Mandy Michelson, the girl who lives on Chet's street, gushes and preens. "You're awesome, Leo. You saved us from another year of Harris's bad jokes."

She laughs and some of her friends join in, but J.C. gasps beside me and my mouth drops open in shock. How could she be so heartless? Fortunately, I'm not the only one who thinks that. Her cheerleader friend, Debbie, looks angry.

"I can't believe you said that, Mandy! Harris killed real people. Kids like us. You could've been one of them."

Mandy looks more offended than remorseful. "I was just joking, girl. Chill."

I look around at the young faces of my peers and wonder how many of them will end up making the world worse, like Harris said. I guess, in his own warped way, like Thanos halving the population of the universe with a snap of his fingers in *Infinity War,* Mr. Harris believed he was doing something good. The thought makes me shiver.

"I'm no hero," I finally say when the chattering over Mandy's comment dies down. "I'm just a guy who stood up for his best friend. I guess I hope everyone would do that." I stop, because there's nothing else I want to say.

But it's enough, I guess, because they burst into applause before filing into the cafeteria for breakfast. I notice many give Mandy the evil eye as they pass and I feel optimistic that most of them will defy Harris's expectations and end up making the world better. We all have a lot of growing up to do, especially me. I think this whole experience has taught me something I already knew, but sometimes forget—being judgmental about people whose shoes I haven't walked in is a wall, not a bridge, and I want to be about building bridges.

Once J.C., Laura, and me collect our food and turn to find a table, kids everywhere are waving at us to sit with them. Out of habit, I glance over at the far corner, to the table where the three of us used to sit before Harris made us eat outside. I suck in a breath of surprise. Chet sits alone, left-arm-cast resting on the shiny metallic surface while he eats his breakfast burrito with his right hand. A single crutch leans up against the wall beside him and he's dressed in a plain shirt with long sweatpants, the left leg sliced open to accommodate his cast.

I glance at J.C. and Laura. "When did he come back?"

"Today, I guess," J.C. replies. "I haven't seen him before."

I glance around at all the kids who disdained me my entire life and notice how they now disdain Chet. No one so much as gives him a look. It's like he's the new invisible kid.

"Come on." I weave my way through the tables past all the gesticulating arms and calls of, "Leo, sit with us," and stop in front of the table where Chet sits. "Can we join you?"

He looks up, his blue eyes wide with surprise. "This is the queer table, remember?"

I smile. "Good, 'cause I'm the queerest kid here."

I sit across from him, while Laura and a scowling J.C. plant themselves at opposite corners, J.C. leaning his crutches up against the wall beside Chet's.

Chet casts guilty looks at J.C. and Laura. "Um, I'm sorry for, you know, everything. I can't take it back, but I would if I could."

Laura and J.C. exchange a look while I watch in silence.

Laura shrugs. "It's all good."

J.C. glances at me, but this has to be his decision. He pauses before giving Chet the chin raise, which is as good as it's going to get for now.

We eat in silence for a few minutes.

Then Chet eyes me, indicating the other kids with a nod of his head. "You have a chance to be popular, Leo. You should take it."

I look at J.C. and then at Laura. I know that, on some level, J.C. loves all the attention he's been getting since coming back to school. But deep down, he knows it's artificial and he'll follow my lead, even though I'd never ask him to. And Laura, she doesn't give a rip what people think of her.

I return my gaze to Chet. "Popularity is overrated. Friends aren't."

His eyes bulge with shock and I swear I see the beginnings of tears forming before he nods and looks back down at his food.

Chet has a long way to go to atone for everything he's done, and I don't expect he'll ever feel like a true friend like J.C. or Laura, but time will tell. For now, the four of us'll stick together and take it one day at a time. In the end, that's what life is all about.

***

ABOUT THE AUTHOR

Michael J. Bowler is an award-winning author of nine novels—*A Boy and His Dragon, A Matter of Time, Children of the Knight, Running Through A Dark Place, There Is No Fear, And The Children Shall Lead, Once Upon A Time In America, Spinner*, and *Warrior Kids*.

His screenplay, "THE GOD MACHINE," won First Place in the 2017 Scriptapalooza competition.

He grew up in San Rafael, California, and majored in English and Theatre at Santa Clara University. He went on to earn a master's in film production from Loyola Marymount University, a teaching credential in English from LMU, and another master's in Special Education from Cal State University Dominguez Hills.

He worked producer, writer, and/or director on several ultra-low-budget horror films, including "Hell Spa," "Fatal Images," "Club Dead," and "Things II."

He taught high school in Hawthorne, California—both in general education and to students with learning disabilities—in subjects ranging from English and Strength Training to Algebra, Biology, and Yearbook.

He has been a volunteer Big Brother to eight different boys with the Catholic Big Brothers Big Sisters program, and a decades-long volunteer within the juvenile justice system in Los Angeles.

He has been honored as Probation Volunteer of the Year, YMCA Volunteer of the Year, California Big Brother of the Year, and 2000 National Big Brother of the Year. The "National" honor allowed him and three of his

Little Brothers to visit the White House and meet the president in the Oval Office.

He has completed three new novels aimed at the teen market, two for middle grade, and is currently writing a new screenplay.

His goal as an author is for teens and middle schoolers to experience empowerment and hope; to see themselves in his diverse characters; to read about kids who face real-life challenges; and to see how kids like them can remain decent people in an indecent world. The most prevalent theme in his writing is this: as a society, and as individuals, we're better off when we do what's right, not what's easy.

***

Website: www.michaeljbowler.com

FB: michaeljbowlerauthor

Twitter: https://twitter.com/MichaelJBowler

tumblr: http://michaeljbowler.tumblr.com/

Pinterest: http://www.pinterest.com/michaelbowler/pins/

YouTube: https://www.youtube.com/channel/
UC2NXCPry4DDgJZOVDUxVtMw

Instagram: michaeljbowler

If you enjoyed *I Know When You're Going To Die*, here's Chapter One in the second book of the Film Milieu Thriller series, *The Horror Film Killer*, releasing October 2021.

CHAPTER ONE

THE FIRST MURDER

Tony staggers and nearly topples before reaching the park bench and collapsing into a seated position. His backpack leaks random food wrappers from a ragged gash up the side and his shoulders slump so sharply he nearly tumbles to the grass at his feet. Exhausted and barely able to stay upright, he lies back the bench and within moments falls into a deep sleep.

Wind kicks up leaves around the bench, and thick shade trees obscure most of the illumination cast by the nearest streetlight. The park is empty, the adjacent street devoid of movement, and no city sounds penetrate this deep in the suburbs.

Tony slumbers on, arms draped across his chest as though he's posing for the part of a corpse in some murder mystery. Shadows surround him, shifting in the meager light, trembling in the wind.

Tony's face is twisted with pain, yet serene, as though this minor respite is the best thing that's happened to him all day. He doesn't look more than twenty-three or four, but the ravages of street life have taken their toll, and he could easily pass for thirty-four if given a cursory inspection.

So sudden it's almost too fast to follow, a gloved hand shoots out from under the bench from beneath and clamps down on Tony's mouth. His eyelids flip open like window shades and the whites glow bright with shock. Before he can even struggle, the sharp tip of an arrow exits his throat from beneath, tearing through the skin with a sound like ripping cloth.

Blood erupts from his trachea as his eyes bug out in anguish and stunned horror. His mouth opens and closes like a fish out of water as the tip of the arrow dribbles dark red blood into a rapidly growing pool, spilling through the slats of the wooden bench beneath him. He twists and flops, but the hand keeps his forehead pinned to the bench until all movement stops and his mouth ceases its desperate attempts to suck in air. The eyes remain open, the pupils etched with terror and disbelief. Slowly, the gloved hand slips off his face and vanishes beneath the bench. The metal spear remains in place, blood bubbling from the jagged flesh around it like lava from a volcano.

Footsteps run away and Tony remains pinned to the bench, finally at peace.

"Cut!" Ashley leans away from the monitor and applauds with gusto. "That's a wrap for tonight, everyone. It looked fantastic!"

The teen who's been filming lowers his camera as the twenty-something actor on the bench sits up and grins.

"Somebody help Grant get that arrow out of his throat," Ashley adds with a laugh.

Grant chuckles as several teen crew members scurry over and set about removing the apparatus that encircles his neck.

"This Karo syrup is nasty, Ashley," Grant says, twisting his face into a grimace. "And cold, too."

Ashley saunters over. "What, you expect me to heat it up for you? You're just an expendable extra so get over yourself."

He sticks out his tongue and she laughs.

The image freezes and then goes black.

"Okay, I'm going to stop here since the bell's about to ring."

Bright light fills the room as Mr. Ketchum flicks on the overheads. Cassie beams with pride as the class of high school seniors applauds. A bank of open windows opposite the door allows a slight breeze to waft through the room, partially offsetting the warm spring temperature outside.

On the white board behind Mr. Ketchum's desk is scrawled in large red letters, *HAPPY FRIDAY THE 13*TH. Also, in the upper right corner are the words Filming Always Permitted in this Classroom, and beneath that two signatures—*Mr.* K and Mrs. K.

Cassie flips an errant strand of auburn hair off her freckled face and tosses Donovan a smile of triumph. That sequence, including the kill, was lensed just last weekend, which means they spent long hours in the school's editing room to have it ready for today. Watching that particular murder on Friday the 13th is especially delicious since the "kill" is an homage to that very movie.

The applause dies down as Kristen Corte, playing "Ashley" in the film, stands and bows. "Thank you, thank you."

Two rows over, attractive brunette Olivia Taylor scowls. "We're clapping for the kill scene, not *you*, Kristen."

Kristen loses her gloating smile. "I keep hoping they'll rewrite the script and kill you off sooner."

Mr. Ketchum holds up a hand. "Enough behind the scenes drama, ladies." He sends each of the girls a serious look that says, "I mean business here," and they back down. Kristen retakes her seat and grabs Diego Bernal's hand, pulling him closer and mad-dogging Olivia.

Cassie sighs to herself. Another typical day in film class. Kristen and Olivia are probably the prettiest girls at school, and that's the problem. Cassie doesn't care enough about stuff like that to be jealous, but the other two girls are so much alike they can't stand one another.

Blonde hair tumbling past her shoulders, small nose, blue eyes, soft features, and a figure to kill for, Kristen is eye candy for every boy who sees her. Olivia is almost the opposite with short brown hair, sharp features, and piercing brown eyes, but her flirting skills are legendary and could easily give Kristen a run for her money if Kristen ever broke up with Diego, her steady boyfriend of the past two years.

"I, for one, am very impressed," Mr. Ketchum goes on, turning his attention Cassie's way. "Your footage looks professional. The lighting and camerawork—great job, William."

Tall, skinny William Webster grins from ear to ear from behind long bangs swept across light brown eyes, his barely visible mustache stretched to pencil thin status.

"And that opening drone shot as the victim staggered into the park and plopped onto the bench was flawless," Mr. Ketchum goes on, his deep voice filled with pride. "Your precision with that drone astonishes me, Baxter. I can't even keep one of those things in the air for two minutes without crashing it into something."

Baxter Jacobs—known as the class nerd for his large glasses and pudgy physique—basks in the glow of the compliment, lowering his eyes in embarrassed pride.

"Your sound was clean too, Baxter," Mr. Ketchum adds. "That's very difficult during location shooting." He scans the class. "Any comments or suggestions for the directors, cast, or crew before we leave for spring break?"

Cassie's least-favorite classmate, Robert Wilkins, leers at her. "Gonna tell us who the killer is, Cass?"

"Not on your life. Not even the main actors have seen those pages."

"I'm the only one privileged to know that secret." Mr. Ketchum grins and pulls an imaginary zipper across his lips. "But my lips are sealed under penalty of death."

The class laughs.

"I'm sure it was Cassie who threatened you." Robert smirks. "We all know Donovan's too feeble to intimidate a fly."

"Ahem!" Mr. Ketchum tosses a ball painted with a frown face to Robert, who deftly plucks it from the air it with his left hand. He eyes the frowning face and shrugs.

"Sorry, Mr. K, but it's true."

Mr. Ketchum is not amused. "If you end up with Mr. Frown one more time, Robert, I'll dock you some serious class participation points."

Robert looks suitably chastised, but Cassie tosses him the dirtiest look she can muster. Tall, dark-haired, handsome, and narcissistic to the max, Robert loves displaying his chiseled physique at every opportunity. Today, he's wearing shorts and skin-tight tank top that might as well be invisible.

Cassie hates arrogance, especially when people flaunt it. Robert has haughtily hit on her multiple times this year, clearly assuming his charm and hot bod are all he needs to conquer her.

Considering he could have practically any girl at school, she doesn't understand his persistence—unless he considers her a challenge. She's turned him down as forcefully as possible and, in his self-absorbed mind, Robert assumes it's because of Donovan.

Donovan lowers his eyes to the floor under the scrutiny of the class. A shadow from his yellow fedora covers his face and gives him a tragic-figure look that sends Cassie's heartbeat into raging overdrive.

How dare Robert!

She bites her lip, fighting the urge to cuss him out right then and there!

"Even I'm not privileged to know the identity of the killer," comes a husky female voice from the back of the room. "And I'm married to the producer." She tosses off a throaty laugh and the class chuckles.

"What did you think of my performance, Mrs. K?" Kristen chirps, her tone indicating she expects a compliment. "Do you think I might play Lady Macbeth one day like you did?"

Mrs. Ketchum, the school's acting teacher, brushes a loose strand of brown hair back over one ear and appears to consider the question.

"I know you've always fancied that performance of mine and I confess I'm rather proud of it. But sometimes I fear you aspire to be like Lady Macbeth in real life."

"Of course, I do," Kristen asserts in her usual take-no-prisoners tone. "She was a take-charge woman, the kind you've modeled for us."

"May I point out," Mr. K adds, "that she was also an accessory to murder. But we're getting sidetracked here."

"I'm proud of every one of you," Mrs. K announces in her most dramatic tone. "The performances are stellar, especially you, Kristen. You are, after all, playing against type as a nice girl, am I right?"

She smiles and everyone joins her, including Kristen, who may be self-absorbed and conceited, but at least makes no pretense of being otherwise.

Cassie has always considered Mrs. K one of the most beautiful women she's ever known, possessing true movie star attributes. Brunette with shoulder-length, wavy hair swept just off the face, full lips accented by understated lipstick, lovely green eyes beneath luxuriously long lashes. Even her high cheekbones give her that star quality, like a modern-day version of Sophia Loren.

Mr. and Mrs. K used to be active in Hollywood—he a director and she an actress—but drinking, drugs, and partying derailed both their careers. They've never tried to keep their pasts a secret—Google has all the dirty details—and Mr. K, at least, has always asserted that he loves teaching more than directing any day. Cassie can't imagine that being true, but she doesn't argue the point.

Mrs. Ketchum looks across the room at Cassie and Donovan. "You two are going places in Hollywood, I've no doubt of that. Perhaps you can convince my husband to produce your next feature."

Cassie's mouth drops open. "Are you thinking of going back to making movies, Mr. K? That would be awesome!"

Dressed in his usual sloppy wrinkled pants and long-sleeved pullover, Mr. Ketchum looks nothing like how she pictures a Hollywood producer.

"That's just my wife's wishful thinking. I prefer nurturing the talent in this room. You and Donovan will do just fine on your own. I agree with Mrs. K on that score."

He nods at his wife and she smiles back. But something about the smile seems off to Cassie, as though Mrs. K thinks Mr. K embarrassed her in front of the students.

"I, uh, I agree about Donovan and Cassie," pipes up a timid voice from the back corner. "It's an honor to work with them."

Cassie turns toward the back of the class.

Jaden Merton slouches in his usual seat, black hoodie partially covering his perfectly woven cornrows, peeking out at them as though afraid he'll be attacked at any moment.

Donovan smiles at the compliment. "Thanks, man," he says in that calm, quiet tone that's soothed Cassie's bull-in-a-china-shop nature since they were children. "You're a great help on the set, and I mean that. You have, like, a photographic memory for details."

Jaden cracks what for him could pass for a smile, but he doesn't respond to the compliment. He seldom says anything at all, but the film crew would be minus its most valuable member if he decided to quit.

It had taken Cassie and Donovan more than a few pleading sessions before Mr. Ketchum agreed to let them co-write and co-direct a feature film for their senior project. Everyone else is making short films, but Cassie and Donovan hope to enter their movie in the local Shriek Festival, one of the oldest and biggest horror film festivals in the country. Final deadline for submissions is in July. Since their film has to be finished and polished before the June graduation date, submitting on time should be a breeze. And they both live in the San Fernando Valley, so attending the nearby Hollywood-based festival will be a cinch.

Mr. Ketchum studies Jaden a long moment, but the lanky African American boy refuses to make eye contact.

"I've heard good things about your work on this film, Jaden, and I'm happy to see you enjoying yourself."

"He enjoys himself too much," Kristen spits out, squinting at Jaden from across the room. "He gets a little too into his role as the guy in the skull mask."

"He's the killer?" a longhaired girl exclaims in shock.

Mr. Ketchum shakes his head. "He's the body double for the killer. That way, none of the other actors know which character is really doing the killing."

The girl nods in admiration.

Jaden withers beneath Kristen's verbal assault.

"Kristen," Mr. Ketchum intones, his voice sounding as annoyed as Cassie has ever heard from him. "I agreed to you not having to make your own film because you're the lead in this one. Don't push me. If I get reports that you're playing the prima donna on set like you do here, you'd better come up with an Oscar-caliber film of your own if you want to pass this class."

Olivia bursts into applause, and surprisingly Jaden joins her. Now it's Kristen who withers—slightly—and Cassie is pleased to note that she doesn't argue or even respond. She merely pulls Diego in closer and he whispers something—no doubt words of comfort—into her ear. That's all he ever seems to do.

Diego Bernal has been called the hottest boy at Performance Arts Academy High School by most of the girls Cassie knows. She agrees that he has that smoldering Latino look and he could easily be a model with his wavy black hair, smooth features untarnished by acne or beard stubble, and soft brown eyes. But he's not her type. He's too… beautiful.

One thing she *does* know—he could do a helluva lot better in the girl-friend department that Kristen Corte. Cassie can't imagine what he sees in her beyond beauty. That must be all he wants.

Kristen is practically a Hollywood stereotype, the obnoxious drama queen everyone hates. That's why it was too tempting to pass up the opportunity to cast her as the "good girl" in this film. She's not joking when she crows about being a great actress. She really is stellar and will no doubt have the Hollywood career she craves if she can keep her attitude in check.

Mr. Ketchum continues the discussion for a few more minutes and then quizzes other class members about the status of their scripts or film projects.

Cassie tunes out to think about the week ahead. She and Donovan have lined up some pretty cool locations and the weather promises to be clear. Since it's already April, Daylight Savings Time is in play. That means longer days, but also a longer wait for night shooting to begin. They've discussed the schedule so often they have it memorized, and plan on making the best use of every shooting moment they have.

When Mr. Ketchum dismisses the class, Cassie gathers up her backpack and smiles as Donovan assembles his stuff. The class files out, several students wishing them success on the rest of the shoot.

Asher, the smallest boy in the senior class despite having just turned eighteen is, in Cassie's opinion, one of the cutest boys in the entire school. He's around five foot five, with a 'fro of thick curly brown hair that wraps itself around his head like a Chia pet, pale blue eyes the color of Forget-Me-Not flowers, and soft, delicate features that make him look much younger.

"See you tomorrow, Cassie," he says in his typically upbeat voice as he passes her desk.

"Yep." She smiles at him as he leaves the room.

Asher volunteered for the cameraman role in the film because he looks up to William, who also aspires to be a Director of Photography after high school. Cassie loves having Asher on set for two reasons: he's one of the nicest kids around and he's gorgeous. Even in a small role, he'll be additional eye candy to lure in female viewers. Cassie is feminist to a point, but recognizes the usefulness of having good-looking people, both male and female, in a film. That's just good business.

She glances around for Jaden, but he was likely the first one out, as always. Jaden isn't like Asher and, if Cassie is honest, he creeps her out a little. He gives new meaning to the word "shy"; he stares a lot and doesn't talk. More than once in class—and now on set—she's felt his eyes fixed on her, or maybe on her and Donovan together.

Could he be jealous of Donovan? She's never seen him show interest in anyone and she isn't exactly the prettiest or most interesting girl on campus with her frizzy auburn hair and brown freckles littering her face like specks of dust. Still, for a timid kid like Jaden, a whirling dervish of energy might seem alluring. With her, he'd never have to talk, just listen.

"Ready?" Donovan is standing beside her, his military green backpack slung over one shoulder, completely at color odds with his mismatched clothes. Cassie loves that he buys everything from thrift stores and then puts on whatever he finds in his closet without bothering to match styles or colors.

Today his red-checkered flannel shirt completely misses the mark against his green and black striped long pants and the yellow fedora resting an angle atop a mop of messy brown hair sticking out from underneath like he's an anime character.

She always describes him as "cute" because of those hazel eyes set beneath perfect brows that most girls would kill for and his dimpled smile, which warms her heart whenever he chooses to share it. However, the truth is he's as gorgeous as Asher and could easily be a model himself, or a professional actor.

Of course, he says the same thing about her, but she gazes into the mirror often enough to know the truth. She's as ordinary as they come, character actor material, at best, if acting was her goal (which it isn't). Not being awash in vanity like Kristen or Olivia, and having little interest in clothes or other teen-centric superficialities like makeup or fancy hairstyles, she and Donovan complement one another perfectly, even to the point of hating how they look on camera, all of which has fused their friendship over the years into an unbreakable bond.

Mr. Ketchum steps over to them. "Now, I know I'll see you here tomorrow for the school scenes, but you also have my cell number in case any complications arise throughout the week."

Cassie nods. "No worries, Mr. K. D-Boy and me have it all covered."

"D-Boy?" Donovan raises quizzical eyebrows. "When did you come up with that one?"

"Just now." She grins. "Like it?"

He shrugs. "It could grow on me."

Mr. Ketchum laughs. "Go on, you two. I'll see you tomorrow at noon."

They laugh and Cassie leads the way to the door, turning as Mrs. Ketchum stands and offers a smile. "Thanks for training such good actors, Mrs. K."

"That's my job, Cassie. Enjoy your week off."

As they cross the campus toward the student parking lot, dodging excited teens itching to start their spring break, Cassie feels penetrating eyes fixed on her back. Maybe it's a lifetime of watching horror flicks, but her sensitivity to being surreptitiously watched has always been ultra-high. As is Donovan's ultra-sensitivity to her moods.

"What's up, Cass?"

She stops and he halts beside her. "I'm being watched. Or we are." She spins like a pirouetting dancer and spots a black hoodie duck behind the large shade tree in the center of the quad. "It's Jaden again."

Donovan squints against the bright afternoon sun. "I don't see him."

"Behind the shade tree. Come on, let's go."

She grabs his arm and turns him around, leading him back toward the parking lot. As they walk, she marvels as always at her amazing school, how it looks like something out of a sci-fi film. They stroll past the Performing Arts Center; having no windows, it resembles a massive upside-down golden funnel that leans to one side and sports a flat roof. She loves watching plays in the Center because the acoustics are perfect, whether you sit in the orchestra section or up in the nosebleed balconies.

"I've noticed him watching us a lot lately, especially on set," he remarks, but he doesn't sound as creeped out as Cassie feels. "I figured maybe it was because he was waiting for us to need him for some job or other. He's so dedicated."

"He's been watching us at school too," she says, keeping her voice neutral as they brush past chattering groups of students near the Dance Building, which looks like a Star Destroyer from *Star Wars* crashed into the ground with the "engine" portion bending back at an angle toward the sky.

"Maybe he has a crush on you," he adds, giving her a friendly nudge.

"I've considered that, but it doesn't seem likely."

"Why not? You're stupendously awesome."

She considers a moment. "I don't notice him watching unless I'm with you."

"He's probably jealous of me like every other guy who's into you. They all think we're gonna get together, even though we keep saying we're not."

"Yeah, that's possible."

He pauses a moment, eyeing her uncertainly. "We aren't, are we?"

She studies his tentative demeanor, seeing in him what she always sees— the only boy she can ever imagine dating, even though they never have, at least not in any romantic sense. They've talked about it in a roundabout sort of way, but never decided on anything.

She grins. "Not at the moment."

He returns the grin as they pass through an open gate into the student parking lot, where they skirt milling students and moving cars until they arrive at Cassie's powder blue Civic.

Donovan tosses both of their backpacks into the rear seat and plops into the passenger side while she slides behind the wheel. Somehow the car's interior always smells new after it's been sitting in the sun, and the pleasant aroma makes Cassie smile as she slips on her seat belt. She likes the car and the boy sitting beside her. The smile remains as she eases out of the parking lot.

They swing by Donovan's white, two-story house to drop off his school stuff and grab the shooting schedule and storyboards—shot by shot drawings of the entire film, drawn by Donovan—and to remind his mom that he'll be at Cassie's for dinner. Dinner at Cassie's is a regular "thing" for them because Donovan's mom works a lot of nightshifts, and if she doesn't have time to prepare food ahead of time, he usually just microwaves frozen dinners.

Short and stout and dressed in her Caribbean blue nurse's uniform, name badge firmly affixed to the upper left side, with dark hair tied back off her face, Marjory Quinn greets them as they enter. "Hi Hun. How was school today?"

"Great," Donovan replies, grinning. "Everyone loved our footage."

Her brown eyes cloud over with distaste and she frowns, but then shifts to a partial smile. "Yes, the horror stuff. Hopefully, you'll outgrow it one day."

Donovan sighs and Cassie touches his arm as a gesture of comfort.

"Mom, I'm eighteen and you know I plan to make horror films my career. You'll just have to deal."

"You'll change your mind," she says in that condescending tone Cassie hates. "Children always do."

Donovan glances at Cassie and shrugs. This is standard procedure for his mom, which is another reason he spends so much of his time at her house.

Marjory scoops car keys out of a colorful wicker basket sitting atop a small round table near the door. "I won't be home till morning and I know it's Friday, but don't stay late at your girlfriend's house again."

Cassie and Donovan exchange another glance of consternation. "She's my best friend, mom, not my girlfriend."

She smiles knowingly. "Your late father was my best friend until he became my boyfriend. It'll happen."

She turns her cheek, and he dutifully leans in to kiss it.

"Don't work too hard, Mom."

"How can I not? It's a hospital." She swooshes past him out the front door.

Cassie and Donovan lock eyes for a long moment before shaking their heads and heading upstairs to his room.

Cassie loves the retro feel to Donovan's room. Just like his clothes, he loves collecting old pieces of furniture, bedding, lamps, and other stuff from thrift stores. He's especially fond of 80s items and often buys them off eBay if he finds a good deal. He has a huge vinyl collection, while everyone else she knows listens to digital music on their phones. Even CDs are pretty much out these days. But Donovan keeps the needle on his turntable in perfect condition and she enjoys listening to his oldies.

He's even got a tube television that still works. It's in color, but the picture quality is nothing like her flat screen at home. His bedcover is a muted pink and his pillowcases are purple and red. His walls are adorned with horror movie posters (what else?)—all films they've watched together, including his all-time favorite, the original black and white Universal classic, *The Wolfman*.

Her current favorite is the 2018 *Halloween* because Jamie Lee Curtis portrayed such a kick-ass woman who determined she would not be victimized ever again. That poster adorns *her* bedroom wall.

He tosses his backpack on the desk chair and rummages around on his neatly-arranged desktop for the storyboards and shot sheets. He likes writing everything down, while she stores notes, locations, shot and call sheets in her tablet. Both of them, however, have contact info for cast and crew in their phones, just in case.

He spins a few ABBA tunes on the turntable, and they sprawl out on the bed side by side to listen. Cassie enjoys ABBA's chirpy, catchy style, which is different from other Pop music she's heard. She's bursting with excitement about the week to come, but senses Donovan needs a few minutes of downtime, maybe because of the "mom" thing. She's a nice lady overall, but has always wanted him to be someone he's not. She doesn't push super hard, but like the incident downstairs, she implies that he's still a child and will outgrow everything he likes. It hurts him deeply, so Cassie does her best to be supportive.

Without warning, he sits up and hops off the bed.

"We better go."

Edward Stewart is laying out ingredients for dinner when Cassie and Donovan stroll into the kitchen. "How's my favorite scream team?"

Cassie smiles as he engulfs her in a hug, reaching out a long arm to pull in Donovan, as well.

"Okay, daddy, you're crushing us, as usual."

She laughs and he releases them.

Donovan tosses her dad a lopsided grin and doesn't look the least bit embarrassed. "Hi, Pop."

Edward winks and turns back to the kitchen counter, which is laid out with veggies, chicken strips, and large tortillas.

Cassie loves how her dad treats Donovan like a son, and Donovan truly thinks of him as his dad. Never having known his own father, and with Edward always having wanted a son, it's worked out perfectly for them both.

Cassie's mouth begins to water. Her dad makes the most amazing chicken burritos she's ever eaten. For such a big man, he's almost delicate when he manipulates utensils and sprinkles ingredients into his dishes. She's often encouraged him to go on one of those cooking shows because his talents are so amazing, but he refuses.

"So, how did everyone like your footage?"

Wearing the bright red apron sporting "Kitchen Elf" in green letters that she gave him last Christmas, Edward looks like a cartoon character, especially with his wide shoulders and old-school flat-top buzz-cut tinged with gray around the temples. He chops the chicken and veggies so hard and fast that the rapid *thunk thunk thunk* against the cutting board sounds like muted machine gun fire.

Cassie and Donovan slip onto barstools, which line the counter that serves as one side of their kitchen. The stove rests dead center and the sink sits beneath double windows looking out into the decent-sized backyard. Cassie typically eats breakfast in here—because there's also a dinette set—and dinner too if her dad has to work nights and doesn't have time to cook beforehand.

"They loved it," she announces proudly.

"Not a single dig on our footage," Donovan adds, looking relaxed, elbows propped back on the countertop. "I think we have a winner."

"You think?" Cassie tosses him a chastising look. "We wrote and directed it, so of course it's fantastic."

He chuckles. "Now you sound like Kristen."

She snatches a potholder off a metal rack behind her and chucks it at him. "That's a low blow."

He ducks to one side, dislodging the fedora, and the potholder strikes her dad in the back. He tosses them a look of mock annoyance.

"Hey, time-out back there. You kill the cook, you don't eat." He grins and returns to his chopping. "I'm glad it went well. You still planning to enter it in that competition?"

"Of course," Cassie and Donovan spit out simultaneously as he replaces the fedora onto his mop of hair.

Hat securely in place, Donovan hops off his stool. "Let us give you a hand, Pop."

Normally, Cassie's dad begs off their help, but this time he asks them to heat up the tortilla warmer—a round machine resembling a waffle iron that's strictly for tortillas—and to warm up the black beans on the stove.

As always, dinner is a relaxed affair as Cassie and Donovan regale Edward with the goings on at school. Being a performing arts high school in Southern California, it seems to Cassie that the kids are even more dramatic than those at regular schools, being performers on the cusp of Hollywood, and all. Every little thing becomes a major "I'm ready for my close up" moment.

"Just today, Dad, this girl in the cafeteria acted like she would die because she got cheddar cheese on her burger instead of Swiss."

Donovan nearly spits out his water. "Oh, my God, that was funny. She deserves an Oscar, seriously. Best performance by an entitled brat."

Edward laughs and takes a bite of his burrito. The salsa dribbles down his chin and onto his plate. Cassie laughs and hands him a napkin.

He wipes away the dripping salsa. "So, everything set for filming?"

They nod simultaneously.

"My buddy over at Star Security will have the key for the warehouse. Just text him the day before to remind him. I gave you his number, right?"

Cassie nods. "Yep. Bob Washington. I've got it."

"We're so stoked you snagged that set for us," Donovan blurts, barely containing his excitement. "That creepy warehouse is perfect for our finale."

Edward grins. "Just make sure to give me a credit at the end—'creepy warehouse location snagged by Edward Stewart.'" He swigs from his glass of beer.

"You got it," Donovan exclaims, holding up his hand for a high five.

Edward slaps it.

The *Theme from SWAT* blasts through the room like a blizzard, startling the kids. Edward looks sheepish as he pulls the phone from his pocket.

"Sorry, I forgot to put it on vibrate." He glances at the number and frowns. "It's the sergeant. Sorry, I have to take this." He stands and steps away from the table. "Yeah, Sergeant, what's up?"

Cassie and Donovan exchange a look. Using electronic devices at the table is forbidden in the Stewart home, but then, the sergeant doesn't usually call Edward at home. They watch as he listens, phone pressed to his ear, standing a few feet from the table in front of a painting of an enormous wave breaking against a pristine beach. Cassie loves that painting. Her mom completed it shortly before she died.

Edward ends his call and absently slides the phone back into his front pants pocket.

When he looks troubled, but doesn't speak, Cassie says, "Dad? Everything okay?"

"I have to work after all."

"You promised we'd hang out tonight, the three of us." Cassie can't hide her disappointment. He's been working too many nightshifts lately and she misses having him around.

Edward nods, his expression grave. "That was before somebody decided to take Friday the Thirteenth too far."

"What do you mean?" Donovan asks, his smooth brows knitted with confusion.

"Somebody was spotted in one of those hockey masks and overalls leaving Pierson Park just after dark."

Cassie shrugs. "So? I'm sure lots of fans dress up like that every Friday the Thirteenth."

Edward nods. "But most of 'em don't commit murder."

"What?" Shocked, she glances at Donovan, whose olive skin pales.

"Sergeant didn't give me all the details, but the killing was pretty brutal, like in one of those Jason movies you guys watch. He wants every officer out on patrol tonight, cruising the parks and keeping a lookout for weird stuff going down."

Cassie locks eyes with Donovan. "We just filmed there last weekend."

"Which is why I'm happy you're not filming tonight because it would've been canceled," Edward asserts, his no-arguments tone in full timbre. "You keep the doors and windows locked."

"What about taking Donovan home?"

He shakes his head. "I don't want either of you out tonight. Donovan can crash on my bed. I won't be back till morning anyway." He glances at Donovan. "That work for you, pal?"

Looking rattled by the development, Donovan nods. "Uh, yeah, sure. Thanks."

"I need to suit up and get down to the station." Edward hurries from the dining room and Cassie hears the door to his bedroom close with a *click*.

A heavy silence settles over the dining room, and despite the pleasant odor of freshly cooked food, it chills her to the bone.

"That's so weird, a Jason murder right after we…" Cassie lets the thought trail off.

Donovan, as always, is on the same wavelength. "Filmed a murder inspired by *Friday the 13th* in that same park."

She nods, brushing some reddish curls away from her eyes. "Except we didn't film the kill scene at the park. We used your backyard."

"Yeah, but it's supposed to take place in that park."

"I wonder if my dad'll find out exactly how the person was killed."

"Are you thinking it could be the same? That's not possible."

She considers a moment. "Ordinarily, no. But what if…?

"What?"

"What if someone was spying on us when we filmed that scene and then decided to act it out for real?"

That's…" He meets her wide-eyed gaze. "Scary as hell."

Here's a preview of
THEY KNOW WHEN THE KILLER WILL STRIKE,
(which wraps up the storylines begun in *I Know When You're
Going To Die* and continued in *The Horror Film Killer*)

PROLOGUE

THEY SAT HUDDLED TOGETHER IN the darkest corner of a seedy smoke-filled lounge, finalizing their plans.

The loud voices all around ensured that no one overheard them.

"Just remember that you want to kill quite a few of the cast and crew. If even one or two 'accidents' happen, it will shut down the entire production, and you'll lose your chance."

"I know. What about your target? What's your plan?"

"That's my concern. You're the amateur here, remember? *I'm* advising you."

"I know. I was just wondering."

"Well don't. You have enough to worry about. After all, killing eight people during a film shoot is unprecedented. Everything must be perfect or some of them will slip through your fingers."

"They all deserve to die for what they did. And they will."

"That's the spirit. Now, let's go through the plan one more time and then get out of this hellhole. The smoke is killing me."

As the noisy patrons laughed and drank and surrounded them with foul-smelling smoke, the conspirators once more laid out their plot to commit mass murder.

CHAPTER ONE

I DON'T THINK IT WAS AN ACCIDENT

LEO SAT AT THE BOTTOM of the steps leading up to his expansive Victorian home, wondering if his mother's desire to fictionalize his brush with death at the hands of a serial killer might end up bringing real-world horrors back into his life. He knew his dread seemed crazy, and yet he couldn't shake the gut feeling that this movie was jinxed from the get-go. Still, he'd agreed—reluctantly—to be an advisor/consultant to appease his persistently pushy producer mother who, he knew, never would've stopped asking until he said yes. Fortunately, he wouldn't be alone on the set. His three—make that *only*—friends had also signed on in the same capacity, seeing as how they were fellow serial killer survivors and, like Leo, sought to ensure that their fictional alter egos were accurately portrayed on screen.

They all sat together on the steps awaiting the arrival of the actors who would portray them. That was another of his mom's "brilliant" (her own word) ideas: the actors portraying the four main protagonists would live with their real-world counterparts while the film was shot on location in La Costa, their small coastal town west of Los Angeles. Knowing his extreme shyness would pose a problem, Leo had objected, but his mother insisted, especially after she saw the actor portraying him.

"He's gorgeous, Leonardo," she'd gushed effusively. "Perfect for you."

Leo didn't even want to ask what she meant by that (though he was sure he knew), and he didn't have a chance anyway because she'd raved on about the pending production and how much fun it would be for them to work on something together for the first time in his seventeen years. She seemed to have forgotten that only a few months prior, he'd nearly died during the actual events she was now so eager to turn into the next hoped-for hit designed to generate box office gold.

Oh well, that was his mother.

"Aren't they supposed to be here by now?"

Leo glanced over at his best friend, J.C. Rivera, looking hot and uncomfortable in the designer shirt and pants he'd worn despite the eighty-plus degree July temperature surrounding him. Unlike J.C., who loved to show off his fancy clothes, Leo sported a plain tee shirt and old board shorts.

Blonde and petite Laura Benson, wearing a light summer shirt and shorts, glanced at her watch. "They still have five minutes, J.C."

J.C. grunted with disgust, causing Laura to toss Leo and Chet a grin. Leo had only met Laura that spring when she'd transferred to La Costa High, but she'd already proven to be a great and loyal friend, especially during those terrifying weeks when she, Leo, and J.C. sought the identity of the person who planned on murdering J.C.

Surfer blond Chet Hamilton, on the other hand, had been a bully most of Leo's life. Only his narrow escape from death at the hands of that same killer, and Leo's part in saving his life, had reformed Chet, folding him into their nonconformist group of oddballs who didn't fit the trendy, partying, self-absorbed mold of La Costa High School students.

Chet shrugged but said nothing as he relaxed beneath the warm sun in a tank top and board shorts. He used to arrogantly show off his ripped physique every chance he got, but that was before he'd nearly died. Leo knew he wasn't wearing the tank to impress the newcomers, but only because it was more comfortable in the hot summer weather.

"At least there won't be thirty-year-olds playing us teenagers like they usually do in movies," Laura commented, wiping perspiration from her lightly tanned forehead.

"I insisted on that," Leo commented dryly, "*and* those script changes I told you about."

"Thank God you got that garbage taken out of the script," J.C. spat, his handsome face twisted with anger. "I already get enough crap from my mom on that front."

"Me too," Leo agreed, noting Chet frowning beside him.

"I guess my part in the story couldn't be changed much," he said, his deep voice tinged with regret. "I don't know if I can relive what happened, and how I used to be."

Laura took his hand in hers and squeezed gently. "You don't have to be there when they're filming something painful, Chet. None of us do." She glanced at Leo. "Especially you, Leo, when they film the part where you almost died."

Despite the heat, Leo shuddered at the memory. "I guess. I'll take it one day at a time."

Laura offered a reassuring smile just as a black SUV rounded the corner and approached Leo's house.

Laura released Chet's hand and sat up. "Looks like they're here."

J.C. grunted, "'Bout time."

The SUV eased to a stop in front of the house. Leo and the others rose to greet their onscreen counterparts. Since his mother was the producer, Leo felt obligated to approach the newcomers first, despite his social anxiety screaming at him to run and hide. As he rounded the rear of the large vehicle, the driver's side rear door popped open, and out stepped a tall guy with sleek side-parted brown hair followed by a shorter guy with a thick head of curly hair. Leo started forward, but then whirled at the sound of screeching tires approaching from behind.

A dark sedan with tinted windows careened toward the two young men standing beside the SUV. They turned at the tire noise, but Leo was faster. He darted forward and tackled both guys toward the sidewalk. Just as they tumbled to the grass separating the sidewalk from the street, a smashing of metal against metal filled the air. Sprawled on the grass with the two guys beneath him, Leo saw from the corner of his eye the dark sedan speeding off down the street.

"Leo!"

Laura rushed forward, J.C. and Chet on her heels. They reached out to pull Leo to his feet and then helped up the young actors, who looked stunned but unhurt. The driver of their SUV leaped from the car and joined them, visibly shaken by the event. He was a young man, probably just a driver who worked for the studio.

"Are you guys all right?" The driver looked terrified, as though he might get blamed for this incident.

The shorter boy with the curly hair broke into an amazing smile that caught Leo's eye. He looked directly at Leo and said, "Yeah, thanks to Leo. You move fast."

Leo was so captivated by that smile he almost made eye contact but quickly looked away, confused by what had happened, and how this guy knew his name. "How…how do you know me?"

The curly-haired guy dusted himself off, while the taller one did the same. Leo found a hand sticking out for him to shake.

"I'm Asher King," the curly haired one said, his voice firm but not especially deep. "I'm playing you in the movie."

Leo shook his hand, still avoiding eye contact but thinking how much his mother's description of Asher fit the young actor. Just then he found himself surrounded by another guy—tall and Latino, wearing a tank top—and a gorgeous girl with shoulder-length blonde hair, dressed in stylish summer attire. Both looked horrified.

"Are you all right?" The girl leaned in like a doctor to examine Asher and the other guy whom Leo had tackled.

"Yeah, Kristen, we're good," said the broad-shouldered, short-haired guy. He faced Leo and stuck out his hand. "Thanks, Leo. I'm Robert."

Leo shook his hand and Chet stepped closer. "Oh, you're playing me. I'm Chet." He shook hands with Robert, who grinned.

"You're obviously Kristen." Laura offered a warm smile.

The long-haired blonde, looking relieved that no one had been hurt, shook her head in amazement. "You always greet visitors like this?"

Laura shrugged. "Only actors."

Kristen chuckled. "I think we'll get along just fine."

The tall, well-built Latino noted J.C. staring at him as though in awe and stuck out his hand. "And you're J.C. I'm Diego. I've been looking forward to meeting you."

Caught off guard, J.C. composed himself and shook hands. "You have, huh?"

Diego smiled, another photogenic show of pearly white teeth. "Sure. I'm hoping you can show me some dance moves during the shoot. I saw some of your vids on social media."

J.C. offered up a smile equal to Diego's. "You got it, man." He eyed Leo. "Here's a guy who knows good dancing when he sees it."

Leo glanced quickly away from Asher, who'd been staring at him the entire time, and gave J.C. a shove to the shoulder. Then he led the group around the front of the SUV where the young driver stared in hopeless abandon at the missing rear door.

"The studio'll kill me for this."

He sounded so morose; Leo placed a hand on his shoulder. "We got your back on this one."

"Yeah," the others chimed in.

"It wasn't your fault, Ron," Asher assured him in a gentle but firm voice. "We'll tell 'em what happened."

Diego sprinted on long legs into the middle of the street and retrieved the mangled rear door. Trotting to the back of the SUV, he waited as Robert lifted the hatchback, and then he slid the busted door into the storage space.

"For a small town, you have some crazy drivers," Kristen commented to Laura.

"I've only lived here about six months, but I've never seen anything like that."

"Me either, and I been here my whole life," J.C. put in, directing his comment to Diego, rather than the girls.

Diego and J.C. made momentary eye contact before Diego glanced down as though uncomfortable.

Robert stepped forward and grabbed two suitcases, one in each hand, from the back of the vehicle and set them on the asphalt. That caught Diego's attention and he grabbed a third. Before either boy could reach for the remaining baggage, Kristen darted forward and reached past them to pull out her two bags, both of which were larger than any of the others. Laura stepped forward to help.

"The boys have been razzing me for bringing two bags for only one week," she told Laura with a heavy sigh. "They just don't realize what it takes for us girls to look gorgeous, right, Laura?"

Laura chuckled but didn't comment. Leo knew Laura wasn't into fashion or makeup, relying instead on her natural beauty, which in his opinion was considerable. He tossed her a smile when Kristen wasn't looking, and she returned it.

Looking like he was headed for his own funeral, Ron, the youthful driver, waved goodbye to his charges. "I'll see you next week. If I'm still employed."

They all assured him he would be and, looking slightly less disheartened, Ron drove off in the SUV, leaving the the group behind on the curb.

"Well, this is definitely a strange way to meet," Kristen announced to the group, "but I, for one, am excited about this shoot." She faced Laura. "I can't wait to get to know you, Laura, and pick your brain for details."

Laura shrugged. "I'm not sure there's much in there to pick."

J.C. stifled a laugh as Kristen eyed Laura quizzically.

"We can head over to my house," Laura told Kristen, pointing at a two-door coup parked across the street. "Later, guys," she added, casting a look back at Leo and the others as she strode across the street. Caught off guard by Laura's abruptness, Kristen grabbed her two large suitcases to follow.

"I can help, Kristen," J.C. blurted, stepping forward with a grin on his face.

She gave him a stony look and he stopped. "I can handle my own bags, thank you." She hefted the bags and waddled across the street after Laura.

J.C. shrugged and turned back to the others. "Well, I tried."

"Kristen's kind of the antisocial type unless she needs something from you," Diego said with a shrug of his own. "I know her pretty well. Where's your house, J.C.? I love the retro feel to this neighborhood, all these old-school homes."

"I'm around the corner. My car is the blue Beemer just over there." He pointed at a shiny new BMW coupe parked in front of the Queen Anne-style house next to Leo's. "You ready to go?"

"You know it. I can't wait to start picking *your* brain." Diego grinned, and it was an infectious grin that Leo found quite appealing. So, apparently, did J.C., because he laughed.

"I think you and me'll get along great, Diego." He reached for Diego's large suitcase. "Let me help you with this." He grabbed the leather handle and tried to lift the bag, but it barely rose a few inches off the pavement before J.C. grunted and let it drop. "What you got in there, rocks?"

Diego laughed. "Naw, just a few dumbbells so I can keep up my workout."

J.C. glanced at Leo. "Another fitness nut like you, Leo."

Leo couldn't help but smile. Other than dancing, J.C. had never been into fitness.

Diego grabbed his bag with one hand and lifted it with ease. The short sleeve shirt he wore stretched at the biceps and prominent veins bulged on his forearm. "I'm ready, J.C."

Looking sheepish, J.C. waved for Diego to follow and started toward his parked car. "I'll check in later, Leo."

"Okay." Leo watched them a moment before turning to Chet, Robert, and Asher.

Robert eyed Chet's physique and grinned. "I bet you got some weights at your place, Chet."

"Oh yeah. I don't surf anymore, but I still work out."

"Awesome," Robert said. "I'll be your workout partner while I'm here."

"That'll be cool." Chet glanced at Leo. "I guess we'll head to my house. See you tomorrow, Leo."

"Later," Leo replied as Chet led Robert toward his shiny black Z4 parked just up the street. Then he turned to Asher, who was gazing at him intently. "Well, Asher, let's go in and I'll show you around."

Caught off guard staring, Asher quickly smiled and reached for his old leather suitcase. "Awesome."

Perturbed by the other boy's ogling, Leo led the way up the stairs toward his front door.

* * *

Cassie Stewart sat at on a barstool in her kitchen, sipping coffee and reviewing the call sheets for the first day of shooting. As assistant director to Mr. K, her job was to make certain everyone was where they needed to be throughout the shoot. Donovan Quinn, the love of her life, sat beside her, reviewing costuming and other details for his script supervisor role on the film. In many ways, his job was harder than hers because films were shot out of order, and he needed to keep track of every detail to make certain scenes or partial scenes shot on different days looked identical.

She glanced over at him, relishing the soft features, mop of brown hair stuffed beneath one of his signature fedoras, and his mismatched retro clothing choices. Donovan was one of a kind, and she loved him with all her heart. Feeling her intense stare, he looked up and smiled. She blew him a kiss and he blew one back. Then they returned to the work at hand.

This film, as yet untitled, was their first foray into Hollywood, thanks to their former teacher, Mr. Ketchum, who, when hired as director, chose Cassie and many of her graduating class as cast and crew. They were all excited to be working together on a professional project. She and Donovan never had a chance to finish the feature film last spring that was to be their high school graduation project because of the copycat killings that had occurred, killings based on those in their script. With that case wending its way slowly through the courts, their unfinished film was considered evidence and had been confiscated by the police. The entire experience had been devastating, especially for Donovan, who was more sensitive and in touch with his feelings than herself.

Cassie shoved these thoughts aside to focus on the project before her. This film was a fictionalized version of a real serial killer incident that had happened earlier in the year down in the South Bay. She knew that four of the surviving teens, including the one dubbed "Hero Boy" by the press, were consultants on the film, and she wondered how they would feel reliving their worst nightmare. She could relate somewhat, but these kids had almost died, and that was worse than what she went through.

"Hey, D-Boy."

Donovan looked up from his paperwork, perfect eyebrows raised questioningly. "What's up?"

"How do you think the others are doing, you know, meeting their real-life counterparts?"

Donovan shrugged. "I know Asher was super excited to meet Leo. I think he's almost nervous about playing him."

"From what the media said about him, Leo sounds pretty amazing. I'm looking forward to meeting him too."

"Yeah."

She paused to collect her thoughts. "Does it seem kind of, I don't know, heartless, maybe, to make a movie so soon after something horrific happened?"

He nodded, his face clouding over. "I agree. Kids died and Leo and the others almost did too. I don't think I could be part of this film if I was one of the victims."

"Mr. K talked to the survivors and their parents and assured them he would not try to make the story anything other than a fictionalized version of what happened."

"I know. It still feels…wrong."

"Leo's mother is the producer. It was her idea."

He grimaced. "Like I said, wrong."

"Do you think we'll get a credit for those rewrites we helped Mr. K with?"

"Doubtful. Writing credits require a certain percent of the script to have been written, and we didn't do that. Plus, we're not in the guild."

"Well, we changed the two boys' relationship from boyfriends to just friends. That took a lot of tinkering."

"I don't think it's enough." He paused. "I wonder why the producer wanted that changed. It worked for me."

"You heard Mr. K. The real Leo and J.C. aren't boyfriends, so this makes it more accurate."

"That's true, but this isn't a docudrama."

She considered a moment. "Maybe the boys objected. Since everyone who knows them will realize the film is based on them, I'd probably want that part changed too."

Donovan nodded. "That's true. Kind of makes you wonder what sort of mother would want the world to think her son is gay if he's not."

"Even if he is, it's not her business." She fell silent. Neither her dad nor Donovan's mom would ever do such a thing to them. While she disagreed with the timing of the film (so close to the actual events), it was a chance for her and Donovan to make their mark in Hollywood, and she trusted Mr. K more than any other adult except her dad. So, she overlooked the unsavory aspects.

"Mr. K'll make sure the shoot is as painless as possible for those kids."

He tossed off a small smile, which practically melted her heart. "For sure."

They kissed, pressing their lips gently together for a few lingering moments, before reluctantly returning to their work.